INDIGO: CASE FIFTEEN

A LT. KATE GAZZARA NOVEL

THE LT. KATE GAZZARA MURDER FILES
BOOK 15

BLAIR HOWARD

For my ever-loving wife Jo

1

Sunday Afternoon 1:45 pm

JEFF STUMBLED UP THE FOURTH-FLOOR RAMP OF THE parking garage, shooting a glare back at the ragged concrete wall. He glanced at the sunlight spilling down into the shadowed lower levels. He paused, breathing hard, adjusted the taser on his belt, then rolled his shoulders and started up the final incline to the top floor into the bright sunshine. He stood for a moment, looked around and sighed.

As if on cue, his cell vibrated and he glanced down at it to see a picture of his roommate and three women. They were all lounging on a beach somewhere. Jeff was supposed to have been with him, but he'd forgotten to request time off for the trip and was now stuck working ten-hour shifts. The parking garage was just a part of his patrol. It was attached to a run-down, mostly empty business building. Jeff shivered despite the heat of the afternoon. Just the thought of patrolling those desolate hallways at night was enough to freak him out. Luckily, he'd be home in an hour or two, with the empty apartment all to himself.

"I'd rather deal with this," he muttered, glancing around the sunlit top floor. It could easily have housed a hundred vehicles, but there were only four. The nearest, an old beat-up Bronco, had two flat front tires and a pile of parking tickets under the wiper. Jeff shook his head and began to walk toward it. He'd barely taken a few steps when he stopped, frowned and sniffed the air.

He shook his head, took a few steps more, and stopped again. The smell was stronger, much stronger.

"Geez! What the hell is it?"

He raised his elbow to cover his nose and mouth, trying not to breathe in the rank smell. Whoever had reported it to Escobar hadn't been kidding—the smell was enough to make his eyes water. *Weird,* he thought, looking around at the expanse of concrete around him. Only three more cars; two Honda sedans and a Lexus that seemed out of place.

Where the hell can it be coming from?

The headset in his ear crackled for a moment before a man's voice came on the line. "Sullivan. You good? It's been, like, fifteen minutes. Shift change is coming up soon."

Jeff took a look at his watch as he hit the button to the mic. "Yeah, I'm good, Escobar. Whoever you talked to, they weren't kidding. There's one hell of a smell up here. Let me do a lap and I'll head back down."

The Lexus. That's where I'll start, he thought and

stepped resolutely toward it. It glinted in the sunlight, freshly washed. He paused a few feet away and brought a hand to his ear again.

"Hey, Escobar. The guy who reported it to you, he look well off?"

It took a moment for Escobar to get back to him, but when he did, Jeff's shoulders slumped.

"Yeah. Said he just bought out the fifth floor of the building for his law firm. Why?"

"Never mind," Jeff muttered. He walked around the car, peering through the windows. There was a stack of banker's boxes and a potted plant on the back seat. *Hah*, he thought. *No detective work needed to tell the car belongs to the guy who complained about the smell.*

It was hot enough on top of the parking garage that he was starting to sweat under his uniform. Another glance at his watch told him the next shift would be there by now. He considered leaving the investigation to whoever came on duty next. It wasn't a job he was serious about, but unfortunately, his parents had pounded a decent work ethic into him. So he ground his teeth and started toward the two Hondas, less than ten feet apart.

As he neared the pair of cars, he had to stop and take deep breaths through his mouth. He was salivating, sour, like he was almost ready to vomit. The smell was overwhelming, something he couldn't place, but not something he ever wanted to smell again. He turned away and braced his hands on his knees.

"Hey! You here to check on that?"

Jeff looked up, squinting against the sun, and saw a figure in a suit walking toward him. *Must be the lawyer.*

"You report it to the front desk?" he called, trying hard to keep the contents of his stomach down. The guy walked a few feet nearer but stopped, grimacing.

"Yeah. Hard to miss, right? Maybe a stray dog or something died up here. Whatever it is, try to get it taken care of before Monday, okay? I don't want my staff to get scared away from the place."

The lawyer grabbed the two banker's boxes from his car and left in a hurry, his high-end shoes tapping out a rhythm on the way to the stairs.

Jeff took a moment to calm himself before radioing down again.

"Hey, Escobar. Do me a favor and run these plates." He rattled off both Hondas, waiting as Escobar confirmed that they'd both been up there for almost a month. A fresh wave of saliva filled his mouth, sour and sick. "Okay, you need to bring a crowbar up here."

He could hear Escobar speaking in his ear, but he was still bent over double in the middle of the parking lot, head down, his hands on his knees, trying not to vomit. It only took a few minutes for Escobar to arrive with the tool in hand. He was young, lean, but not impervious to the smell. As he approached, he opened his mouth to ask Jeff what was up but then stopped short as if he'd walked into a wall.

"Holy crap! What *is* that?"

"That's what I said," Jeff replied.

Escobar took in their surroundings as Jeff stood upright, his hands on his hips and pulled himself together.

"Here, gimme that," Jeff said as he walked over to Escobar.

Jeff grabbed the crowbar, took a deep breath and strode quickly toward the two Hondas before he lost his nerve.

A quick glance through the windows told him there was nothing in either one, so he wedged the crowbar under the trunk lid of the one nearest to him and strained. When it became clear he wasn't getting anywhere, he motioned for Escobar to give him a hand, which he reluctantly did. And between them, in less than thirty seconds, the trunk lid popped open with the sound of protesting metal and they found themselves staring at... two beach chairs, an umbrella and a set of jumper cables.

Jeff looked at Escobar and tipped his head toward the other Honda. Before Escobar could protest, he walked over to it and wedged the crowbar into the gap between the trunk lid and the frame, breathing heavily through his mouth. Escobar had to stop to gulp and dry heave, but then they put all their weight on the crowbar, grunting and cursing, bouncing and straining until, with a loud crack, the trunk lid flew open. Jeff stumbled backward, the crowbar clattering loudly onto the concrete. Escobar immediately wretched and turned away.

The smell was impossible, ungodly, like rotting meat, rotting fruit, sweet, rancid. His eyes were watering and he didn't want to look inside the trunk, but he had to. And he did.

Escobar was crawling away as Jeff fumbled for his phone. He spun, unbalanced, and staggered away as he tapped three times for emergency services. When the dispatcher got on the line, he was gulping with nausea.

"I need the police," he breathed heavily into the phone, dropping into a crouch, his eyes watering. "We just found a body in a car."

2

Sunday, November 24

Afternoon 3:30 pm

I COULDN'T HELP GRINNING AS SAMSON LOPED ALONG ahead of me, his body stretching easily as his legs worked in a furious rhythm. This dog would be the death of me, but I'd die happy. We'd been running nonstop for more than two miles and I was beginning to feel it, trying to keep up with him. I didn't want to slow him down; he looked so happy, his mouth open, his tongue flapping as we took a particularly sharp turn through the park.

Fortunately, it was late enough in the day that we didn't have to deal with the heat. It was late November, but it had been unseasonably warm for the last week or two.

The music, keeping a steady rhythm in my ear as we

ran, was suddenly interrupted by two beeps, and I slowed, touching a button on the side of the earbuds.

"Gazzara."

"Kate," Chief Johnston said, "I'm sorry, but you're going to need to come in. I know you were supposed to be off tonight, but something's come up, down on Wyatt Street."

I frowned as Samson circled on his leash, impatient with having to wait. "Wyatt usually goes to the rookies, doesn't it?" I asked.

Wyatt Street was in an industrial part of town, not too far from the water, but not anywhere you'd want to stick around. It had been named after George Wyatt. Not exactly a town hero, but he had a way of making the money circulate so well that authorities back in the 70s turned a blind eye to whatever it was he got up to, and he was up to a lot. The street was notorious for questionable businesses, occasional sex workers and domestic violence calls. Not my usual beat.

The chief's tone was tight when he answered. How had I already gotten on his nerves?

"That's right, it is, but I need *you* there, Gazzara. I have a feeling this one is going to be... big. Corbin's already on his way."

I could hear in his voice that it was frustrating to him that he'd had to call me in. Probably because he knew how much of a pain I'd be to corral on anything "big." But also because he knew I'd get the job done. So, knowing better than to question him further, I got the address, then told him I needed to go home and change. He told me not to bother but to go as I was, so I told him I would and put a finger to the earbud to end the call.

It was just as I was about to turn and run back to my car when a middle-aged guy with an amazing head of hair and a perfect running gait jogged by. He shot me a crooked smile and called out "Nice dog!" as he passed. My heart pattered a quick little rhythm as I turned to return his smile. We'd seen each other quite often on the running path, but I'd never tried to get his name.

The last few years for me had been unlucky for love —or maybe I was the unlucky one, and love was just another victim. Either way, there wasn't any time to lament my lack of a love life.

Pulling my cell out of the pack at my hip, I quickly autodialed Corbin's number.

"Hey, Captain," he greeted me, the echo of him being on speaker telling me that he was in his car and likely on his way to the scene.

"I just got off with the chief. I'll be heading your way as soon as I can, but what can you tell me?"

There was a moment of silence. Sergeant Corbin Russell was a few years younger than me, but his gravity aged him. He was thoughtful, his process a little slower than I was used to, but I'd learned to trust him and if anyone could fill me in properly, it was him.

"I spoke on the phone with an Officer Christine Robertson a few minutes ago. She and her partner answered the call. The location is a four-story parking garage on Wyatt. The victim, a young girl, was found in the trunk of a car on the top floor. The rest of our team is en route."

"Any leads? The victim?"

"No, Captain, sorry. I'm about two minutes out, though. I believe Doc Sheddon arrived a short while ago."

My brows rose in surprise. We usually beat Doc to the scene. He was known for taking his time, which always brought results, but almost always made him the last one to arrive.

"Interesting. I'm on the Greenway but heading back to my car now. I'll see you soon."

Lips pursed, I wondered what else was going on there. Chief Johnston kept me and my team in reserve for the most serious crimes, which meant there was something about this one that had thrown him a red flag. Not that all homicides weren't serious, but there was almost always another layer to the crime when we were assigned a case.

The chief and I didn't always get along, but there was enough respect between us that I trusted his instincts. There was something different about this one, and I had to wonder just what I'd be walking into.

I sighed and jogged backward a few steps, beckoning to Samson. "Come on. Let's go, boy. We've got work to do."

And so, with a backward glance in the direction the cute jogger had been running, I reminded myself that I had a full life, a great career, a busy schedule, and a canine companion I loved who helped me fight off those inevitable lonely moments. So why settle for a stranger?

3

_____

Sunday Afternoon 4:10 pm

THE CRIME SCENE TAPE GAVE THE PARKING GARAGE
away immediately. Otherwise, it looked just like every
other parking garage I'd ever seen: a giant concrete block
of angles and shadows. An ambulance was parked near
the entrance, with back doors open and a stretcher
waiting to the side. The lights were off, indicating that
there was no chance of saving whoever had been found.

"Come on, boy," I told Samson as I grabbed his leash
and then stepped out of the car and looked up at the four-
story monstrosity. There was something about parking
garages that was off-putting to me. Always has been.
They were the perfect place for crimes to be committed,
especially at night: deep, dark shadows, dark stairwells,
and... echoes.

A cop stationed just inside the tape lifted it for me as
I ducked under, nodding. I didn't know his name, but I'd
seen him around here and there. There were other faces I

recognized as I approached a small group. Corbin and two uniformed men. Each of the trio looked a little green around the gills.

"Sergeant." I nodded, waiting for him to introduce me. He did, then gestured at the two men before him.

"This is Jeff Sullivan and Angel Escobar. Both security guards for Whitlow, Incorporated, the company that owns the office building attached to the garage."

I looked at the two men, both about ten years younger than me and not looking so hot.

"Which one of you found the body?" I asked. Jeff and Angel looked at each other, but Jeff was the one who answered.

"Both of us did," he said. "I called Escobar up to... help open the trunk."

I raised my eyebrows and said, "You opened a vehicle on the lot? Is that normal practice?"

Angel Escobar shook his head as Jeff took a few deep breaths through his mouth. "No, ma'am. But we were aware that the car had been parked there for several weeks. So we checked the logbook and saw that other guards reported it unmoved. And there was this guy, a lawyer. He just moved into the building and was complaining about the stink. And our instructions are to take matters into our own hands if there seems to be any signs of distress or harm. Usually, we tow abandoned cars, but..."

He was professional, but still looked a bit nauseous. I watched him closely as I asked, "Was there something about the situation that made you think someone was in distress?"

It was Sullivan who replied, "No, not exactly. Just that it was abandoned. Normally we'd just have it towed, but... the smell. So... we opened it, and the other Honda."

That made sense. I glanced at Corbin. Even he looked a little pale and clammy, which surprised me. "You should probably head up there," he said with a grimace, tipping his head toward the ramp and stairwell. "I'll radio ahead and let them know you're coming, then finish up here. I've already talked to Officer Robertson."

He seemed to have the interview with the guards almost wrapped up, so I nodded and started toward the ramp, Samson at my side, thinking how funny it was that, after such a short time, everyone seemed to take him for granted, even the chief.

The stairwell door was open and Mike Willis' team was already going over every inch of the concrete steps and walls. Apparently, I was the last to arrive.

My eyes scanned each floor of the garage as I hiked up the ramp, looking for anything out of place. But nothing stuck out, and soon I reached the top floor, sunlight breaking over my face and shoulders. Carol Owens was waiting for me.

"Captain," she greeted me. "You're going to need this," she said, holding out a small round bottle of Vicks VapoRub, something I wasn't used to seeing on-site.

"That bad?" I asked, wrinkling my nose. I wasn't a fan of Vicks. It reminded me of being sick as a child, bundled up in bed with a stuffy nose and rattling lungs. I dipped a finger in anyway and smeared a thin layer under my nostrils.

"That bad," she confirmed, turning to lead me across the lot.

I looked down at Sam seated at my side and then looked around for an officer. There wasn't one handy so I kept him with me, on a short leash.

There were four vehicles, three in close proximity to one another. We walked right by a Bronco. Doc and three paramedics were gathered near a Honda, a body bag ready on the stretcher I'd seen downstairs, and there were other tools I didn't recognize. I glanced at Carol but didn't ask.

"Doc," I said, surprised by the unusual gravity of his face.

"Just hold off for a minute," he said to the two paramedics. "I need the captain to see this. Sorry, Kate," he added. "It's not pretty."

I handed Sammy off to Carol, assuring her he was a good boy. She took the leash from me gingerly and backed away. Sam went obediently with her for several feet, then dropped his backside on the cement and refused to move.

I nodded to Doc, stepped forward, leaned in and looked into the trunk, realizing suddenly that I'd been walking into the smell for the last twenty feet. The Vicks helped take the edge off, but the overpowering scent of hot decay was... oppressive.

I could tell immediately that the body had been in the trunk for quite a while. It had somehow both bloated and sloughed at the same time. The carpeting of the trunk was darkened with dried blood, and the victim's hair was matted into it, a dark nest. The parts of her face, right arm, and bent right leg I could see were the color of week-old oatmeal.

"Blood has pooled in the other half of the body," Doc recited as if by rote. He was a short man, heavy and usually jovial with a gallows sense of humor, but not that day. Still leaning forward, I looked up at him. The late afternoon sunlight glinted off his glasses.

"She's been hog-tied, throat cut." He stood with his hands behind his back and shook his head. "It's enough to make a man want to skip his next meal."

"Been here a while?" I asked, finding it harder to breathe between the sharp scent of Vicks and the rot.

"Hard to tell how long," he said. "I'll know more when I get her on the slab, but judging by the state of decomposition, the recent heat and the lack of insects, I'd guess a week, ten days, maybe. Decomposition has probably been sped up at this point. Go ahead." He motioned to the paramedics, who began to carefully maneuver the body and stepped away with me. It was a good thing, too, because my stomach churned at the sight of the skin shifting so easily under their fingers.

"We don't have an ID yet, Kate, but this is a young woman," Doc said quietly. His eyes caught something over my shoulder, and I turned to see Corbin walking toward us, resolutely avoiding looking toward the car. Doc continued, speaking to both of us. "I would guess she's in her mid-to-late teens."

"Out for a night of fun," I mused. The girl was wearing a slinky, black sequined dress.

Doc nodded. "That's about all I can tell you right now. The sharp force trauma to the throat is the obvious cause of death, but when Carol and I get her back to the Center, we will, of course, check for other injuries. Now, if you'll excuse me, I need to talk to Carol and Mike."

I followed him, relieved Carol of Samson, who jumped to his feet, wagging his tail.

"What next?" Corbin asked.

I was surprised to see him so thrown off, but then, the state of the body was pretty bad. My heart ached for the victim... and her family.

"The poor kid," I muttered, more to myself than to Corbin. "She had her whole life stolen away from her."

And I knew at that moment that I would do everything in my power to find her killer and bring him, or her, to justice, although I knew a knife to the throat was rarely a woman's MO.

"Anything suspicious going on with the guards?" I asked.

Corbin shook his head. "Not that I picked up on. They were badly shaken. They confirmed the car has been here a while, and they're willing to hand over security footage, but the car is actually parked in a blind spot."

I stared at him, then at our surroundings, noting the evenly spaced pillars and light posts.

"Are you kidding?" I said. "That's a little too convenient." Was it just a coincidence, or was someone familiar with this area?

"Do we know who it's registered to?"

"Not yet," Corbin replied. "I—"

"That's kind of sloppy, isn't it?" I said. "What about this Officer..."

"Robertson," he replied. "Maybe she was... a little overwhelmed."

"I want to know who owns that car, Corbin. Come *on.* This is basic stuff."

I walked over to the outer wall of the parking garage, looking down the four stories to the street. Most of the businesses were shuttered, but there was some activity further on down the street, and a few spectators indicated that there was still life in this area.

"Let's get some people out here and have them do a survey of the surrounding streets," I said, pulling back from the wall. "To start with, we'll need a list of the businesses in the immediate vicinity. And let's talk to the Whitlow company. Have them get the rest of the guards together. I want to know more about when and how this car got here and who has access to this area."

Corbin nodded, tapping some notes into his phone.

"Look, I need to go home and change. You wait here for me. We'll talk to the guards together," I said, then Samson and I headed back down the ramp.

4

Sunday Evening 6:20 pm

Samson breathed heavily, happily, over my shoulder when, a little more than an hour later, I pulled into the front drive of the Whitlow building. I sighed, glancing at his big, wedged head in the rearview mirror.

"You're a lucky boy," I murmured, grazing a hand over my chest and hip to make sure I had everything. Badge, gun...

I'd gone home, grabbed a quick shower, put on a pair of tan pants, a white top and my favorite hunter-green leather moto jacket. Then I fed Samson, ate half a buttered bagel, made myself a large coffee to go and told Samson to behave himself. But it took only one look at his big brown eyes and I knew he'd be coming with me. Since we'd be meeting only with a group of security guards, I figured it was okay for him to be there. The big old boy was turning into something of an asset. Everyone at the department loved him, even my arch nemesis, Henry Finkle. And I thought that maybe... Hell, I don't know what I thought. All I knew was I didn't want to leave him home alone. So, protocol be damned, I took him with me.

I parked my unmarked cruiser on the street, wrapped Samson's leash around my wrist, and together we walked toward the front doors. I noted the badge scanner just to the right of the doors and thought, *So you need access to get in, then.* Fortunately, the light on the scanner was green and the doors were unlocked, so I stepped inside, into the atrium, and couldn't help but look upward.

The ceiling was arched, almost church-like, painted dove gray and navy blue. Stained glass windows decorated the wall to my left, spilling in colored light. The white-tiled floor had dark gray veins lacing through it, and the floor of the reception area was covered with a deep emerald carpet.

Overall, it wasn't a bad looking atrium, though obviously empty and disused. And... a bit dated. The building must have been a hive of businesses back in the 70s and 80s, but most of it had trickled out into different parts of the city.

A young woman was seated at the front desk watching me. She appeared timid, her eyes flickering from me to Samson nervously. *Okay... so maybe not everyone's susceptible to loveable dogs.*

"Captain... Gazzara?" she asked, sounding unsure.

I nodded and stepped over to her desk, my badge on a chain around my neck. She swallowed and nodded and then said, "They're all in the first-floor conference room.

First pair of doors to your right." Then she pointed back toward a darkened hallway.

I thanked her and left her staring after me, hearing the murmur of voices as I turned the corner. About ten feet down on the right were two big glass doors, and behind them, a large room filled with people, including Corbin and Detective Anne Robar.

I'd called Anne in for the interviews. With a group this big, I figured we'd need all the help we could get. Anne was a great detective and an intimidating figure with her sharp hazel eyes and cropped hair. Having raised two boys, Anne didn't mess around. She looked out at the crowd of mostly males with a no-nonsense expression. Her partner, Hawk, was on his way to meet with Doc Sheddon. One look at Corbin earlier and I didn't think he'd make it through an autopsy.

Also present among the crowd were Jeff Sullivan and Angel Escobar. Both seemed reluctant to talk to anyone but were surrounded by curious coworkers. Corbin cleared his throat, and the guards mostly quieted and shifted in their seats.

"Hello," I said. "My name is Captain Catherine Gazzara. You're probably all aware, by now, of why we're here. For those of you who aren't, the body of a young woman was found in the trunk of a car on the top floor of the parking garage. And because you're all familiar with the parking garage and its patrons, we wanted to speak to you and see if any of you noticed anything odd or... just unusual during the last several weeks. That would be between October twenty-fifth and yesterday."

A young man in a blue uniform seated near the front

snorted. Anne's eyes flared, but I cut her a quick, restraining look. When I looked back at the man—more of a boy, really, who couldn't have been older than twenty-three or four—he shrugged and spoke up.

"We see a lot of odd stuff around here. There's never a lot going on here at the Whitlow." He gestured grandly, earning a few chuckles from his coworkers. "But 'odd' covers a lot. Drunks, drug deals, men dressed as women, you name it, we see it almost daily."

I frowned. I was annoyed. This guy obviously wasn't going to make it easy for us.

Samson, sensing my attitude, shifted into a standing position with his head low, his ears flattened. The young guard's mouth clapped shut pretty quick.

"I see," I said. "Maybe it would be more helpful if we broke you up into groups."

Anne, as always, was quick to latch onto the suggestion, directing the guards to break up into groups of five. There were fourteen of them in total, so one group of four. I told Corbin to handle that one, as I could tell he still hadn't quite recovered after seeing and smelling the severely decomposing body.

I took my group and gestured to Anne and Corbin that I'd be down the hall.

The room was smaller but still accommodating. Samson slipped into the room first and the motion-activated lights came on. The five guards with me crowded around a circular table and sat down, all of them seemingly uneasy. Me? I told Samson to sit and dropped his leash. Then I leaned against the wall, my head tilted to one side, watching them. I took my notebook from the inside pocket of my jacket, flipped it open in my palm and took out a pen.

"Before we start," I began, "I want to make it clear that this isn't an interrogation. We're just looking for some help. Maybe you saw something that struck you as off, or maybe it was a person that triggered you as someone who needed watching. We're trying to figure out how this girl got up there, in the trunk of that car, and when. We know it was abandoned more than a month ago. We also know she hadn't been in the trunk much more than a week. Any thoughts, anyone?"

One of the guards raised his hand. I nodded, and he introduced himself as Dylan. "Wouldn't the security footage tell you that?" he asked a bit nervously.

"It might, and we're in the process of retrieving it. But you guys are the eyes and ears around here. Like your friend in the other room said, you see it all. So, I'm asking you now; what have you seen that seemed… unusual during the last few weeks?"

The small group gazed around at one another. A slightly older man, closer to his mid-forties and who appeared to be less shy than the other members of the group, spoke up.

"I can't think of anything off the top of my head, but a new nightclub opened up down the street about two months ago, and there's been an increase in activity since then. A lot of people walking by the garage at odd hours of the night and morning."

That set me back a little. I hadn't been expecting it to be easy, but I knew that high foot traffic in the area would make it a whole lot more difficult. And I tried to drown out the voice in my head telling me, *Geez, this could have been anyone.*

"Do you know who the person in the trunk was?" another guard asked, a female. She was the only other woman in the room. I lowered my head a little and looked at her. She was cute and already knew that in a position like hers, she had to play it down. She wore no makeup and kept her blonde hair tied back in a low bun.

"I'm sorry, I can't reveal any information other than what I've already told you."

She looked crestfallen, petting Samson's head. He'd wandered around the table and was snuffling her thigh.

"Sorry," she murmured, "I was just thinking that... we might know her."

Her words immediately struck a chord with me. After all, the other guard had just pointed out that there had been a lot of new people around in the area. *So what,* I wondered, *would make her think she might know the victim?*

"Your name is?" I asked, remembering that Corbin had the list of security guards employed by Whitlow.

"Carolyn Brown," she replied, face heating with a blush. I quickly gathered the names of the other guards and made a note of them.

By then, Samson had nosed his way under the table and I saw several hands disappear, and I had to fight the urge to grin, knowing he was looking for affection wherever he could find it. The effect was almost immediate; the nervous edge to the room softened noticeably.

"Can one of you please explain the process to me?" I asked. "With regard to abandoned cars. Jeff Sullivan mentioned that the one on the roof had been abandoned for almost a month. What happens to them?"

The older guard I now knew as Ted spoke up again. "In those situations, we reach out to Whitlow management and wait to hear back. They're not in the actual building, so..."

There was a bitterness in his voice that I well understood. Waiting on superiors could be frustrating and time-consuming.

"Usually, we end up calling a tow company to come get the vehicles. Our go-to is Baldacci Brothers. A few more days and that's what we would have done." He shook his head, seeming far away. "I feel bad that Sullivan and Escobar had to see that," he continued, "but it would've come out in the end. I doubt the tow would've taken the car stinking like that. One way or another, we would've been calling you."

His cool eyes cut back to me, and I didn't see anything in them that made me suspicious.

"But wouldn't you try to contact the owners first?" I asked.

He shrugged. "That's not what we do. We report it to Whitlow, as I said, and leave that to them, but I doubt they even try to trace the owners. They just order them towed and leave it to Baldacci to track them down."

"How often do you guys break into the cars?" I asked. "Jeff Sullivan said you're allowed to do so when there's harm or distress concerned." *Harm and distress?* I thought. *In an abandoned car? That seems a little ambiguous to me.*

Another guard, Oskar Pope, spoke up. "Last summer

I broke a window out when someone had left their dog inside." He glanced down at the table, where Samson was still lingering beneath. "The owner asked me to. She'd dropped her keys in a storm drain and it was hot." He shrugged. "Other than that, I can't think of any time we've ever had to."

There were murmurs of agreement around the room.

"I'm surprised Sullivan remembered that part of the manual," Ted added. "That's a rule I never even think about."

I tried once again to prompt them into thinking of anything strange that had happened recently, but the room stayed silent. After stepping outside for a moment to check in with Corbin to see that he had everyone's contact information, I stepped back into the room and sighed.

"Well, that's all we need for now. I want to thank you all for your cooperation. I know this is jarring, but I just want you to know that we're doing everything we can to find whoever did this."

The group slipped out of the room one by one, and Samson emerged from under the table, looking sad to see his new friends go. My eyes were on him when Carolyn surprised me by waiting by the doorway.

A quick glance at her told me that she was anxious. She was shifting her weight from foot to foot, her fingers laced together in front of her. I let the door swing shut slowly behind the last guard out and waited, locking eyes with her.

"I have a friend," she began, looking down, picking at her nails. "I haven't seen her in a while. I thought it might be... because her dad is strict, and she's not really supposed to be out here."

Trying to keep my expression stoic, I asked, "What's her name?"

Carolyn was hesitant to tell me, but eventually she blurted out, "Indigo Salazar."

Not wanting to worry her by whipping out my notebook or phone, I simply nodded and asked, "How do you two know each other? And why exactly are you worried?"

She took a deep breath, self-consciously touching her hair before leaning against the table. "I don't want to think it's her... I'm sure it's not. But... We met here, actually. See, sometimes, after my shift if it's late, I'll go to some of the clubs and just let loose a little. Nothing crazy. They drug test here, so..." She shrugged.

I nodded and smiled at her to show support. Now that she was talking, it all came out in a flood.

"I met Indigo at one of the clubs maybe a year ago? She's really nice and fun and doesn't get up to anything bad other than a drink or two, so we got along. We met up once or twice a week to hit the clubs, but... I haven't heard from her in a couple weeks. It's not like her."

"Okay, Carolyn. I see where you're coming from. You said her father is strict, so I assume she still lives at home with her parents?"

She nodded. The nerves had suddenly returned. "Yes. I don't know where exactly. I've never been there. I know you said the person in the trunk was a woman, and I'm really hoping it's not her."

She broke off, her eyes brimming with tears.

"It's okay, Carolyn. You're doing the right thing by telling me. At the least, we can confirm she's at home. Can I reach out to you if I have any more questions?"

She nodded. I made a note of her number and slipped the notebook back into my pocket.

Samson huffed and nuzzled Carolyn's hand, making the young woman smile. I reassured her I'd be in touch and waited for her to leave the room. I followed her out and watched as she jogged to the entrance doors and out of the building.

Corbin and Anne were waiting for me in the hallway.

"Anything useful?" I asked, wanting to see what they had before I revealed my possible tip.

Corbin shook his head. "My group was pretty close-mouthed. I'm getting a sense it's a boy's club, but nothing specific."

Anne shook her head. "I got that, too. It seems like there are cliques in their group. One of the guys in my batch mentioned that there are two employees who aren't here: Monica Larenta and Lewis Massey. I called the manager and he confirmed they're both out this week on PTO—personal time off."

"All right, let's get their contact info and bring them in as soon as they're available. One of the female guards in my group mentioned that she has a friend she hasn't seen in a while. An Indigo Salazar. We need to check her out."

Corbin's eyes lit up with recognition, and Anne and I waited for him to explain. "We should head back to the department," he said seriously, already moving toward the door. "If it's who I think it is, I know why the chief wanted us involved."

Anne and I, both caught off guard, hurried to catch up with him. Corbin was a straightforward kind of guy, and his lack of a full explanation and sudden hurry didn't bode well for Indigo Salazar, whoever she was.

5

Sunday Evening 8:15 pm

THE SITUATION ROOM WAS MOSTLY EMPTY, AS WERE most of the offices and hallways—not unusual on a Sunday night. Part of me liked the privacy; the other part always got a little creeped out by big empty buildings.

I'd stopped off at home to drop Samson off and then went back to the department, where I found Corbin and Anne waiting for me.

"The chief's wanting to know where you are, Cap," Corbin said. "He's waiting for us."

Us? I thought. Now that was unusual.

I entered his outer office to find that Grace, his new secretary, was absent, also not surprising since it was, after all, a Sunday evening

Chief Wesley Johnston was in his office, seated behind his desk. Also present was Captain Henry Finkle —not my most favorite person.

What the heck's he doing here? I wondered as I set my

jaw and stood to one side for Corbin and Robar to enter. Then I shut the door behind me and remained standing.

"Kate, Corbin, Anne," the chief said, taking a file from his desktop and holding it out to me. "Sit down. I had a feeling something like this would come up. It's too quiet these last several weeks, and this city never stays quiet for long."

I stepped forward, took the file from him and sat down in the chair in front of his desk, alongside Finkle. Corbin and Anne sat in chairs alongside the walls on opposite sides of the room.

I opened the file to find the face of a young woman... no, a girl, staring up at me. She was pretty, with dark hair spilling over her shoulders and a sweet smile that told me she was probably a little naïve. The name on the jacket, in heavy bold, read, INDIGO SALAZAR.

The first section below the photograph listed her as a seventeen-year-old high school student with a local, high-end address. It also listed her physical details and mentioned a reward substantial enough to take my breath away.

I looked at the chief, then glanced to my right at Finkle.

"She's the daughter of a prominent pediatric surgeon," Finkle explained. From the look on Corbin and Anne's faces, I could tell they'd already heard as much. "She's been missing for a little over two weeks. She was last seen on Saturday, November 9th. One of my officers took the report and didn't... handle it well."

His jaw worked in a tight knot, indicating his displeasure. Johnston didn't look too happy either.

I frowned. Finkle was the head of Vice and was usually involved in prostitution, illegal guns, drugs... *How did Indigo end up reported to them?* I wondered. I could have asked him, but I didn't. Finkle was always combative when I was involved, and I knew an argument between the two of us would tempt me to take a swing at him. So I decided to start with the easy questions.

"Why didn't this get followed up?" I asked. "If her father is such an important guy?" None of us missed the chief's glare.

Finkle crossed his arms over his chest. He was a small guy with a Napoleon complex. I was pretty sure I could take him if I had to, and I wasn't convinced that it wouldn't come to that someday. Finkle also happened to be a bigot and misogynist. And we'd already had a few run-ins, now in the distant past.

Finkle rolled his tongue around the inside of his cheek, then said, "The officer marked it as a likely runaway and pinned the poster up on the board but didn't do much else. He figured she was... offering herself up."

Oh, was I ever angry when I heard that. Of course Finkle and his team would assume that a missing young woman was a prostitute. Don't they always? And they'd been sitting on it for weeks, and now we'd found her in the trunk of a car. What if we'd started looking for her right away, when she was first reported missing? Would she still be alive? It's doubtful, but at least she'd have had a chance. As it was...

I hated it when my mind went to that place, trying to re-work the narrative. It didn't matter. Indigo Salazar was dead, and now it was my job to find the person who killed her. And worse, that oh-so-important forty-eight-hour window had closed almost two weeks ago.

Corbin caught my gaze, but it was Anne who spoke up. "Two weeks, two days," she said, shaking her head. "Her father..."

"He's not going to be happy," Chief Johnston said. "In fact, I'm expecting him to tear us apart. I've already spoken to Doc Sheddon and he's certain it's her." He heaved a huge sigh, shook his head and said, "We'll have to have Dr. Salazar identify the body, of course."

My stomach churned at the memory of the state of Indigo Salazar's body, and the thought that her father might have to see enough of it to positively ID her made it even worse. No parent should ever have to see a child pass before they do, and especially not under these circumstances. If he was smart, he'd be okay with a DNA match. But I knew that wasn't going to happen; parents always wanted to see their children. I could only hope that Doc would try to hide her hideously slashed throat.

"Carolyn Brown," I said, fingering my notepad in my back pocket, "one of the security guards. She told me that she and Indigo frequented some of the clubs on Wyatt."

Corbin nodded. "We had officers canvas the area and get the names of the businesses and owners. There are four clubs on Wyatt."

"We'll start there tomorrow," I said. "Anne, I want you and Hawkins in on that, too. I'll get Cooper and Tracy on the security footage. Do we know if they found her phone?"

"Not yet," Corbin said. "I'll check with Mike Willis in the morning."

"I need to go through this," I said, lifting the file off my knee and dropping it back again. "I'll do it first thing in the morning."

Chief Johnston nodded. He looked too tired to even try and argue with me about how I ran my investigation, or my team. Not that he ever did, much. Instead, he usually pushed for a quick closure, and I had no doubt that this case would be any different.

Working out the details, we decided to start in on Wyatt at midday. It was unlikely they'd be staffed any earlier. That would give me time to talk to Mike Willis and make some calls. And then there was Dr. Salazar to consider. Fortunately, it wasn't up to me to arrange for him to ID the body, but sooner or later, I knew I had to talk to him and that, I wasn't looking forward to.

Throughout the quick conversation that secured the plans for opening the investigation, Finkle sat with his arms crossed, sullen and resentful. *His own fault*, I thought. Finkle oversaw more than thirty officers, some of whom I knew were particularly valuable—a few were quite the opposite.

"I'll stay and read through the reports we have so far," Anne offered.

"No," Johnston said. "You three, all of you, go home and get some rest. Make a fresh start in the morning. Eight-thirty sharp!"

I nodded, told the chief and Finkle goodnight, and we left them both sitting there, and I couldn't help but think how I wouldn't have wanted to be in Finkle's shoes at that particular moment. Chief Johnston was not a man to cross.

"I have a feeling this is going to be a rough one," I murmured to Corbin as we walked the halls to the exit to the parking lot. He didn't answer, nor did Robar. What could they say? They knew I was right.

It was only the beginning. We had a body, a cause of death, and a probable ID of the victim. But who had killed Indigo Salazar? And what was the teenage daughter of a prominent children's surgeon doing strutting her stuff on Wyatt Street?

Whatever we were about to face, I had a restless feeling deep in my gut, and I knew I wouldn't be getting much sleep that night.

6

_____

Monday Morning 8 am

Monday mornings were always rough for me. It didn't matter how my schedule for the week played out; I just couldn't seem to get it together on Mondays. As I walked into the situation room that particular Monday morning with Samson at my side, I was well aware that I looked like crap. I was exhausted. Samson had slept like a baby all night, as he always does, but not me.

I'd been up most of the night thinking about Indigo. Cases involving kids are always tough. It was impossible not to think about those cases during every waking moment. Their terrible experiences, the terror they must have endured during their last few moments, the life they would have had had it not been snatched away from them. Luckily—and I don't know if that's the right word— these thoughts only fueled the fire inside me: to do better, work faster, to catch whatever sick person had tied that poor girl up, slit her throat and left her in a car to rot in the Chattanooga heat.

Anyway, as I said, I arrived at the PD just before eight that morning and took the elevator to the second floor, where my office was located on the east side of the situation room, and was halfway across the room when I literally bumped into Lieutenant Mike Willis.

"Ah, there you are," he said, holding out a Styrofoam cup of coffee.

My eyebrows rose. "That for me?" I asked.

It was, and it was an uncharacteristic gesture for him. The supervising CSI tech for the CPD, Willis had been around for a long time, even before I joined the force. I looked at the coffee dwarfed by his massive hand... and I took it.

He reached down and scratched behind Samson's ears. "I know yesterday was rough, and I thought it might help," he said by way of explanation.

I nodded and took a sip, waiting for him to cut to the chase.

"Your team find anything in the garage?" I asked finally.

Willis shook his head and said, "If you'll come with me."

And he turned and started powerwalking toward one of the conference rooms used to lay out the evidence. I had to hurry to keep up with him. Willis was a man always in a rush, despite being the most methodical and patient tech in the building.

The long, low table was laid out with an assortment

of... junk, garbage. My heart sank, knowing that the majority of it would be useless.

"Despite everything you see here," Willis said, staring at the organized mess, "there's not much I'd say is indicative of who your perp might be. Parking garages are the petri dishes of the city."

One by one, he pointed out multiple scrapings of gum, swabs of what was apparently spit, used tissues, coins, an unopened tampon, several used condoms, a half-dozen or so needles and... the list goes on. Willis went over each area of possible evidence and told me why it wasn't viable. I tried to be patient but couldn't help cutting him short.

"Okay, so what about the car?" I asked. "Did you find her phone or her purse? She had to have had one."

He took a long sip of his coffee, throat bobbing, before answering. "No, and no. But I'm digging into the car this morning, actually. I was on my way there when I saw you through the window in the parking lot, so I figured I'd catch you up."

Okay, so not all hope was lost. Maybe Willis would find something in the car that would help us out. If anyone could... I'd already had a brief report texted to me from Cooper and Tracy Ramirez that morning on the way in. They were able to track the car arriving at the parking garage, but it had no plates to run, and we wouldn't have the VIN until Mike was done with it.

The only glimpse they'd gotten of a possible perp was a figure in a hoodie rushing through the garage. The hoodie suspect hadn't even taken the stairwell, which confirmed everything Mike said about all this evidence essentially being trash.

I thanked him for the coffee again and told him to call me with whatever he found and the VIN. He nodded but seemed to be lost in a world all his own, his eyes glued to the table as if he was reading a book. I left shaking my head. He was an odd duck, but he'd come up with something; I just knew it.

Me? I walked first past Corbin's desk, then Hawk's, then Robar's on my way to my office. None of them were there, which was unusual, especially in Corbin's case. So I entered my office and closed the door. Samson went to his bed under the window, lay down with his front paws alongside his nose and stared up at me, his eyes following me around the room.

I hadn't been seated for more than a minute when my cell phone rang. I looked at the screen. It was Corbin.

"Good morning, Captain. I'm at the McDonald's across the street. You want some coffee?"

I looked inside my now half-empty cup and said, "Sure, large and black. And when you get here, I need everyone in my office ASAP. Oh, and bring Samson a chicken biscuit. I'll pay for it."

"You got it, Cap. My treat," he replied and hung up.

I looked at the empty whiteboard, then I opened the Indigo Salazar file and stared down at the image of the pretty young woman, and my stomach turned. *How could someone do something like this? How could someone take a fellow human being's life?* They were the eternal questions, questions I'd asked myself a thousand times over the years I'd been a cop. And the answers were always the same: there were no answers.

A knock on the door jerked me out of my morbid reverie. I looked up. The door opened and Corbin stepped inside, two coffees and a McDonald's bag in hand. He was followed closely by Hawk, Robar, Cooper, Ramirez and Jack North.

We got through the usual early Monday morning chatter unusually quickly. The mood was somber. It seemed Indigo's horrifying demise had affected everyone deeply.

Eventually, inevitably the chatter soon died away to an uncomfortable silence; it was time to get to work.

I opened the file again, took out the photo, ran it through the copier on the credenza behind me, stood up, and taped it up on the top center of the whiteboard.

"Indigo Salazar," I said as I wrote the name below the image. "Seventeen. High school junior. Lived with her father. Mother not around."

"Carolyn Brown," I said as I wrote the name next to Indigo's image. "Friend of the deceased."

I turned to face the group around the table.

"These two," I tapped the tip of my dry erase pen on the board, "according to Brown, regularly frequented the night clubs on Wyatt. Labyrinth, Bongo's, Urban One and Electric Blue. That's it. That's all we've got. So that's where we'll begin. Jack, I want you to go to the high school and make inquiries. I want to know who her friends were, her teachers. Was she romantically involved? You know what I'm talking about. The rest of you are with me. We'll hit Wyatt at midday. Most of them don't open until then anyway.

"Corbin, you and Anne will take the Labyrinth and Bongo's. Hawkins, you and I will take Urban One and Electric Blue. Any questions? No? Good, then off you go. Find something constructive to do for the next couple of hours. We'll gather in the lobby at eleven-thirty, except for you, Jack. The school is open now. I want you to talk to every one of her classmates and teachers. Don't leave anyone out."

7

Monday Midday

Anne, Hawk, Corbin and I stood on the sidewalk a short distance away from the Whitlow building, going over our gameplan. A quick glance at my phone told me it was just after noon. The streets were quiet at that time of day, but I was hoping the clubs were staffed and getting ready for the evening.

There was a focused air about the moment. I'd told the team about the lack of evidence, and we all knew we needed more to go on. The interviews we were about to conduct had to give us something, if only a suggestion of where to turn next, because if not, we'd find ourselves at a dead end.

"Anne and Corbin, you take the Labyrinth and Bongo's. Hawkins and I will take Urban One and Electric Blue. Everyone has a copy of Indigo's photo?"

When it was confirmed that each of us had a copy of Indigo's missing person flyer, Hawkins, Samson and I started off in one direction as Anne and Corbin headed in the other. I didn't really like splitting up partners, but Hawkins would be able to deal with my bad attitude today and Anne would balance out Corbin's wait-and-watch approach.

Sergeant "Hawk" Hawkins was close to retirement, but that hadn't slowed him down. He'd met Doc Sheddon for the autopsy no questions asked and, though it couldn't have been easy for him, he'd returned with a detailed and clear report and a stack of autopsy photographs.

Even in the heat of the day, Hawk wore a dark blue suit with a white button-down shirt and suspenders.

"When are you going to bring the pup around?" he asked as we strolled along the street. "I bet he'll get along great with the girls."

Another thing about Hawk was that the man had been swimming in a pool of estrogen for most of his life. He lived with his wife and one of his three grown daughters, plus two female dogs. The thought of Samson playing with their little devil of a chihuahua and the aging golden brought a smile to my face as we approached our first stop, Urban One.

"How about after all this is over?" I offered. "We can do dinner. Jenny and I have to catch up anyway."

Urban One was a hipster type club, minimalist and clearly "above" their surrounding competitors—or at least they thought so. We introduced ourselves and were directed to the owner, a man named Theodore, who couldn't have been more than twenty-five. He was tall, skinny and wearing a pair of thick-framed glasses on his upturned nose.

"Dogs are not allowed in..." he said loftily, then trailed off. "Oh, I see," he said, looking back and forth between the two of us, taking note of Hawk's badge clipped to his jacket breast pocket. Hawk did a better job than I did at keeping his face straight.

I took in the open floor plan with its all-black concrete walls and dark wood. Plants hung from every available surface, and a staff member was wheeling in a humidifier.

"Have you seen this young woman?" Hawk began, taking Indigo's photo from his inside pocket and unfolding it. "She's been reported missing."

Theodore squinted as he stared at it, then shook his head, looked down and away to his left—a sure indication he was about to lie—and said, "You think we want to get shut down?" he scoffed, crossing his arms over his chest. The shirt he wore, I realized, was patterned with cats.

"Why would I think that?" Hawk asked.

Theodore gave him a side-eye look, clearly intimidated by the older and much larger man. He shoved his glasses up nervously.

"Well, she's obviously underage, isn't she? Urban One has a good reputation, and we're trying to keep it."

"Theodore," I said, locking eyes with him. "If you don't tell me the truth, I'll have Vice and the Beer Board all over you. Now, tell me, have you *ever* seen this girl in here?"

He hesitated for a moment, then said, "Maybe... once or twice. Look, she looks old enough and... I don't want any trouble, okay? Hopefully, we'll be moving out of this rat's nest to a new location in a few months."

That last statement pinged on my radar. Was it just coincidental that Theodore was moving his entire club weeks after a girl went missing?

"But you've only been open a few months. Not happy with the location?" I asked. "Why the sudden need to move?"

He looked at me as if I was stupid.

I took a deep breath and glared at him. His attitude was beginning to grind my gears.

"Have you *seen* Wyatt Street?" he asked. "Half of my clientele are too scared to even come down here."

Out of the corner of my eye, I saw Hawk's arms go taut and knew he'd taken an interest in that claim, too.

"Why are they scared?" he asked casually, obviously trying his best to look less intimidating, though Theodore didn't seem convinced.

"Well, being cops an' all, I'd think you'd know that better than I do." He looked at Hawk, then Samson, then me, then back at Hawk. "There's just so much crime on the street. Only last week, my dishwasher got mugged on his way out. Some of the other clubs go a little further in their entertainment offerings, too, and that's not something I'm interested in getting mixed up in."

Inwardly, I sighed, fed up with the way he beat around the bush. "And just what d'you mean by that?" I snapped.

Apparently, Theodore wasn't used to straight-talk, because he looked as if I'd slapped him. "I..." He shrugged, then continued, "there's a lot of... prostitution," he finally spit out, his face flushing. "And drugs. You know, dealing. I heard one of the clubs basically has an open bar for whatever you're looking for."

He looked anxiously back and forth between Hawk and me, as if we might arrest him for simply hearing about such things.

"And which club would that be?" Hawk asked.

Theodore glanced around to make sure no staff were nearby and then practically whispered, "Bongo's. The owner is this old guy from California. Kind of a hippy. Our last dishwasher used to stop by there before his shift, and he'd always come in with his eyes unfocused and barely able to function." He scrunched his nose. "Had to let him go only a few weeks after."

I jotted down a few notes, to his dismay, and hoped that Corbin and Anne were knee-deep in whatever Bongo's had going on right now. Although nothing about Indigo's situation indicated drugs were involved, we couldn't rule it out yet.

Seeming a little more comfortable now that he'd gotten that off his chest, Theodore rambled on: "I mean, we're lucky down our end. There are some people who keep an eye out for us, and they let us know what's going on. Who's doing what, you know. It's been nice getting some insider information, but it's time for us to move on." He lifted his chin again and I almost rolled my eyes.

"Who have you been hearing this 'insider information' from?" I asked.

"Some of the people who work in the area. They come to us for a nightcap, you know, somewhere *relaxing* to hang out after work. And that's when they fill us in."

Hawk and I shared a quick look. We asked for names. He blanched, hesitated, then reluctantly gave us two, Lewis and Oskar. Oskar, I remembered as one of Whitlow's security guards, but it took me a moment to recall that Lewis was also a guard and that he'd been one of the two that hadn't been present at the interviews.

"And the girl?" I asked, staring him down.

He stared back at me, then looked away and said, "I don't know. They had a girl with them sometimes, but I don't know if it was her." He nodded at the flyer still in Hawk's hands. "She hasn't been in for... I dunno, several weeks, more than a month... It could have been her, I suppose." He raised his hands and his shoulders. "I don't know, okay? You're not going to report us, are you?"

I ignored the question and instead replied, "If you don't mind, Theodore," I said, "we'd like to talk to the members of your staff. You know. Show them the girl's photograph. See if anyone remembers seeing her." I looked around, noting a man working behind the bar and a young woman cleaning tables.

He pushed his glasses up again and said truculently, "Be my guest, but you'll have to do it without me, I'm afraid. I have work to do, so I'll bid you goodbye."

We thanked him and let him know that we'd be in touch, and Hawk gave him his card in case he remembered anything that might be helpful. *Wishful thinking*, I thought.

We spoke to both of his employees, but it turned out to be a fruitless fifteen minutes. Neither of them recalled seeing Indigo. And neither of them had anything helpful to add to what their boss had told us. So we left and stepped out of the dark cavern into the weak November sunshine.

Back outside, with the sun high overhead, we stood for a moment on the sidewalk. I glanced at Hawk through my sunglasses. He picked up on my train of thought immediately.

"The girl? Not Indigo?" he asked, referring to the girl Theodore had mentioned. "Someone else?"

"Carolyn," I said. "I'm going to give her a call later. I have a few more questions for her. For now, let's head for Electric Blue. Then we'll see what Anne and Corbin dug up, if anything."

8

Monday Afternoon 12:55 pm

Electric Blue was, from the outside, a nondescript, red brick building almost as old as Chattanooga itself. The neon lights over the double glass doors were turned off and inconspicuous. If I craned my neck and stood on tiptoe, I could see the Whitlow building, within walking distance, maybe a ten-minute hike away.

The doors were unlocked. Hawk held the left one open for me and we slipped inside, Samson leading. We stopped in the foyer and took in our surroundings, and I have to tell you, I was surprised by how much it appealed to me.

Clubs weren't my thing, but this one... It was dark inside, of course, but tastefully decorated with a long, classic bar with stools. The ceiling was painted entirely black, with several of the constellations picked out with pretty blue lights.

Two women, probably in their late twenties, were

seated at the bar, while a third was behind the bar. All three were laughing together, but they quieted down when they saw us and stared at us through their eyelashes.

"Can I help you?" the one behind the bar called out.

"I'm Captain Kate Gazzara. Chattanooga PD," I replied as we approached the bar. "This is Sergeant Hawkins. We're here to see the manager or, better yet, the owner."

All three women gave Hawk appreciative glances. One flinched when Samson poked her thigh with his nose. She looked down at him and drew her foot up onto the stool's rail. He took the hint, backed away and sat down, looking up at her.

A quick look at their drinks revealed they were sipping hot tea. I found that a little strange. It was, after all, a nightclub we were in. But I weighed my priorities and turned my attention to the woman behind the bar who'd turned her back to us and was picking up the house phone. She pressed a button and spoke quietly into the phone.

She put the phone down, turned again to face us and said politely, "He'll be down for you in a few minutes. You can have a seat if you'd like."

Like Urban One, the layout was largely open, though the ceilings were much higher—close to fifteen feet, so I thought. Hawk strode toward a sitting area on the far side of the big room furnished with a dozen or so black couches and armchairs and settled comfortably into one of the latter. Me? I opted for the couch and perched on the edge, Samson at my feet, not wanting to get too comfortable.

I was flipping through my notes when a slightly nasal and more than slightly annoyed voice asked, "How can I help you?" Samson was already up on all fours.

I looked up to see standing before us what I initially thought was a homeless man. He was wearing baggy, ragged brown pants and a shirt that was buttoned off-center, so one side hung lower than the other. A sprinkling of sparse chest hair showed at the collar, and the hair on his head was dark but thinning. His eyes were small and sharp. They set off a warning inside of me, but Samson seemed okay with him, so I stood and introduced myself and Hawk.

"Rat Nelson," the man said, holding out his hand to me.

I opened my eyes wide in surprise and stared at him. "I'm sorry. What did you say?"

"My name. It's Rat Nelson. I run this place. That's who you wanted, isn't it?"

Fighting the urge to glance at Hawk with a *He has to be kidding, right*? look, I took his hand and shook. His grip was surprisingly firm.

What do I call this guy? Rat? Mr. Rat? Mr. Nelson?

He smiled at me as I repeated the question in my head. "So, how can I help you?" he asked and walked to the armchair next to Hawk's and sat down, sprawling both arms and legs out. There was a tense moment of silence before he asked, "Well?"

Hawk and I took our seats and I forged ahead, wondering what the hell we were getting into.

"Have you seen this young woman?" I asked. "She's... missing," I lied, taking the flyer from my inside pocket and handing it to him.

I watched his face closely as he took it from me, unfolded it, and Rat's eyes moved over the page.

He tisked, then looked at me. "She's missing?" he asked, with just a hint of hoarseness in his voice.

"She is," I lied again, sensing he knew something. "Her father's a prominent surgeon in the city. He reported her missing on Sunday the tenth. It's been two weeks. I need information. Now."

I could feel Hawk's eyes on me. Leaving out the fact that Indigo was actually dead was a gray area, and one I intended to play for as long as I could.

This was my thought process: I figured if the people we spoke to knew that Indigo was dead, they were more likely to get scared and clam up. If they thought she was just missing, they might be more inclined to talk to us. At least, that's what I hoped.

But Rat Nelson wasn't biting.

"She looks vaguely familiar," he said in an off-hand sort of way. "She's probably been in here before, but I'm not down on the floor a lot, so..."

I looked around quickly and spotted a concealed iron staircase leading to an upper level. Then I noticed that the female bartender was watching us. She caught my eye and dropped a glass, her gasp loud in the empty room.

Rat looked at her sharply. "Lara. You okay?"

The woman nodded, keeping her gaze on the counter as she cleaned up the mess. Hawk and I shared a look.

"Do you usually let girls this young into your club?"

Rat ground his teeth before biting out, "No. Of course not. It's twenty-one or older for bar service, eighteen or over for the floor."

"How do you differentiate between the two?" Hawk asked curiously.

"We use stamps, like most clubs. If they can drink, they get a stamp."

My annoyance was cooling. I looked down at Samson. He was lying down facing Nelson, his tongue hanging out, panting gently. He seemed happy enough, which was good enough for me. He's an excellent judge of character, but me? I just couldn't get a good read on Rat. Something about him raised my hackles, but despite that, I just didn't peg him for a murderer. Grimy, sure. But not a killer.

"The thing is, Mr. Nelson," I said, adjusting my belt as I shifted, "Indigo—the girl in the photo—she was seventeen. So if she's been here before, that could put you in a heap of trouble."

His face reddened immediately. Despite his relaxed posture, it was easy to see he was tense as he answered, "If she did, the doorkeep would have checked her ID. You wanna arrest me for something; go ahead. Do it. If not... well, look. I won't deny there are some girls that age that slip through the cracks. And not just here at Electric Blue. Maybe you should be checking in with the other nightclubs, too."

He spit out the suggestion. Hawk leaned forward, elbows on his knees, hands clasped together in front of him.

"We are," he answered. "We've already talked to the guy that runs Urban One."

Rat snorted at that and grinned, "You mean that twat Theo? Lot of good that did you, I'm sure."

"Rat," I said, the name sticking in my craw. "If we find out that Indigo was here the night she went missing, we're going to be back. Do you understand?"

He shrugged. "So if she was reported missing on a Sunday, you're assuming it was Saturday, right?" He shrugged again, then continued, "I'm not saying she wasn't in here that night, and I'm not saying she was. I've seen her several times, but that night? Two weeks ago? Hell, how would I remember? I see so many."

"Those three at the bar," I said, turning my head in their direction. "They all work here?"

"Nah! Well, Lara does. The other two work at Provident. They just come in at lunchtimes, now and then."

"Is it all right if we talk to Lara?" I asked.

"Sure. Knock yourself out, but she doesn't know anything. She works noon to seven, when we're quiet."

"Well," I said, rising to my feet and taking the flyer from him, "it's worth a shot."

The man nodded, his small eyes unfocused as he stared in Hawk's direction. I snuck another look at the bar and saw Lara tinkering with an assortment of lemon slices and cherries. She had that far-away look of someone who was eavesdropping, and my gut told me that she knew something. No one would be that nervous if they weren't involved.

"Like I said, knock yourself out." And with that he turned away and walked back up the stairs.

He was right. All three women looked at the image and all three shook their heads, though Lara did give a funny look and sucked on her bottom lip.

I nodded to her and took the flyer from her, discreetly exchanging it for my card. Our eyes met, and when they did, I knew I didn't have to tell her to reach out. She would, sooner or later, whenever it finally caught up with her, the guilt, the shame, or whatever else it was that was eating away at her.

Back out on the street, Hawk didn't seem overly worried about Rat.

"He's a weird guy, but I think it just comes with the territory." He shrugged, shook his head and changed the subject. "Kids. I dunno."

"What about them?" I asked.

"My oldest went through that rebellious stage. We got lucky though, and she'd call home for a ride. I always picked her up and got the lay of the land. You can't stop them. If you try, it just makes a bad situation worse," he grumbled.

Further down the street, we could see Anne and Corbin walking toward us, the sunlight glinting off of Anne's cropped hair.

"So you don't find it strange?" I asked. "That he obviously knows who Indigo is but didn't budge? And what the hell kind of name is Rat?"

Hawk frowned as he considered what I'd said. "Honestly, no. He's a product of the night, learned the hard way that he needs to keep his mouth shut. Sure, he knows something, but Kate, I really don't think he's involved the way you think he is. As to the name. It's probably something he picked up as a kid and it stuck."

Anne and Corbin had done no better than we had, and they were quick to fill us in. They'd spoken to both owners, and both came up with similar stories. Indigo looked vaguely familiar, but no one really remembered her. She could have been any one of a number of young women who flocked to Wyatt Street on Friday and Saturday nights.

I was deflated.

"What now?" Anne asked as we strolled back to our cars.

"Willis is working on the Honda," I replied. "I need to catch up with him. And the chief said he wants to be there when we talk to Salazar. Tonight."

As if by fate, my cell pinged and I saw a text from Doc.

DNA result confirms the body is that of Indigo Salazar. Also found this.

I stared at the screen. It was a photograph of what looked like the inside of Indigo's wrist, discolored because Doc had been using an ultraviolet light. On the skin, which was badly discolored and disturbingly loose, was the unmistakable image of a stamp in purple ink.

I held the phone out for Hawk, Anne and Corbin to see.

"This look familiar?" I asked.

Anne and Corbin shared a look, but it was Corbin who spoke. "Labyrinth. That's their logo."

9

Monday Afternoon 4 pm

THERE'S NOTHING LIKE A LEAD TO GET ME BUZZING,
and as I drove over to Salazar's house on Ooltewah-Ring-
gold Road, I felt more awake than I had all day.

I glanced at the manilla folder that lay on the
passenger seat, a thin and relatively short dossier on Ivan
Salazar, Indigo's father.

His family had emigrated to the east coast forty-five
years ago when he was ten. Ivan was a smart kid and
skipped two grades, once in middle school and once in
high school. He attended college at age sixteen—a year
younger than his deceased daughter.

My heart ached for him, but I had to keep my guard
up. After all, Ivan Salazar hadn't made it this far without
a reputation. He was known to be tyrannical, methodical,
intelligent and hard to work for. He ran a tight ship at the
hospital, and dozens of fellows had dropped out from

under his watchful gaze. *I guess you have to be that way if you're a pediatric surgeon; there's not much room for error.*

I wasn't intimidated by his reputation or his wealth, though wealth usually equaled hissy fits, and rarely intelligence. Hopefully, Salazar was smart enough to let us do our jobs and track down his daughter's killer.

The chief's car was already parked in the circular drive, and I pulled up behind him, cracked the windows—though the sun was shining, it had turned quite chilly—told Samson to be a good boy, and stepped out onto pearl-white gravel. As I did so, Chief Johnston also stepped out of his car and gifted me with a solemn nod. His uniform was, as always, impeccable; the four stars on his collars glistened in the weak afternoon sunshine.

Rarely did the chief leave his office and, for me, it was a first. I didn't know what to expect from him. He and I didn't always see eye-to-eye, but we'd established early on an understanding between us that this particular situation called for a team effort.

A short, balding man waiting at the top of the stone steps greeted us and held the front door open. He gestured toward the open doors of what I took to be a sitting room.

The loveseat and chairs were all beautifully upholstered in deep navy blue and gold. *Oh dear*, I thought, *do I really have to sit down?* I knew I had Samson's hair all over my backside, so I didn't, and neither did the chief.

It was less than a minute later when a tall man appeared in the doorway.

"Hello," he said tightly but politely.

Ivan Salazar was in his late fifties, a handsome man

with a head of thick, salt-and-pepper hair and an aquiline nose. The chief shook Salazar's hand and introduced me.

"Captain Gazzara is heading the investigation into your daughter's death, but we wanted to talk to you today to discuss the details and see if you could help us in any way."

Salazar nodded but didn't reply. Instead, he stepped past us, sat down in one of the chairs, propped an ankle on his knee, tilted his head and looked both the chief and I over slowly, making us wait in silence before saying, "Please. Sit."

We did as he asked, and I shifted uncomfortably on the edge of my seat, not used to giving up my authority. But I had to play by Johnston's rules, and he wanted me to take a more submissive role. I wasn't so sure it would get us anywhere, judging by the bored expression on Salazar's face.

"I've already been filled in on most of the details," he informed us. "I know my daughter's body was found tied up in the trunk of an abandoned car on Wyatt, and she died as a result of sharp force trauma to her throat. I also know you have no leads."

It was hard to keep the shock off my face, and I almost got whiplash from looking to the chief quickly. He appeared surprised, too.

"Can I ask who gave you that information?" Johnston asked quietly.

Salazar steepled his fingers under his chin. He had long, thin fingers, almost womanly but large. His skin and nails were immaculate: the mark of a surgeon.

"I have contacts in your department," he said flatly.

"Though they didn't help much when I reported my daughter missing two weeks ago."

Again, I shifted my backside on the edge of my chair, eager to pursue the next part of our investigation since Salazar apparently already seemed to know as much as we did, but Johnston held up two fingers, warning me to wait.

"I'm sure you're aware that's against department protocol," he said evenly. "And I'd like the name, or names, of your informants."

"You know better than to ask me that, Chief," Salazar replied, smirking at him.

The chief simply nodded, unwilling to be drawn into an argument, saying instead, "Then I'll apologize on behalf of our Vice department. They dropped the ball, and there's no excuse for that."

Salazar's eyes burned as he looked at the two of us.

"Do you think my daughter would still be alive if you hadn't 'dropped the ball,' as you say?"

This wasn't good. He was coming at us with the calm reasoning of a predator, someone who knew he had the upper hand. Part of me wanted to hope he would cooperate, but I knew we were past that now. Neither Chief Johnston nor I answered his question. There was no point in speculating, but I couldn't tell him that; it would be unprofessional. Instead, I cleared my throat as delicately as I could and readied my pen to take notes.

"Dr. Salazar, what you may not know is that Indigo was in the habit of frequenting the nightclubs on Wyatt. Any comment?"

The doctor's face was suddenly a thundercloud, and for a moment, I thought he would lose his temper. Instead, he said benignly, "My daughter wasn't allowed out, detective."

"It's been confirmed that she did indeed visit several of the nightclubs. So how do you think she got there? Could someone have picked her up? Did she have a driver's license, her own car?"

"I will repeat, my daughter was not allowed out. Not after seven PM," he said carefully. "Not to those nightclubs. Not to the mall. Not... If she was there, as you seem sure she was, I wouldn't know how she got there or who took her. Indigo did not have a license or a car. I wouldn't allow it, not until after she graduated from college."

I frowned and wanted to say something about how ridiculous that was, but I held it back. Carolyn Brown hadn't been kidding when she said Salazar was a strict parent.

"My daughter was a good girl," he continued angrily. "She would never willingly stoop to socialize with those kinds of people. She must have been kidnapped and... murdered."

I sat back in my chair and glanced at the chief. I'd briefed him earlier that afternoon, so he knew that Indigo was known around the clubs on Wyatt Street and had been for at least a year. But he didn't say so to Salazar.

"I'm sorry," I offered, trying to sweeten my tone when what I really wanted to do was bang some sense into his stupid head. "I appreciate what you're saying, of course, but we're trying to build a picture of what happened that night. You say you don't know how Indigo got to Wyatt Street and that she wasn't allowed out. The fact is, she did go out and she did go to Wyatt Street. But let's put that aside for now. Was there anything going on in Indigo's life that you would consider... stressful? A recent breakup, perhaps, or could she have been having a hard time at school?"

Salazar snorted, surprisingly inelegant. "No, of course not. Indigo wasn't allowed to date. And she was a straight-A student. I fully expect her to get into Johns Hopkins."

Oh, no.

The three of us froze for a moment as the realization that he'd used the present tense sank in. It was always hard for the victim's family to internalize the fact that their child was gone, and even for us, it wasn't easy to see them grapple with the sudden change from then to now. Salazar glanced up at me, his annoyance plain on his face, and I saw for the first time that his eyes were rimmed red. So he'd been mourning in his own way, despite the professional shell he'd adopted.

He stood abruptly. Chief Johnston also stood, shooting me another look. I could practically hear him telling me to "Keep it down, Gazzara."

"Until you have more information," Salazar snapped, "I don't think there's any point in us talking further." And with that, he turned on his heel and walked quickly out the door without a backward glance.

"Thomas will show you out," he said over his shoulder. "Don't come here again until you know the name of my daughter's killer."

"I can't believe him," I muttered, leaning my elbow against the chief's car. He motioned for me to get off of it. "You'd think, as the parent, he'd want to help."

The chief shook his head. "It's harder than you think, Kate. You don't have kids of your own. Salazar comes from a different world; this is a terrible blow for him. Privately and in the public eye. His daughter was found on a disreputable street, rotting in the trunk of a car. People are going to have questions, and Salazar doesn't really want to know the answers."

"But we need the answers," I insisted, starting to pace, the gravel crunching under my shoes.

Johnston tapped the roof of his car. "And you'll get them, I'm sure. That's why I put you on this case. Willis told me he'd found something in the car that might help. You can pick up his report first thing tomorrow." He paused before getting into his vehicle. "Don't screw this one up, Captain."

I nodded, then went to my car where Samson was waiting for me. The drive home took less than twenty minutes. And, with Willie's Roadhouse playing in the background, I ran through a quick to-do list in my head:

Get the report from Willis.

Call Carolyn Brown.

Revisit the Labyrinth with Corbin to find out what Indigo was doing there.

Check with Jack to see what he found out at Indigo's school.

Try to get at least five hours of sleep.

The last item on the list was unlikely, but if I could make it happen, maybe tomorrow wouldn't be a total loss.

10

Tuesday Morning 8 am

I WOKE TO MY ALARM BLARING AND SAMMY groaning in grumpiness at the end of the bed. He'd been sleeping on the floor the last couple of weeks, but he'd snuck up onto the bed sometime during the night. So I patted his head, gave him a bleary-eyed, apologetic smile, turned over, picked up the phone and tapped the screen to turn off the alarm.

There were several notifications on the lock screen informing me I had text messages, so I sat up in bed and scrolled through them, absently petting Sam as I read through them, but the one that caught my eye was from the chief.

Salazar is holding a press conference at eight-thirty. Don't be late.

There were others. One from Corbin and another from Tracy Ramirez; they'd heard the announcement, too, and were giving me a heads-up.

I rolled out of bed, took a quick shower, threw on my clothes, grabbed a cup of coffee to go, my Glock and my badge, and then my keys and told Samson, "Come on, big fella. We've got work to do. I'll stop by McDonald's and get you a chicken biscuit."

He snapped his jaws and gave a barely audible woof, but his tail was wagging, so I knew he was happy enough with that.

In less than ten minutes, I was—almost—speeding toward the PD. I glanced at my phone as I drove and saw that Corbin had sent a message asking where I was. I dictated a short reply telling him I was on my way and would be just a few minutes and then pulled into Mickey D's across the road from the PD.

Seven minutes later, we stepped out of the elevator into the situation room, which was oddly empty, but then I saw everyone at the far wall, watching the big-screen TV. Salazar's presser must have begun, so I joined the group, standing at the back, craning to see over Hawk's big shoulders.

On the screen, a reporter, mic in hand, was standing in front of the familiar residence. Ivan Salazar was standing on the top step, looking solemn and professional. He was wearing an immaculate pair of trousers, a light blue button-down shirt that enhanced the silver in his hair, and a doctor's coat, unbuttoned, of course.

I caught the chief's eye. He was standing just a few feet away and didn't look at all happy. I grimaced.

He took a step back and came to join me. "He's really playing this up," he commented dryly once he was at my side.

"He's using his position and reputation to draw attention," I said in a low voice. "But what's he hoping to achieve, Chief?" I was frustrated. I ignored Sammy who nudged my hand. His food bowl and chicken biscuit were in my shoulder bag, but I had a bigger fish to fry. He'd have to wait.

"We're at the home of renowned pediatric surgeon Ivan Salazar. Earlier this week, it was announced that Dr. Salazar's teenage daughter, Indigo, had been found murdered in the business district on Wyatt Street. Salazar has called a press conference today to raise his concerns about the competence of the Chattanooga police and to ask the public for help."

The officers, detectives and admin staff present all began to murmur and shift. Most of them looked displeased with what they'd heard, but I noticed that Janice Toms, one of the front desk administrators, pursed her lips and gave an approving little nod.

The scene on the screen changed. Salazar cleared his throat, indicating he was ready to speak into the microphone someone had handed him. The reporters surged forward to surround the bottom of the steps.

"Thank you all for coming today," he began, his slight accent noticeable. "As you're aware, my daughter, Indigo Marie Salazar, was found dead and mutilated on Sunday morning."

As we watched the reporters vie for a better spot, I muttered, "Mutilated? Way to go, Ivan."

Johnston exhaled heavily through his nose. "A slit throat isn't too far off. But, yes, 'mutilated' will give the wrong impression."

"And gain attention," I added.

Salazar went on to drag our department through the mud for a few minutes, stating that we seemed to be taking our time with the investigation. I kept my mouth shut as everyone around us began to complain. Until I heard my name.

"Captain Catherine Gazzara, in particular, didn't strike me as a woman intent on, or even capable of getting the job done," Salazar said casually, his blue eyes scanning the crowd of reporters.

I felt my hackles rise, my mouth falling open.

"Which is why I'm tripling the reward I initially offered when my daughter first went missing. Anyone with any information should call the tip line my lawyer has set up. If the police department won't take the case seriously and bring my daughter's killer to justice, I, as a parent, will take on that responsibility. I will hunt down the person who murdered my daughter and make sure he's brought to justice, with or without the help of Kate Gazzara and her team."

Saying those last words, Salazar stared into the cameras. My heart was thumping I was so angry. The officers and staff were turning, sending me awkward glances. Salazar, meanwhile, was answering questions from the press, mostly about what his daughter was like.

"Stay calm, Kate," Johnston whispered so only I could hear him.

Samson, still at my side, whining, his ears flattened, could tell I was upset.

Blood rushed to my face. *Who the hell does this guy*

think he is? I thought. *He has no idea what we go through every day trying to solve these cases. Son of a bitch!*

"A tip line," I scoffed. "You know what that means, right?"

"It's a huge problem," Corbin said, appearing out of the crowd. His solemn expression matched the chief's. "That reward he's offering is no joke, and people will call his tip line instead of ours."

Johnston dragged a hand down the side of his face. He looked... pissed, would not be too strong a word.

Late fall wasn't exactly a slow season for the PD. There were plenty of open cases on the books, a tangled mess of shootings, some of them fatal, assaults, drug deal-ing, domestic violence, larceny, you name it, and Salazar, with his tip line, had suddenly become a royal pain in the ass and actually interfered with my investigation. And there was nothing we could do to stop him.

"Have we even gotten anything useful from the line?" Johnston asked finally.

Sgt. Tracy Ramirez, who was in charge of compiling the tips and notifying me of anything that looked promis-ing, shook her head and said, "A lot of people clubbing out on Wyatt Street who can confirm that Indigo was in the area, but nothing hinting at who took her and killed her, or why."

I noted Johnston's expression. He wasn't happy. It never felt good to get behind on a case, and Salazar's press conference didn't put the team—and more specifi-cally, me—in a good light.

The presser ended and the chief turned to me and stared me down, his great mustache twitching.

"What's the plan, Gazzara?" he asked.

I straightened my back and rattled off an update I'd meant to give him, until this bombshell dropped.

"We're still waiting for the surveillance footage, and we're heading back to Labyrinth. Indigo had their stamp on her wrist, so we know she was there the night she was taken. Willis should be around here somewhere and he finished up the car last night. I need to get his report." I glanced at Corbin, silently asking that he do so; he nodded and dipped off to find the CSI. "I also want to talk to Carolyn Brown again and bring in Lara Crump, the bartender from Electric Blue. I think she knows more than she's letting on."

Johnston nodded, but he didn't look any happier. "Keep me informed," he said as he turned and left.

Ramirez gave me a sympathetic look and said, "Cooper and I will get you a list of any relevant tips in a few, okay?"

I asked her to send Anne and Hawk to my office and she left, and then I was alone as the other officers churned around me, heading back to their respective departments and desks.

Sammy whined again, sitting on his haunches.

"Sorry, boy," I murmured, ruffling his ears. Even he couldn't take the edge off. I headed to my office, digging around in my bag to retrieve his food bowl. Sitting behind the desk, I watched him devour every last piece of his chicken biscuit and kibble.

Next, I added the names Lara Crump, Rat Nelson, Oskar Pope and Lewis Massey to the whiteboard and began adding autopsy photos. That done, I stood back and looked at it, dismayed at the lack of anything substantial.

A light knock on the door announced Corbin's arrival. He entered with Mike Willis close behind. "Thought you should hear this for yourself," Corbin said.

Willis looked out of place in my office, his shaved head shining under the fluorescent lights. He was, is, a strange little guy, a CSI wizard, who's been in charge of his department since even before I joined the force. And he's become somewhat eccentric over the years. He's short, overweight, a little on the scruffy side—clean but untidy—a round face with a pair of brown eyes hooded by a set of thick and bushy eyebrows. A man, despite his eccentricity and untidy appearance, who was also, somehow, incredibly organized. And having him visit me in my office with something important enough to report personally lifted my somber attitude, a little.

"We found something in the car," he began, handing me his report. "A joint, or most of one, tossed on the passenger side floor."

I raised my eyebrows. "DNA?"

Willis nodded. "Yes, and a very specific wrapping paper that we're trying to nail down. Chocolate and cherry scented."

I wrinkled my nose. It was something, but I knew it would be tough to track down, but the DNA? Yes! That gave me some hope.

"And there's something else," Willis continued. "It's odd—the car was wiped clean of fingerprints, which isn't unexpected if this is a career criminal. But it's rubbing me wrong. Why wipe the car clean but leave DNA evidence? I'm thinking it may be a plant."

Corbin and I made eye contact, and I knew we were both on the same page with Willis. It didn't make any sense.

"See if you can ID those wrapping papers and the weed, too," I instructed. "The rest of the car was clean? No trace evidence? Hairs, fibers, anything?"

Willis shook his head. "There was nothing in the trunk that didn't belong to the victim."

I exhaled, reliving again the image of the teenage girl in that trunk; the decomposition, the dried blood, the ragged void of her cut throat.

All right, so maybe I couldn't blame Salazar for coming at this thing like a pit bull. But I still had the bitter taste in my mouth at his distrust of me and my team.

"Okay, Mike," I said. "Keep me updated."

Willis nodded and disappeared back into the situation room on his way back to his lab. Corbin lingered.

"You okay?" he asked.

I shrugged, not wanting to let on just how *not* okay I was. I never doubted my skill, but, damn... the day was starting out to be a rough one.

"Listen," I said. "That guy Theodore, at Urban One, mentioned that Oskar Pope and Lewis Massey were frequent visitors. We need to bring them in for quest—"

The phone on my desk trilled, interrupting the thought. I picked it up. "Gazzara."

"Kate, it's me, Hawk."

"I was wondering where you were," I said, remembering that he'd disappeared halfway through the press conference. "Where are you?"

"Oh, you're going to love this, Kate. I'm at the Electric Blue. They found Rat Nelson this morning out back, behind the club. He's dead. His throat cut. You'd better get down here."

"I'm on my way," I said and hung up.

I turned to look at Corbin and said, "Come on. There's been a development. I'll explain on the way. Oh, and don't forget to have someone bring those two security guards in for questioning. I have a feeling they must have known Indigo."

I slapped my thigh and said, "C'mon, Sammy."

11

Tuesday Morning 9:30 am

LESS THAN THIRTY MINUTES LATER, I WAS STANDING in the alley behind Electric Blue looking down at Rat Nelson's body with Doc Sheddon at my side. Rat was a dirty shade of pale. His eyes were open, vacant, and there was a look of shock or anger on his face. The cut across his throat was deep and extended almost from one ear to the other. It was a violent, vicious slash deep enough for me to see glistening white tissue, though whether it was windpipe or tendons, I didn't know. Inwardly, I blanched at the vision I had of what I thought must have happened.

"Body temp is ninety-four-point-seven," Doc said reflectively. "So, time of death would be between five-thirty and seven-thirty this morning, I'd say." Doc sounded chipper. The way he kept patting his paunch made me suspicious that he'd managed to grab breakfast on the way in. Doc was no stranger to mediocre diners, and there were plenty of those around.

So Rat had died early that morning, and I couldn't help but wonder, *How come?* Though I'd only met him once, Rat had struck me as a creature of the night, lurking among the shadows. Out there in the early morning with the sunlight exposing his secrets, his chest hair looked gnarly, his body oddly twisted, and his clothes dated.

"Aside from... the obvious," I began, shoving my hands in my pockets so I didn't fidget in frustration, "what else can you tell me about what happened here?"

A few feet away, Mike Willis grunted, presumably in annoyance. He was trying to work the scene with the body still in it. Not entirely uncommon, but I could tell he wanted to get into the dumpster, and Rat's body was blocking the way.

Doc gave a slight eye roll and told him, "Just a few more minutes, Mike. I can't control the team having to switch out vehicles on the way over."

Doc had come straight from home; it was his day off, and Carol and an intern were on their way with the Center's transport vehicle. Willis huffed but kept his eyes on the asphalt, scouring the cracks and crevices.

"The fatal cut itself was deep," Doc began, the chipper edge back to his voice as he went into lecture mode. "From left to right, indicating a right-handed assailant. It severed both external carotid arteries. He would have bled out quickly. Hence, the obscene amount of blood. It's not a coincidence that your victims were killed the same way. I'd bet my dinner on this being the same murderer." He grinned at me. "Where's the pup, by the way?"

Doc was an odd little man, but I was fond of him.

Somehow, he was always in a good mood, despite dealing with the dead day in and day out. He talked about torture, assault, open wounds, and atrocities that would make most people cringe as if he were relaying last night's football game. And his sense of humor... well, would you believe his personal license plate read DOA and that he had one of those green street markers outside the rear door of the forensic center that read, "Dead End"?

Be that as it may, he was right; the amount of blood soaked into the ground around Rat and draining away under the dumpster was more than I'd seen in a long time. There had been blood in the trunk with Indigo Salazar, but her throat hadn't been cut as deeply.

"Samson? I left him in the car," I said. "Anything else you want to tell me?"

"The difference here," Doc said, his brows furrowing in a frown, "is that there are also several stab wounds to the body, which your first victim didn't have." He struggled to crouch down a bit, gesturing toward Rat's chest and flank. Rat had been wearing a dark shirt, and it obscured the oozing wounds.

I crouched down beside the body and, now that I knew what to look for, I could see two thin wounds to his right pectoral. The stab wounds on his flank were more obvious, the shirt and flesh torn.

"How many?" I asked.

Doc tipped his head, made a face and said, "Hard to tell until we have him on the table and washed, but from what I can see, at least five."

"I'd say whoever did this was kinda pissed," I mused.

"Very angry, yes. Mr. Nelson," he said, looking down

at the body, "you must have really ticked off whoever did this to you." He glanced at me and said, "I'd say it was personal, though there was little point to the stab wounds. His throat was slit first, and judging by the amount of blood around the throat area and the minimal amount around the stab wounds, he must have been close to death when they were inflicted."

"Well, at least it must have been relatively quick," I said. Why did I suddenly feel bad for Rat Nelson? My brief interaction with him hadn't shown him to be a hallmark of generosity or compassion. No, he'd been uptight, secretive, and grimy.

Even so, he didn't deserve to die the way he did. And I couldn't help the niggling feeling that Rat had been murdered because he was doing something... good.

I looked over my shoulder and spotted Corbin directing several of the officers to hold down the area until Willis and his team were done. The younger CSIs, training under Willis, had arrived with grim expressions on their faces.

"Hey, Mike," I called to him. "I need photos ASAP, please." He gave me a look that would have caused Samson to back away. Me? I just grinned at him.

I thanked Doc, asked him when he intended to do the post, told him I'd have someone there to observe, and joined Corbin and filled him in on the major details. Then I thought for a moment and said, "I think we need to talk to Lara Crump. She works here."

"She called it in," he replied. "We're holding her, two members of the kitchen staff, and a couple of cleaners until we can clear them. Ramirez and Cooper are inside, but I'm not sure who they've talked to yet."

We headed back inside, and again I was struck by the aesthetic of Electric Blue. But my eyes zoned in on Lara, seated in the same area Hawk and I had been when we'd talked to Rat. I waved and made my way over to her.

"Hello, Lara," I began and sat down beside her. "You may remember me. I'm Captain Kate Gazzara, and this is my partner, Sergeant Corbin Russell. I'm sorry about the timing, but I need to ask you some questions."

She sniffed, looked at me and nodded, her cheeks tear-stained, a tissue crumpled in her hand. Corbin's face softened as he sat across from her. It was typical of him— and not always a good thing. I was well aware that I could come across as a little harsh, but in most cases, that's what it took to get the job done. Corbin's approach was more "softly, softly catchee monkey," and it could be annoying. At least, I sometimes found it so. That aside, he's a good cop and I was happy enough to have him for a partner.

"So, Lara," I began as Corbin surreptitiously took out his notebook. "I understand that it was you who called it in this morning. Is that correct?"

Lara nodded again, unable to speak as fresh tears streamed down her cheeks. She was a pretty woman, and I couldn't help glancing at Corbin, wondering if he'd noticed.

"Were you also the one who found him?" I asked gently, leaning forward to watch her expression. It was impossible to forget my last interaction with Lara. Remembering the feeling that she knew something more about Indigo Salazar and what had happened to her than she was letting on. I wanted to trust Lara the way that Corbin so easily trusted the people we interviewed, but... something was stopping me.

"I did," Lara choked out, swiping at her face. "He's been training me on doing the accounting and payroll, so I can move to an administrative role here. We do that in the mornings and then I come back at around two to set up for the night."

"Okay. So the two of you were here working on accounting this morning, and...? Then what happened? Did Rat leave at some point? Did you hear something? What?"

She shook her head. "We weren't working on the books, not then. We hadn't started... See, I got here around seven, maybe a little after. Rat's usually here before me, but he wasn't up in the office or down here." Her eyes glanced up to the second story, where I assumed Rat's office was.

I asked her to give me a minute, then retrieved my phone from my jacket pocket and texted Willis to let him know that both the office and the club itself would need to be processed next. Then texted Cooper to have the front entrance taped and to make sure he didn't let anyone up there.

"I'm sorry for that, Lara," I said. "What happened next? How and when did you find him?"

Her eyes glistened, but there were no tears. Instead, she heaved a huge sigh, began to tear at the tissue with her fingernails and said, "It was... maybe... seven forty-five? I noticed the back door to the alley was open, but I didn't think anything of it. Not at first. Sometimes the cleaning crew comes in that way if Rat isn't here yet, so I went out to see if they were here and ask if they'd seen him. But instead I found..."

She choked on her words, unable to finish, bringing a hand to her mouth. Corbin and I were all too aware of what she'd found.

Corbin quickly confirmed that she hadn't touched anything, and she explained that the 911 operator had asked her to check for a pulse, but she hadn't. "I just couldn't," she said, her voice breaking on the words. "There was so much blood... It was obvious that he was gone." The tears were streaming down her cheeks. "He wasn't a bad man," she said, wiping at her tears. "He didn't deserve..."

Rat Nelson couldn't have been all bad if his staff loved him as much as Lara apparently did. It was obvious that Lara, as well as the other members of the staff Ramirez and Cooper had corralled in another nearby seating area, were distraught and upset. I figured I must have read the man wrong, which didn't happen often, but then, I wasn't infallible.

"Lara, this is important: did you notice anything about Rat the last few days? Did he seem worried about anything? Did you see him arguing with anybody?"

She immediately shook her head but then sucked on her bottom lip, half closed her eyes and frowned. "He did get a text last night just as we were closing up. I think it upset him, but he didn't talk about it."

"Ask Willis if they found his phone," I said to Corbin. He nodded, stood up and left.

I took a deep breath and turned to focus my attention

on Lara. It was time to ask the questions I really wanted answers to.

"Lara, I want to talk to you about Indigo. Did you, or Rat, or anyone else here, know Indigo?"

I maintained eye contact with her, and though she tried to break it, I could see her walls crumbling. Was I about to get an answer that might break the case wide open? Probably not, but I was hoping we'd get something we could work with. She hesitated for a moment, and then I got lucky. She broke.

"Indigo... Yes, we know her. Knew her," she corrected herself, closing her eyes tightly. "We all thought we might get in trouble since she was underage, so... but, yeah. Indigo came here pretty regularly. Maybe two or three times a week?"

"Nights?"

She nodded.

"Lara, I need you to be honest with me. Was Rat involved with her? Was she drinking, or—"

Lara cut me off, shaking her head vigorously. "No! Not at all. No, Indigo... Sure, she snuck in a few times about a year ago and security caught her. She didn't have a good fake, so it was obvious she was too young to be in here." She sighed with a faraway look in her eyes.

"But Rat was a good guy," she continued, "and he could tell that she was going to get herself in trouble if she wasn't careful." Her voice broke again, and I wondered what she was thinking.

"Anyway, she'd come in the back way and Rat let her stay here, usually up in the office or the break room. She wasn't allowed on the floor, ever. Usually, she'd just do homework. She always had so much homework! But she was a smart kid. Just a few weeks ago she was telling me about the colleges she was looking at."

I leaned forward, trying to figure out how this all fit together. "So you all knew Indigo and let her hang out here, but why? Why let an underaged teen in if it could result in the club being shut down?"

Lara shrugged. "Rat could be a little rough around the edges, but he had a good heart. He grew up in foster care so he knew how hard it could be at home. He knew her dad was a tyrant." She shrugged, then continued, "I think he saw something in Indigo and wanted to protect her. Even here, she was always trying to push the envelope. We all did what we could to keep her on track and encourage her."

My heart softened a bit more toward Rat Nelson and the loss of a man like that. But something was bothering me.

"You said he 'knew how hard it could get at home.' But Indigo wasn't a foster kid; she had a father and, from what we can tell, a stable home. So why would Rat feel the need to protect her, and give her space here?"

Lara scoffed. "Yeah, she had a home, but... from what she told us, her dad was insanely strict. Did you know she doesn't, I mean didn't, even have any friends? He wouldn't even let her have a phone." She seemed disgusted by the idea and rambled on, "A teenage girl! Not allowed to hang out with anyone her age. There was so much pressure on her to do better, get scholarships, and go to the best college, so of course she was going to escape at some point. She just happened to end up here.

Like Rat told you when you talked to him, our competitors... they're not great."

A snippet of memory replayed Rat's words from that day: *I think you'll find that here and there some girls that age slip through the cracks... Maybe you should be checking in with the other nightclubs.*

Frustration made my jaw grind as I tried to make the leap. What had Rat been getting at? We'd talked to the other clubs on Wyatt. We were checking in with Labyrinth again later today; but like Rat had said, girls slipped through the cracks. So the stamp on Indigo's hand that gave away her entrance at Labyrinth wasn't surprising. I needed more.

"How did she get here?" I asked. "More to the point, how did she get home?"

"Oh, she was smart. She'd get an Uber to bring her. Rat took her home and dropped her off just around the corner from her house. Then he'd watch to make sure she got in all right. She'd climb in through the mud room window."

"But how did her father not catch her?" I asked.

"I told you. She was smart. She'd get out when he was at the hospital."

"The text he got last night," I said, "you have no idea who it could have been from?"

Lara shook her head, but I saw the slightest hesitation and waited her out.

Eventually, she broke.

She heaved a sigh and said, "Okay, so I asked him, but he wouldn't tell me anything. He actually yelled at me, something he never did, and told me to keep my nose out, that the guy was dangerous."

"Guy," I repeated, puzzled. "You're sure he said it was a guy who texted him?"

She hesitated again, then said, "That's exactly what he said, 'this guy's dangerous.'"

I could see she was getting antsy, tired, upset. I thought I'd gotten from her all I was going to, but then, it came spilling out, just as her tears had earlier.

"Indigo was seeing someone," she said, looking down at the shredded tissue. "She wouldn't tell us who it was, but Rat must have figured it out and confronted him for some reason. I think that's what the texts were about. That's all I know... Can I go home now?" And she gave me one of the most pitiful looks I think I've ever seen.

I nodded. "Thank you, Lara. You've been a great help and I really appreciate it."

I gave her my card, again, and told her to call me if she remembered anything else. Then I went looking for Corbin.

12

Tuesday Afternoon 12 pm

"Anybody seen Sammy?" I asked Cooper, Ramirez and Anne, craning my neck to see out into the situation room. I'd brought the big guy into the office with me, knowing he'd help me decompress as we caught up on the details and what we had so far on the Indigo Salazar case.

But Samson had other ideas; he'd hung out in my office for about twenty minutes before huffing, getting off of his dog bed and wandering out into the situation room to find some affection.

"There, I think?" Anne said, pointing toward a small gathering of officers and staff near the coffee pot. I couldn't see Sammy but figured he'd be somewhere in the middle of the crowd, lazily wagging his tail and giving everyone that big goofy smile.

Shaking my head, I turned my focus back to the whiteboard.

"Anyone heard back from the team running the car's VIN number?"

Cooper cleared his throat. "We should have that info done today. They busted a parts ring yesterday, so that got priority, unfortunately."

I'd heard about that bust; it was a big one and had tied up a lot of resources. I'd thought about going to the chief to see if I could get my request expedited, but decided not to. I really didn't need to aggravate him further, especially as my case was dragging. But that was before my interview with Lara Crump. Now, I figured I had something positive to tell him.

I was just running through that interview in my head when there was a tap on the door. It opened and Corbin ducked into the office.

"Captain, we've got a problem—" he began, but before he could explain further, I heard a loud commotion out in the situation room. Through the panes of glass, we watched as Ivan Salazar stormed across the room, shouting angrily at two officers who tried to tell him he couldn't just barge in.

"...deserve an explanation!" he shouted.

I caught the tail end of his rant and sighed, pushed myself up and out of my chair, opened the door wide, took several steps and stood there, feet apart with my hands on my hips.

Samson was trotting along the far wall, his dark eyes on me. He reached me just as I started toward Salazar and I let my fingers ruffle his scruff. I took a deep breath and set my jaw. I was not going to let this guy get the better of me... again.

"Can I help you, Mr. Salazar?"

Ivan whipped around to face me, his eyes stormy.

"There you are," he snapped. Actually, it was more of a bark. He was clearly a man used to being obeyed, and I couldn't imagine what working under him must be like. But I was on my own turf this time, and while I fought back a scowl, Sammy emitted a low growl from deep in his chest.

"I suggest you might want to watch your tone," I warned the towering man. "Samson doesn't take kindly to aggression, of any sort."

Salazar's mouth snapped shut as he stared down at him. He was showing his teeth and not because he was smiling; it was a threat.

"Is that thing allowed in here?"

"Samson is a part of the team," Ramirez said, coming up behind me. Cooper and his large body right behind her, Corbin too, though he usually tended to hang back and observe.

Salazar's jaw worked, but he didn't offer any accusations or demands.

"Why don't you come to my office?" I offered, turning on my heel. "We can talk there."

In the reflection of the TV screen, I saw Ivan Salazar scoot warily past Samson, and I bit back a smile. The big dog trotted just behind the man, his nose low to the ground.

Was I surprised that Ivan Salazar didn't like dogs? Not in the least, and that told me all I needed to know about the man. And Samson backed up my suspicions. It was easy to see he didn't trust him.

"Give me a minute, guys," I said, then turned and walked back into my office, followed by Salazar with Samson on his heels. He went to his bed and sat down, his eyes never leaving Salazar, not for a second.

Me? I closed the door, then offered Salazar a seat at the table and sat down opposite him.

Salazar continued to eye Samson nervously. Out in the situation room, Cooper and Ramirez each gave me a small nod through the window to let me know they'd stick around.

I wasn't sure where Corbin was, or Anne, but she rarely disappeared without a good reason, so I wasn't bothered.

"Before we start," I said, linking my hands together on the tabletop, "I'd like to remind you that any disrespectful behavior will be taken care of accordingly. I have no problem transferring this interview to an interrogation room if you can't conduct yourself in a proper and professional manner."

Ivan Salazar's eyes were shooting daggers at me, but he managed to keep his thoughts to himself. Instead, he came right out with his reason for being at the PD: "That dirtbag I saw on the news this morning, the one running a club. Does he have anything to do with my daughter's death?"

Ah, yes; despite his busy surgery schedule, he'd somehow found time to watch the news that morning. The one morning they showed footage of Rat Nelson's crumpled body, his slit throat barely visible before it cut out.

More often than not, the media could be a useful tool

for us, but in this particular case it was being used against us. First, Salazar's press conference, and now this; Nelson hadn't deserved to have his death exposed that way, raw and uncensored. I promised myself I'd make it a point to talk to our legal department about that particular media outlet.

Rat Nelson didn't have any family, that we could find. He was a lone wolf, and maybe, partly because I'd misjudged him, I felt a certain responsibility to protect him.

"Yes," I said honestly, knowing it was pointless to shade the truth. Any fool could see the connections between the cases, the bodies discovered only days apart, with the same cause of death. "We think so, Mr. Salazar, but I'm afraid I can't discuss an ongoing investigation."

Yes, we now had some leads, and yes, we knew where Indigo was the night of her death. And I intended to go to Labyrinth myself that night to do whatever it took to find more answers, but I wasn't going to tell him any of that.

There was a tense moment of silence between us as Salazar considered my words. He didn't intimidate me, far from it. I stared at him, thinking to myself it was Indigo who mattered. She was the victim. Not him. She was the one who demanded justice.

"My daughter was a good girl," Salazar finally said, his voice breaking at the last moment.

Samson, satisfied he was no threat, lay down and lowered his head between his paws, his eyes flitting this way and that.

"You need to know, Captain Gazzara, that... yes, I was strict. I had to be, but I only wanted the best for her...

Indigo was a good girl," he repeated. "She'd never do anything to put herself in jeopardy like this. Whoever did this to her was a sick, sick person, and I need you to find him."

His conviction found strength as he spoke, and I found myself nodding, feeling that finally we might be on the same page. Well... maybe. For the most part... because while I did believe that Indigo was a good kid, and too young and naïve to consciously take part in anything that would get her killed... Well, that was just it; she was young and naïve.

Unfortunately, that wasn't uncommon when it came to teenage deaths. Most were caused by a moment of poor decision. Just think of all the car accidents, currently the number one cause of teen fatalities. All it took was one quick text, one phone call, one underaged beer too many, and lives were ended and for no good reason. It makes my heart ache just to think of it.

So while I could understand where Salazar was coming from—let's face it, every parent believes their child is perfect—I knew that all it would have taken was one split second for Indigo to make that one bad decision that ended her life and put her in the trunk of that car.

I was angry at her killer. I was angry at the VICE department for dropping the ball on her missing person's report, and I was angry at the world that something like this could happen to a seventeen-year-old girl. But mostly, I was angry at myself because I was beginning to feel that Indigo's killer was slipping through my fingers.

"Mr. Salazar," I said quietly. "I never make promises I can't keep, but what I can do is assure you that I will do my best to hunt down Indigo's killer and bring him to justice. But I need you to trust me and my team to do our job."

With a deep sigh, Ivan Salazar suddenly looked like he'd aged ten years. He stood up and nodded. "Thank you... Captain. I... apologize for... my actions."

So I lied and told him he had nothing to apologize for, that I understood. But, yeah, he'd been a real jerk and had probably hurt my case more than he'd helped it. I stood up, then asked him for access to his tip line, after which a gesture brought Ramirez to my door. She escorted Ivan Salazar across the situation room to the elevators.

I looked at Sammy. "Got a little iffy for a second there, huh, boy?"

He snapped his jaws, tilted his head and stared up at me.

But the moment of peace and quiet didn't last long. Anne knocked on the doorframe and stepped inside, her face grim.

"I just heard back about the Honda," she said. "They traced the VIN to a Victor Franklin, now deceased. He passed about seven months ago. His son reported the car stolen a week later. It was taken right off the front driveway while they were clearing out the house. That was in Macon, Georgia."

"Any security footage on the person who stole it? Ring cameras, CCTV, traffic cameras?"

"No, nothing." Anne shrugged. "They checked when it was reported, but all they found was a short section of footage from a doorbell. The driver was wearing a hoodie, so..."

"Damn," I muttered, leaning back in my chair. "Another dead end."

"The owner's son said we can scrap the car; he'll take the loss. So there's no need to return it. Everything okay here, Kate? I heard Salazar stirred things up a bit."

"Yeah, turned out okay. He's upset, and no wonder. He saw Rat Nelson on the news and, unless you knew the guy, it's easy enough to make the leap that Indigo might've been involved in something unsavory."

Anne shook her head, frowned, and said, "Yeah, I get it. If either of my boys were ever in that kind of situation —God forbid... Kate, it's hard for a parent to come to terms with the fact that their kids are capable of making mistakes. Something as simple as being in the wrong place at the wrong time."

I made a face and said, "I know, but Indigo frequented Electric Blue by choice. And we know, at least we think we know, she was visiting the other clubs regularly enough that Rat provided her with a safe space to hang out. Salazar just can't accept that his daughter had another life he didn't know about."

The look Anne gave me wasn't a pleasant one. "Maybe someday you'll get it, Kate," she said before excusing herself.

Anne was one of my closest friends, and while I knew she meant well, it was still a stark reminder of where I was in my life. I was forty-one years old, without a love life. Did I even want kids? It was a question I rarely considered, and one to which I had no answer.

Besides, I had Sammy now to keep me company.

Maybe not exactly the body I wanted in my bed, but he'd keep my feet warm when the cold nights set in.

Pushing intrusive and worrying thoughts from my head, I stood and decided that it was time to check in with Jack North. We had found Rat's cell phone, and we had his computer. But what I wanted to know was who he'd been texting when he warned Lara to stay out of it.

I found Jack in the IT room messing with the exact item I needed to talk to him about. Sammy lumbered up to Jack and happily laid his head in his lap.

Like most men, Jack was slightly shorter than me. Not a stunner by any means but better than average looking and, overall, a decent guy. Crazy as it sounds, he was dating a single mom he met while working a case. He was good at his job—sharp and better at computers and tech than anyone else on the floor. I was happy to have him on my team, especially on this case.

He had Rat's cell phone, a beat-up old android, plugged into a laptop. I had no idea what the codes and numbers running on the screen meant, but Jack did, and it apparently wasn't good. He looked at me with a grim face.

"Well, Miss Lara was right about the content of the messages, at least." Jack handed me a sheaf of papers, about five pages, detailing the texts. He'd highlighted the conversations between Rat and the person of interest. A quick glance told me that Lara had been right in her assumption that Rat had been talking to Indigo's beau.

The responses to Rat's accusations were masculine, aggressive.

Rat: if I find out you had anything to do with her death, I will hunt you down.

Anonymous: I'll make it easy for you Nelson. I had everything to do with it.

Rat: you won't have long then. Between me and the PD, one of us will track you down and you'll regret the day you ever set foot in my club.

Anonymous: Whatever happens, it was worth it just to get a taste of her.

Rat: I'm going to kill you the moment I lay eyes on you.

Anonymous: If I don't get you first.

Rat's texts were clunky, full of anger and boiling rage, and I felt myself responding to them with just as much anger. The suspect had given himself up, unless confessing to a crime he didn't commit was some weird kind of brag.

"What are your first thoughts on this?" I asked, still processing.

Jack stroked Sammy's head gently, absently. "I've looked through his history several times, but Rat never uses the other person's name so we're out of luck there. If you read from the very first text, it seems like they're continuing a conversation that I'm assuming started in person, since there's no other text chain."

"The number, it traces back to...?"

Jack grimaced. "No one. They used an app. Not Rat, obviously, but whoever was doing the texting."

"Okay," I said slowly, taking a seat in the dim room. "What kind of app, exactly? Is it traceable?"

With a sigh, Jack explained, "No. Not yet, anyway. The app they're using isn't uncommon. There are quite a few of them, actually, that generate false numbers and let you text people."

"Wait, I've heard of this. Didn't an app like that feature pretty big in a recent case?"

He nodded, turning away from the laptop. "Yup. I know which one you're thinking of. A woman kept harassing her ex and the girls he was dating. Eventually ended up shooting one of them and killed another."

"Exactly. So they were able to figure out she was the one sending messages from the app. What's the hold up here?"

"Well, this is a much newer app. It only came out a few months ago and the company isn't US based. They don't seem overly concerned with consequences, either. I'm betting if the legal team reaches out to them, they'll ignore us or won't budge on giving up whoever sent these messages."

I sank back into the chair, frustrated. "So what are our options?"

Jack tipped his head back and forth. "I can try and dig in behind the scenes. Get into their software from this end, see if I can trace it back to a number. But it's going to take time," he said apologetically, giving me a sad smile.

"We don't have much of a choice, do we?" I said. Both Jack and Samson gazed at me, silhouetted by the light from the laptop's screen.

13

Tuesday Evening 5 pm

A FEW HOURS LATER, AFTER I'D DROPPED SAMSON
off at home and fed him, Corbin and I were at the
Forensic Center, side by side opposite Doc at the autopsy
table, gazing down on Rat's naked body. Doc had done an
amazing job cleaning him up and there was an odd sort of
peace on his face now that he was at rest.

"My initial guess was off," Doc told us, pushing his
half-glasses up his nose. "There are twelve stab wounds
in all, made by what appears to be a kitchen knife. Willis
and his team confirmed that there was a knife missing
from the kitchen. It's located at the rear and just inside
and to the right of the exit."

"That means the perp must have been in the kitchen,
then?" Corbin said.

Doc looked up at him over the top of his half-glasses,
gave him a small nod, and replied, "Yes, but we can't
know for sure. Not until we find the knife, but the stab

wounds are deep and, as you can see, are about two inches at the widest point, which suggests a larger blade."

Corbin lifted two fingers in acknowledgment before asking, "But he died from the wound to the throat, correct?"

"Yes. Absolutely. The wound is, as I mentioned at the scene, from left to right, indicating a right-handed assailant and is similar to the one that killed Indigo. I compared my notes on her wound and believe both wounds were inflicted by the same person. They both would have bled out in moments. As to the stab wounds... deep, angry. Whoever did this to him had some issues."

"Huh," I muttered, "that's putting it mildly."

"I'm sorry?" Doc said, leaning forward across the body.

"Nothing. I was just making an observation. Time of death?"

"Between six and seven."

"Well," I said, "that narrows it down. Anything else we should know? Anything under his fingernails, defensive wounds?"

"Nothing under his nails, no. There's a bruise to the left side of his face, again indicating a right-handed assailant. But no defensive wound to the arms or hands, which again suggests the stab wounds were inflicted after his throat was slashed. Other than that... there's not much more I can tell you."

I nodded, stared at the gaping void in Rat's throat, heaved a deep breath, shook my head and said, "I'm trying to picture what must have happened, and I can't. We know the attack must have taken place outside by the dumpster, and we know the weapon must have been taken from the kitchen. That means the killer must have, at some time, been inside. Did Rat let him in? Or what? And how did they end up outside? Not that it really matters, I suppose."

"Maybe Rat left the back door unlocked... and the killer snuck in, grabbed the knife and hid and waited until Rat took something out to the dumpster," Corbin said.

"I don't think so," I said, shaking my head. "Doc, could the wounds have been made by... say, a hunting knife?"

"Yes... perhaps a skinning knife. In fact, that would make perfect sense. The wounds were made by a wide, thin, exceedingly sharp blade."

"But what about the missing kitchen knife?" Corbin asked.

"That could have gone missing anytime," I said. "But let's say the killer brought the knife with him and he caught Rat taking something out to the dumpster. That makes a lot more sense. Maybe they argued, and the killer punched him hard enough to render him defenseless. That would account for the bruise, right, Doc?"

Doc nodded thoughtfully but said nothing.

"Oh well," I said. "As I said, it doesn't really matter, and it's all conjecture anyway." I checked the time and said, "Gotta go, Doc. Thanks."

We were in Corbin's car on our way back to the PD when my phone dinged. I glanced down and read the text from Anne, confirming that she and Hawk had Oskar

Pope in one interview room and Lewis Massey in another.

I'll be there in five, I texted back, then turned to Corbin and said, "It's already after six. You can drop me off at the front door and go home, but would you mind stopping off at my place and checking in on Samson for me? I'm not sure how long I'll be, and he's probably going a little stir-crazy by now."

"No problem, Captain," Corbin said, pulling up in front of the entrance. "Let me know how the interviews go."

I RODE THE ELEVATOR UP TO THE SITUATION ROOM and checked in. Hawk and Anne were in an interview with Lewis Massey. I stepped into the observation room and settled down to watch.

Massey was Caucasian, tall and lean, with sandy blond, close-cropped hair. He was lounging in the chair, his legs outstretched, and he had one of those I-couldn't-give-a-shit smirks on his lips. I could tell that it was rubbing Anne the wrong way; her lips were tight, her brow furrowed, and her eyes narrowed. She was annoyed.

"Let me repeat myself," Anne said in a tone that made me wince. I could tell she was quickly losing her patience and, with two teen boys at home, that wasn't easy. But Lewis seemed to be doing the job. "You were seen at Urban One with a young girl. You and Oskar Pope. Who was she?"

Lewis shifted in his seat but didn't seem particularly

bothered by Anne's intense gaze. "Let *me* repeat *myself*," he responded sarcastically. "If you've already spoken to Oskar, then he's told you who the girl is, unless... he has a reason not to. I think, at this point, I should ask for a lawyer."

Hawk sat back with a sigh. Anne stood up and walked out of the room, obviously beyond done with his attitude. I looked at the timer on the recorder. Apparently, they'd been having this circular conversation for almost ten minutes. Was it the first time Lewis had brought up a lawyer? I didn't know, and the request didn't necessarily make him guilty; neither did his attitude.

Anne knocked on the observation room door and stepped inside.

"Can you believe this jerk?" she asked, nodding to the screen.

I smiled and nodded, then asked, "How did it go with Pope? Did he tell you who the girl was?"

"Yeah. He confirmed it was Indigo they were with that night. He says Carolyn had been with them earlier in the night, but she had a five-AM shift and had headed out early."

She sat down next to me, her expression changing from one of annoyance to one of contemplation. "He also said that the 'vibe' was off between the three of them. He said they didn't know each other well, but Pope felt like something was definitely off. He didn't know what, but he said they all left together and that he and Massey walked Indigo back to Electric Blue, then called her an Uber."

That lined up with what we'd seen on the footage, and we knew she didn't have a phone. So why did it feel like we were missing something important?

"So, what d'you think?" I asked. "Did either one—or both of them—do it?"

She thought for a few seconds, looked at me and said, "Who the hell knows? Pope? I doubt it, not by himself, anyway. Massey? He's an arrogant son of a bitch... Yeah, I think he has it in him. But proving it is another story."

I nodded and stood up, deciding that I needed to see Carolyn again. The last time I'd spoken to her, over the phone, hadn't revealed much more than our initial conversation. But now that we had more information, I decided it was time to talk to her again, face-to-face.

"Let him go," I said, nodding at the screen. "We can always bring him back in if we need to. I'll be in my office if you need me."

I was halfway down the hall when my phone rang. Still walking toward the elevators, I took it from my jacket pocket and glanced at the screen. It was Mike Willis.

"Captain, I just sent you a video of the alley where Rat Nelson was killed. Do you have a minute to take a look at it?"

Frowning, I replied, "Didn't we already comb through that footage?"

"Yes. But not well enough, apparently."

Telling him I'd get right back to him, I hung up and pulled up my email on my phone. The secure attachment opened and I read Willis' short note: Bottom right, at 3:56.

The entire clip was just over four minutes long, taken from a security camera across the alley. I'd already seen it before, watched it several times, and had dismissed it as unhelpful. The camera had recorded someone, possibly a suspect. Unfortunately, whoever it was on the footage was unrecognizable.

I stopped walking, hit play, and squinted hard.

It was the same scene I'd seen over and over. The camera was located across the alley, screen right with a full view of the dumpster. Rat's body lay partially hidden by the dumpster. The suspect, if that's what he was, was hooded and wearing a gaiter up over his nose, and could be seen bending over the body. The recording had missed the attack entirely as it must have been hidden by the dumpster. There was no sign of a knife, either on the floor or in the suspect's hands, so the analysts had assumed that he must have put it away before stepping into the shot. He moved around a bit, tilting his head this way and that to see if anyone was coming down the alley, then he straightened up, turned and walked quickly away, head down, hands in the pockets of his hoodie.

What am I supposed to be looking for? I wondered. Then I remembered Willis' directions and I played it again, this time paying special attention to the bottom right.

At minute 3:56 the suspect flicked something toward the dumpster.

Closing out the email, I dialed Willis.

"Please tell me you had the team keep the contents of the dumpster."

"Of course I did, Kate," Willis replied, sounding

slightly offended. "We're still going through it, but guess what we found only twenty minutes ago?"

I waited for him to tell me.

"A joint, wrapped in the same chocolate cherry papers we found in the Honda."

I caught my breath. Thinking DNA. *If we can get a match...* But then., as I well knew, in and of itself, DNA rarely helps us find a killer. Only when we have a viable suspect does it help. And then it helps convict said suspect. Still, it was something.

"Good," I said. "Let me know as soon as you get the DNA results back."

By then I was in the elevator and on my way up to the situation room.

14

Tuesday Night 8:30 pm

I<small>T WAS ALMOST SEVEN WHEN</small> I <small>LEFT THE</small> department that evening and went home to feed Samson, shower and change clothes.

Samson seemed a little peeved at being left home alone again, but he perked up after I'd taken him out for a short walk and given him a treat. I left him lying flat out on the couch watching Perry Mason.

Corbin and I reunited on Wyatt, just a block away from the parking garage at the Whitlow building. I shifted from one foot to the other as he approached, somewhat embarrassed by the way he was looking at me. "You and Sammy do okay?" I asked.

He nodded, his round face looking pale under the street lights. "All good. I took him out. We walked, played tug for a while, then I left him on the couch. You clean up nice, Captain."

The compliment was sincere but evenly said.

Corbin's eyes wended their way methodically down my body—the same way he worked a crime scene. He took in the short, navy-blue dress and the snappy heels that I'd had to dig out from the back of my closet.

I imagined him reading off a report to the team based on my appearance: *41-year-old woman, in great shape due to her career choice, occasionally lonely, often frustrated, slightly desperate, with split ends due to a lack of self-care.*

I tried to keep a bitter smile off my face as he reached me.

"Not too bad yourself," I commented, surprised that he had any casual clothes. Neither of us were spring chickens, and we'd probably stick out in the young clubbing crowd, but I didn't think we read as cops. It was good enough.

"Where do you want to start?" he asked, his hands shoved deep into the pockets of his jeans. Well-kept boots gleamed beneath the hems. Corbin wasn't my type, but I could see the appeal.

"Carolyn agreed to meet us at Electric Blue, so we should start there. It'll give Ramirez and Cooper time to get here, anyway, and then we can all head to Labyrinth."

We started the short walk toward the nightclub, lit up in various shades of blue. It had been cleared by Mike and his team earlier that afternoon, and the owners, mercenary to the core, had seen fit to open it back up immediately.

Me? I was in work mode, but still impressed with the turnout. A lone security guard stood out front, keeping an eye and an ear out for rowdiness. He was maybe a decade younger than I was and gave me a questioning glance when I held out my license. Probably wondering what a woman my age was doing out this way when there were plenty of wine bars around.

Corbin he gave a once over and didn't seem too thrilled about letting in, but we both stepped through the door and into the throbbing club.

It was as beautiful as I'd assumed it would be the first day I saw the ceiling, lit up with constellations. The bar was backlit a dark blue, and behind it, I saw Lara, another woman and a man chatting up customers, darting around to reach whoever held up cash.

My eyes scanned the crowd, but it was Corbin who spotted Carolyn and nudged me. She was sitting at a high table, sipping a tall glass of something purple-red.

"Hi, Carolyn," I greeted as Corbin pulled two other seats over. The young woman had let her hair down and her eyes were painted with perfect cat eyeliner. But she looked slightly distrusting. When we'd spoken earlier, I hadn't told her exactly what we wanted to talk about. Bringing her down to the station, I was sure, would've only scared her, and I needed her to talk.

She greeted us with a murmur, lips wrapping around her straw again as she took a healthy sip. And I thought that if it was alcohol, maybe it would loosen her up a little.

"Thank you for agreeing to meet us," Corbin said softly. She scanned him over the top of her straw through half-closed eyes before gifting him with a tiny smile.

Hmm. Maybe I should let Corbin stay at Electric Blue and keep Carolyn company while I head to Labyrinth...

"Carolyn, I know the last few weeks have been tough for you," I said, "but we have a few more questions."

She sighed, seemed to deflate a little, then said, "I really don't know how I can help, but... I already figured out that you wanted to talk about Indigo."

Quickly, I filled her in on what we'd learned from Oskar, that the four of them had been together at Urban One that night. Neither Corbin nor I mentioned that Oskar had said it was tense after Carolyn left, but she quickly became shifty.

"What happened that night, Carolyn?"

The young woman shrugged, flipping her hair over her shoulder. "There's not much to tell, really. Indigo met me at the Whitlow building after I finished my shift. Oskar and Lewis were outside smoking, and they asked if they could tag along."

"Did the four of you normally hang out together?" Corbin asked.

Carolyn scrunched up her nose. "Not really. I mean, sometimes the security team will go out together for nightcaps, but when I go out to the clubs, I go with my personal friends or with Indigo."

Corbin shot me a quick glance, and I knew he was on a trail, but I wasn't sure what had caught his attention. I gave him a small gesture to let him know to continue, trying to ignore the feeling of my heels' straps digging into my toes.

"Was Indigo okay with the guys joining you?" he asked.

Carolyn frowned. "Oh yeah. I mean, Indigo was happy to meet anyone, you know? She didn't really have any friends at school. So out at the clubs, she was always really talkative."

"And did that worry you?" Corbin said.

The look Carolyn shot me was telling, and I understood it immediately. As a woman, outside of being a cop, I was always on high alert. It was part of what I believed made me good at my job. And I recognized that most women had the same kind of radar. *Where did Oskar and Lewis fall on your radar?* I wondered.

"Not usually," Carolyn said, uncrossing and recrossing her legs. "Not all the time. She was pretty good about sticking with me and listening if I didn't think someone was safe. And whenever we were at Electric Blue, she was really careful about who she talked to. Actually, a few times we saw Lewis there and she ignored him completely. I think that night she was just being nice."

"Okay," I said, jumping in as Corbin appeared to be ruminating on something. "We spoke to Oskar earlier today, and he mentioned that you left early. Indigo didn't go with you. Did you try and persuade her?"

"Uh... Umm, yeah." It was obvious to me we were moving into uncomfortable territory.

She took another sip of her drink, blinking up at us through her lashes. Her pretty mouth had a sour twist to it as she continued, "I don't know. They're not bad guys, but I never feel good about leaving one of my girlfriends out alone. Anyway... yeah. I asked her to come with me. She insisted she wanted to stay."

"Did you notice anything odd before you left?" Corbin said, back in the driver's seat. I itched at the heel of one foot with the toes of the other as he continued, "Anything going on between the three of them?"

Carolyn lifted a brow, looking back and forth between us. "No. Not that I can think of. We all got along pretty well. I mean, Oskar and I share Saturday shifts, and Lewis is really outgoing. He spends nights out on the street after work, too, but we run in different circles."

There was a slight pout to her mouth now, and I knew we were pushing our luck. Especially as she'd almost finished her drink. Anything she said to us right now was technically off-record, and we'd have to bring her in to keep this conversation legitimate.

I thanked her for her time, told her we'd be in touch, and tipped my head as a signal to Corbin.

We both stood, but I wanted to stop at the bar quick and say hi to Lara.

She smiled at me uneasily, and I wondered if she was still feeling some guilt about Rat's death.

I wanted to reassure her that it wasn't her fault, that she'd tried, but he'd pushed her away. But the crowd was noisy, a little rowdy, and generally happy.

"Just checking in," I said loudly, leaning over the bar top as Corbin scanned the room behind me.

"Thanks," she said gratefully. "I'm doing okay. It's weird without Rat here to run the place, but... we're making it work. I'm kinda glad your people let us open back up so quickly."

That was all down to Mike Willis. He'd had more than twenty people combing every inch of this building and the alley.

My eyes wandered behind the bar, a habit I couldn't help, and I cataloged my surroundings. At hip-height was a collection of photos. At first, I thought they might be photographs of patrons. You know, funny pictures of people enjoying themselves, drinking a little too much, having a good time.

But the tone of these photos was all wrong. Off. They were oddly cropped, often dark, of only one or two people. And then a familiar face caught my eye.

"Lara!" I called just as she turned toward another customer.

She whipped back, looking surprised.

I pointed, then asked, "What are those photos?"

She glanced over her shoulder, then leaned over the bar top and put her lips close to my ear. "Those are photos of people who aren't allowed on the premises," she explained, her breath warm on my ear. "Troublemakers usually. Security knows to pull them if we see them."

I stared at the collection of ten or twelve photos, wondering why Lewis Massey's face was looking back at me and whether or not it was a coincidence.

"What about him?" I asked. "Third from the right."

She glanced around at the image, then turned back and said, "Him? He got drunk one night and had a big argument with Rat. Rat had him thrown out. What the argument was about, I don't know."

15

Tuesday Night 9:30 pm

Out on the street again, I took a deep breath, then groaned. "Geez, I miss my boots."

Corbin chuckled. "I don't envy you women. You know, you could have come in your boots."

"I'm pretty sure that would've given us away," I said.

Only moments earlier, Ramirez had texted me to let us know that she and Cooper were situated at Labyrinth, also dressed as civilians and playing it cool. Their job was to observe. Our job was to ask questions.

I'd seen photos of the place but had never been inside.

Corbin raised his brows and held the door open for me. Just inside, in the foyer, a blowsy woman about my age, wearing a short red leather skirt and a sneer, looked me up and down, held out her hand and said, "Wrist."

I fought the urge to roll my eyes and held out my wrist, jarred by the memory of Indigo's stiff wrist.

She'd stood in this same place, been stamped with the little dancing satyr. The music, even in the foyer, was loud and threw me off balance. I stumbled back into Corbin, who caught me, holding out his own wrist.

Once inside, my lip curled. The surroundings were so dark it was hard to tell where to go. Somewhere off to the left was what looked like a fountain bubbling out of the wall, though I couldn't hear it. Labyrinth was right. Corbin, who'd been here in daylight, lightly took my elbow and we threaded our way through the crowd.

"There," he said, leaning in close to my ear and motioning toward a circular booth where Ramirez and Cooper were tucked up close together. If I didn't know better, I'd be worried; but Cooper was a couple of decades younger than Ramirez, who was more than tired of men in general, much less youngsters like Cooper. Divorced after just a few years, she'd raised her two daughters mostly on her own. In the dark surroundings her black hair looked like liquid pooling over her shoulders.

They clocked us but didn't show any sign of recognition. Cooper leaned into Ramirez, whispering in her ear. To anyone who didn't know them it looked like a lover's touch.

"Who are we looking for?" I asked, trying to keep a couple of inches of space between Corbin and me. Even in public, where we were supposed to blend in, I couldn't help the office etiquette.

"Alana and Robert Jakob. They're Eastern European, and they're co-owners. Look for an older couple, in their sixties, classy."

Frowning, I scanned the room. "In their sixties?" I asked, glancing at my watch. It was almost nine-thirty. "Isn't it past their bedtime?"

But just as I thought it, a flash of silver caught my eye. A long, lean woman in a silver sheath dress that reached from her neck to her ankles was standing with what looked like a glass of champagne in her hand, laughing near... what I can only call an indoor rose garden. *You have got to be kidding me*, I thought as I tried to figure out how exactly there were full blooming rose bushes in the club, in the dark.

"That her?" I asked uncertainly.

If it was Alana Jakob, she sure as hell didn't look like she was in her sixties. Her skin was flawless, smooth, her thin blonde hair sheared chin-length in a severe bob; the kind I'd never be able to pull off.

Corbin nodded and tugged me in that direction. "Not sure where Robert is," he said, barely loud enough for me to hear. But as we reached Alana and she turned, it was clear from the way her face hardened that she remembered Corbin.

"Mrs. Jakob," he said lightly, holding out his hand for her to shake. "We met the other day. I'm Sergeant Russell. This is my partner, Captain Kate Gazzara. If you have a moment, we'd like to speak with you and your husband."

"I already answered all of your questions," the woman spat, ignoring his hand, and I couldn't help but notice her long, perfectly manicured fingers holding the stem of the champagne glass. "I cannot imagine what more you could want."

I stepped in, ignoring the fact that my dress was riding up my thighs. "Mrs. Jakob, I know this is probably not the best time to talk, but I'd like to ask you and your husband about the stamp Indigo Salazar had on her wrist the night she disappeared. You do know who she was, don't you? You should. It's been all over the media these last couple of days. If you can't make time for me, I'd be happy to ask your patrons."

Her ice-blue eyes widened momentarily before she held out her glass while maintaining eye contact with me. A much younger man stepped forward and relieved her of the glass.

"If you will follow me," she said, her voice low, vibrant. And she turned and walked into the shadows, leading us through an intricately carved door.

I pressed a palm against it to hold it open for Corbin. It was heavy, solid oak, stained dark. I glanced back to see Cooper and Ramirez watching intently from their booth.

Then the door closed behind me.

The room was smaller... well, compared to the club floor, intimate, the music soft, classical, Beethoven, I think. And the room was better lit, so the patrons could see the dancers, I assumed.

Four women moved atop platforms carved with what looked like scenes from the Bible, though the less pious ones. My eyes skimmed the carvings as Alana led us toward the back of the room. I glanced up once more at the women; the one nearest us wore a passive expression. The next one over was really playing it up for the five men in front of her.

I had no problem with dancers, or even sex workers.

Stay in my line of work long enough and you find out the paths that lead to that kind of work are paved with men ready to take advantage of naïve girls or financially unstable women. I didn't judge the dancers, who were mostly clothed, though scantily. But there was something about the room that felt... I don't know... but I know I felt a little uncomfortable.

Alana led us through another door, this one blending seamlessly with the dark purple walls, into a short, brightly lit hallway and into an office.

And oh, what an office it was. Two walls were lined with bookshelves full of not only books, but also expensive-looking trinkets. A taxidermal serval, a wildcat native to Africa, seemed to have launched itself, mouth wide open, fangs bared, from a dark wood bar in the back of the room.

Alana moved to a leather chair behind a long, low desk and gestured with pointed nails to the padded bench before it. I sat down carefully, crossing my ankles, and Corbin joined me.

"Thank you," I began, but she waved a hand.

"It will take a few moments for my husband to get here. I prefer to wait until he arrives."

My blood boiled a little at that, recognizing it as a power play. Alana Jakob wanted to be the one in control of the conversation. I glanced at Corbin pointedly and he took a folded photo from the back pocket of his jeans. And we waited in silence.

It was just a few minutes later when the door opened again, and a man who looked oddly like he could be Alana's sibling stepped into the room. He, too, was long and lean, his hair an unnatural silver and his dark suit luxurious.

He gave Corbin and me a cheery smile and a wave as we stood up and turned to meet him.

"Hello, hello," he said, clapping his hands together. "Welcome. I am Robert Jakob. I do not believe we've had the pleasure of meeting."

He leaned forward, taking my hand and turning it to brush his lips across my knuckles. I tried to school my expression to hide my disgust at the move. What I wouldn't give to see him try that same move on Anne...

Smiling tightly, I pulled my hand away and replied, "If you don't mind, Mr. Jakob, I'd like to skip the formalities. Your wife already knows why we're here. It has to do with Indigo Salazar—"

Before I could get any further, he nodded solemnly and interrupted me. "A sad, sad business. But, to be honest, Miss...?" he said as he lowered himself into the chair next to his wife's.

"Gazzara," I said evenly. "Captain Gazzara."

"Miss Gazzara." He smiled, ignoring my title. "I don't see how we can help. We already spoke to your partner and his companion."

"I understand that," I pressed, holding a hand out for Corbin to pass over the photo, "but we need to inform you that your club has been implicated in Indigo's disappearance. At least, on the night of her disappearance. What d'you make of this?"

I placed the unfolded photo on the desk and in front of them. Alana and Robert Jakob leaned over it together, staring at it. Alana's face hardened once more into a mask; Robert's jaw ticked. I glanced at Corbin and saw that he'd caught the reaction.

"What confuses me," I said, turning over my own wrist on the desk, "is that it appears Indigo's stamp was a different color from the stamps you give your patrons."

The stamps on our wrists were green. A vibrant green that was hard to miss even in the dark rooms. The stamp on Indigo's had been purple—the same purple as the room of dancing women we'd just been in. I hadn't missed that.

Alana's eyes met mine, and I saw that she understood where I was going with this. Out of the corner of my eye, I also saw her put a hand on her husband's forearm. He'd opened his mouth to speak, but she stopped him.

Corbin and I sat waiting for an answer. The silence was uncomfortable, but Alana Jakob underestimated me if she thought I wouldn't wait her out. It was like we were smoking a rabbit out of its hole.

Now that we were closer and under better lighting, the smoothness of her skin looked unnatural. And I had to wonder if she ever got tired of trying to hang onto her youth.

Her lips pursed tightly before she said, "Depending on the day of the week, we use different stamps. I cannot remember much about the case; wayward girls don't interest me. But I would assume she was here on a Saturday."

She was right. Indigo had been reported missing on a Sunday morning and found on a Sunday afternoon weeks later.

I'd never met anyone like Alana Jakob before, but I knew she was lying.

I also knew I couldn't catch her out, not then, anyway. Not while she was in her element. Her husband, Robert, sat frozen as if expecting to be caught out. But I unfurled myself from the bench and stood.

"Thank you. That lines up with what we know so far," I said truthfully. "We'll be in touch if we have any other questions."

Corbin followed, a slightly startled look on his face as we stepped out into the bright hallway. Robert Jakob stood in the doorway behind us, watching as we went back out into the purple room.

Me? I kept my eyes straight ahead, lost in thought and unprepared for the heaviness of the door. I hauled it open, using my frustration for a surge of energy, and then we were back in the club, the cacophonous music drowning out any attempt at communication.

A quick glance and a nod at Ramirez and Cooper told them to follow us.

Outside, we tried to find a quiet spot away from the smokers, but it was near impossible. In the end, we settled under a streetlight to the left of the club entrance.

"How'd it go?" Cooper asked, shifting his weight from one foot to the other and scanning the area.

I took a deep breath. "Well, we didn't catch them off guard. Alana Jakob seems prepared to lie to our faces. Although what she said did make sense. She claims the stamps are different colors for different days of the week."

Ramirez looked skeptical. "None of the other clubs we spoke to do that."

"I know," I said, nodding my head. "I just can't catch her, not here. I need something more." I muttered the last part to myself, knowing we'd hit a dead end.

So far, we had a suspect we had no way of identifying, no prints, but DNA being run through the system. Someone with a habit of smoking chocolate cherry-wrapped joints, but we had no facial features. We knew Indigo had been at Labyrinth the night she died, but no way to connect her murder to the place. The big question was: what had happened between her leaving Labyrinth and ending up in the trunk of the car?

A scraping sound and a huff drew our attention to the alley nearby, between the club and a gated CBD shop. A petite, curvy young woman with frizzy dark hair stood there, stomping out a cigarette. She sent us a sullen look and then did a double-take.

"Aren't you the cops that were in here last week?" she asked, squinting in the bright light of the lamp.

Corbin looked at me, then stepped forward.

"We are," he answered. "I'm Sergeant Russell. This is Captain Gazzara, Detective Cooper, and Sergeant Ramirez."

"Nice to meet y'all," the girl said, a sultry smile curling her lips. Ramirez shot me a look and raised a brow. Women around here could smell fresh meat, and Corbin was getting some attention. He managed not to look flustered.

"Wait," I said, suddenly remembering where I'd seen her before. "Aren't you a dancer here at Labyrinth?"

The girl snorted, digging another cigarette out of the crumpled pack in her jacket pocket. Her legs were short, thick, and sheathed in stockings with runs at the ankles. "You could say that, yeah," she muttered.

Ramirez and I shared another look, sensing gossip. She jumped in. "I didn't get the chance to see the back room. You like it here? Seems busy for a Tuesday."

The girl looked at Ramirez, then at me. She seemed to be considering her answer, then she said, "No. Since you're asking. I don't like it here."

"Why not?" Corbin asked.

"Well, for starters, Alana pays us like waitresses, thinking we'll live off the tips. But Robert takes a twenty percent cut of the tips. So there's that." She met my eyes and stared, as if daring me. If what she said was true, that was illegal. The dancers should at least be making minimum wage.

Her frustration was practically steaming from her oversized jacket, and inwardly I smiled, knowing it was the perfect opportunity to dig around a little.

And then Corbin spoke. "The stamp on your wrist— isn't that just for Saturday nights?"

She looked at him like he was crazy. "The purple? No. That's just for strip... for dancers."

Her cheeks reddened under the streetlight. She knew she'd slipped up. But it was too late. We had her. We had what we needed, and I couldn't help but grin as Ramirez clarified in a sharp voice, "Strippers?"

With a deep sigh, the girl tossed her barely lit cigarette away, seeming to make a decision. "You know what? Yeah. I don't even care anymore. I'm looking for other jobs, anyway. The 'dancers' in there are strippers after hours. All of us. And the purple stamp is only for *us*."

Indigo's purple stamp? I thought. *That means... No! She couldn't have? Could she?*

By then, the girl had picked up on the fact that what she'd said made for a serious turn of events, and she obviously wanted out of there.

"I've got to go, sorry." She started to turn away, but I stopped her.

"Wait," I said, taking the folded flyer from my clutch. "This girl. D'you know her? Is she one of the dancers?"

She glanced at the image, looked at me, shook her head, and looked away.

"I gotta go," she said. "They'll fire me if I don't." And with that, she disappeared inside before Corbin could catch her, and we didn't even get her name.

"Well now," I said. "That's a turn of events I wasn't expecting. The Jakobs need a permit to employ strippers, and the strippers need licenses. I'm willing to bet that none of them have them."

"But this means that Indigo was stripping in there?" Cooper said. "She was only seventeen."

"That girl didn't look much older," Corbin said, tipping his head toward the side door.

He was right. She was young, probably of legal age, but barely.

At that point, I didn't know how I felt. What the hell was Indigo doing taking her clothes off in a sleazy nightclub? I didn't think much of her hanging out at Electric Blue, but at least there she was confined to the office, an act of goodwill on Rat Nelson's part. The man, so Lara

Crump had said, was trying to keep her safe, but from what... Apparently, only Rat knew that. Did he know she was stripping at Labyrinth? There was no way to know. What he did know was that she was seeing someone that he, Nelson, hated enough to threaten openly. I wasn't sure how the two tied together, but I was sure they did, and the combination had sealed the deal for Indigo.

"We should have the DNA results back tomorrow," I said, "and that, I hope, will officially link the suspects to both scenes. For now, we need to focus on the next steps. I want to get a warrant to search Indigo Salazar's room. We need to find out who her friends were—if she had any —and who she was seeing, and track them down."

16

Thursday Morning 6:30 am

But we didn't get the DNA back the following day, and we had to wait a day for the warrant. As I remember it, I rose early that following Thursday morning. Samson had been cooped up in the office all the previous day and was giving me a real run for my money.

It was just after six-thirty and we were on the Greenway. The only sounds I could hear were my heart beating, my breathing, and my shoes slapping the pavement. Samson was loping along ahead of me, keeping the leash almost taut.

Four days had gone by since Sullivan and Escobar had discovered Indigo's body in the trunk of that car, and I hadn't stopped thinking about her since. Neither could I get rid of the image of that dark little room at Labyrinth, with her up on one of the pedestals dancing naked for a bunch of drunken perverts. Had she enjoyed dancing? I had to suppose that she did. But what had attracted her to it in the first place?

The dancer we'd met, whose name I still didn't know, seemed anything but happy there. And I just couldn't imagine that working for Alana and Robert Jakob was enjoyable. Oh, they were a glamorous couple, but beneath all the show, I had the feeling they were running a tight, and cruel, ship and I kept coming back to the same question: How had Indigo found her way there?

Especially when she had a place like Electric Blue. Friends like Carolyn, Lara, even Rat Nelson—people who cared for her. No, it wasn't uncommon for teens to rebel now and then. I was no exception. I'd taken part in some... let's say questionable scenarios back when I was that age. But Indigo had been a top student, incredibly smart and by all accounts, not entirely naïve.

For her to get locked into the Labyrinth, to end up stripping in that small room with men's eyes all over her young body...

Sammy barked and I skidded to a halt, ready to put all my weight on the leash. He was a great dog and almost never pulled, but the one thing that drove him crazy was ducks. And there was a small flock of them nearby on the riverbank. It was then that I realized that, lost in thought as I had been, I'd gone quite a bit further than I meant to.

"Darn," I muttered, realizing I had to be at the department in a couple of hours and I still had a bunch of stuff to do, like shower, dress, eat, feed Samson and... oh, you know, all the usual stuff one needs to do before the day can begin. And that meant I'd get no breaks on the jog back to the car. Samson looked up at me, tongue lolling out, as if he was ready for the challenge.

And then my phone rang and I jumped in surprise. I rarely kept the sound on, relying on feeling the vibration when it was tucked away in my pocket. Tapping an earbud, I said, "Gazzara."

"Hey, Captain," Cooper said. "I know you're heading in soon, but I wanted to reach out and let you know. The DNA came back and we ran it through CODIS. No hits. Sorry."

I let out a breath. It felt like I'd been holding it, my breath, for the last two days.

I was pacing around in a tight circle with a hand on my hip. "Damn it. Okay. Yeah. Whew. If the chief asks before I get there, and he probably will, you can tell him. Yes, and update Hawk and Anne. They should be working on the release of Rat's body."

With no relatives, Rat Nelson would be buried in a plot collectively purchased by his staff. That so many of them were willing to step forward after his death was just another example of how good of a person he'd been, and of how wrong about him I'd been.

Cooper cleared his throat on the line. "I don't get it, Cap. This guy wipes his fingerprints but leaves his DNA. He must have known we wouldn't find anything on him. But what are the chances we have his fingerprints on file and not his DNA? If he's a criminal, we'd have both, right?"

"If he committed a felony, yeah. But there are plenty of other crimes he could have committed that would leave us with fingerprints and no DNA." It was something I hadn't thought too hard about. I'd been assuming we'd get a hit. But Cooper was right; this guy was smart. He wouldn't be stupid enough to leave his DNA if he thought it would get him caught.

"Look," I said. "I have to go. I'll be in as soon as I can, okay? Let everyone know."

I tapped my earbud and hung up, then I looked down at Samson, who slowly wagged his tail. "You ready, boy? I hope I can keep up."

And we took off, running along the Greenway and away from the ducks and the water, heading back toward home. Sammy had filled a hole in my life I hadn't realized needed to be filled, but as the two of us ran, I couldn't help feeling there had to be more to life than this. And that wasn't a good feeling.

IT WAS EIGHT-FIFTEEN WHEN WE WALKED INTO THE PD from the parking lot at the rear of the building. I was barely through the door when Chief Johnston leaned out of his office, chucking his chin at me and said, "Gazzara. A minute please."

I gave Samson one last pet on the head and handed him off to Officer Danielle Kelly, a newer recruit in one of the outer offices in Chief Johnston's suite. Dani had been a dog walker in a past life. And she'd helped me out a couple of times before. She loved Sammy, and he loved her. And I already made up my mind to call her when—and if—I ever took time off and went on vacation.

The chief was sitting at his desk, looking slightly pained and somewhat tired.

I stepped into his inner sanctum and closed the door. He didn't get up. Instead, he waved a manila envelope at me and said, "Your warrant. It just came through. You're good to go to Salazar's residence and search Indigo's room and Indigo's room only. Keep that in mind, Kate. Don't do anything that dirties our hands. Salazar won't be happy about this, and we need to toe the line and do this by the book. You have the authority to seize anything in the room you deem to be relevant, including computers, phones, diaries... well, I don't need to tell you."

I nodded, taking the envelope from him. I opened it, extracted the warrant and quickly scanned it. Then I looked up at him and nodded.

"We'll be careful," I said.

"What exactly are you looking for?" he asked.

"She was seeing someone, and I need to find out who it was."

Johnston sighed, leaning back heavily in his chair. "Girls that age... As you know, my daughter... She..." He shook his head, and for the first time since I'd known him, he looked at me with his emotions laid bare. His eyes were watering. "She... she drove us crazy. She even kept a fake diary."

"Yes. I know... Chief. I'm sorry."

And I did know. Back in 2009, ten years ago, his daughter Emily had been murdered. They'd found her body on Signal Mountain, out of our jurisdiction, so the chief had gone to Harry Starke for help. He, Harry, insisted I work the case with him, and together we solved it and brought her murderer to justice. So yes, I did know, and you've no idea how it felt that morning to sit before him, the chief, and see the raw emotion in his eyes.

But Johnston quickly pulled himself together and said, "Kate, I need you to be ready for Salazar. He's a quirky son... He's quirky. He asked for your help last time he was here, but that doesn't mean he trusts you, or us. It doesn't mean he's going to move aside and let you and your detectives loose to go through his dead daughter's room. He'll fight you every inch of the way and, with our luck, the media will catch wind of it and will be stationed outside within the hour."

I nodded grimly, but a stab of annoyance went through me. First Anne, now Johnston... why did everyone assume I didn't know how to handle parent-child relationships? True, I didn't have any kids of my own, but I'd been a kid once and fought with my parents at the slightest provocation. And I'd investigated a lot of cases involving underage teens. Why was this suddenly creeping up on me, as if no one had any faith in me because I was a single, childless woman? I was good at my job—better than good—and that was all that should matter.

"You need a copy of this?" I asked, trying to keep the chill from my voice.

He shook his head.

I stood, smoothed the front of my button-down and said, "Then I'll go get North and the team. I'd like to knock this out in a few hours and have a name by the end of the day. Umm... I can't take Samson with me, so is it okay if I leave him with Danielle until I get back?"

He nodded, and I turned again to leave.

"Gazzara," the chief called, his voice sounding like he'd worked a 24-hour shift, just as I was about to let the door close behind me. I turned back, waiting.

"I don't want you to get the wrong idea," he said quietly. "You're the only one I trust to handle a case like this. We knew from the start it wasn't going to be easy, and you don't have a lot to work with. But I do know you'll get it done."

I gave him a tight smile, nodded, and let the door close behind me, wondering where I might find Jack North. I should also mention that while I appreciated the chief's sentiment, I also felt as if the man had read my mind, and I couldn't get rid of the needling feeling that I wasn't doing enough. Not just at work, but in other aspects of my life, too.

Samson ducked out from under Dani's desk and trotted toward me, pressing his nose against my pants pocket, the one that held the treats. "Danielle," I asked, coming around to her desk, "I'm going to be heading out soon and can't bring the big guy. You mind watching him? The chief says it's okay."

She nodded eagerly, happy to have the company while she filed paperwork on her in-office day. I patted him on the head, gave him a treat, told him to be good, and then left them to it, Samson staring after me. With Samson taken care of, I went looking for North, trying to quiet my mind, knowing the most important part of the day, maybe the entire investigation, was ahead of me, hidden somewhere in the room of a teenage girl.

17

Thursday Morning 8 am

"I DON'T CARE WHAT IT SAYS. YOU ARE *NOT*. *GOING*. *In. Her. Room*."

Well, that was almost exactly what I'd expected from Ivan Salazar. I stood on his front steps with Jack North and Mike Willis at my side, as well as three officers ready to secure the front drive when the media showed up.

Because we were searching just one room and not the entire house, Willis and I were on the same page; keep it small, keep it tight. No need for any of his team to jump in. We could be in and out in four hours or less... if Salazar ever let us in the house at all.

"Mr. Salazar, you're a smart man. I don't think I need to explain to you how this warrant works," I said slowly, deliberately. Would I be a little smug if we had to remove him from the property? Maybe... Did I want it to come to that? No. Of course not. But he was standing at the front door with his arms crossed and his eyes blazing.

Where had the tired parent gone who I'd spoken to only a couple of days ago? Part of me had hoped Chief Johnston was wrong, and Salazar had accepted that my team and I were his best resource. But so far he'd already managed to spit out the words "defile" and "trample," so I doubted very much that he had.

"Sir!" North said, leaning in closer to the much taller man. "We don't want to have to remove you from your home, but if we have to, we will."

Salazar's phone was in his hand and he was ready to call his lawyer, which he'd been threatening to do for the last few minutes. I hoped that he would. Maybe his lawyer would talk some sense into him. Explain that the warrant was valid and that he had to get out of our way and let us do our job.

Once I'd taken my concerns to the chief, along with the fact that Labyrinth was likely in violation of quite a few laws and statutes, including employing an underaged girl as a stripper, he contacted Judge Daly and asked him to push the warrant through ASAP, and he did. It wasn't often we asked for such preferential treatment, but Indigo Salazar had been a minor and we had multiple people claiming she'd been seeing someone, and that someone could likely be her killer. We needed physical evidence, and I knew it was somewhere in the girl's room.

"Captain."

I turned around to see Tracy Ramirez just a few steps behind me. She'd just dropped her eldest off at band practice and would be overseeing the officers keeping the perimeter in check.

"Ramirez," I greeted, noting the way Salazar took the Hispanic woman in.

Maybe in another lifetime, a run-in between these two would play out differently. After all, Ivan Salazar's wife had run off shortly after Indigo's birth and, as far as we knew, hadn't been heard from since. And Tracy had been divorced for quite a while. She was in her late forties and still very attractive. But Ivan Salazar was in mourning, and his emotions were apparently swinging pretty wildly. Only a moment earlier he'd been defiant and angry; now he appeared deflated and resigned. His fist loosened around the copy of the warrant we'd given him, crumpled now. His other hand, holding the cell phone, dropped to his side. He looked helplessly at the four of us.

"I have a hernia repair in less than an hour," he said, exhaustion tingeing the words. "I can't be here for this..."

From the way his voice broke, I wasn't sure he'd want to be here even if he could. No parent should see the police rifling through their dead child's room, even if it was for a good reason. Who knew what secrets we'd bring to light? Who wanted to know those things about their children?

"Willard will see you to her room," he said, "and escort you out when you're finished. Please don't touch anything else in my home."

"Of course not, sir," Jack promised. "Thank you for your cooperation."

Salazar stepped past us and went to the Lincoln Navigator in his driveway, his shoulders drooping. I caught a glimpse of the white physician's coat hanging on the back of the passenger seat as he pulled a U-turn in the drive and left.

"Good timing," I said to Ramirez, meaning it. "You broke the tension."

She shrugged. "Glad I could help. You know where we're going?"

As if on cue, an older man in the doorway cleared his throat. He wasn't the same man who'd greeted us the first time we came to speak to Salazar. He was shorter, stouter, balding, and wearing a perfectly tailored casual suit.

"Willard?" I asked, holding out a hand. He glanced at it for a moment before taking it with an air of distaste. "I'm Captain Gazzara. This is the rest of my team: Detective Jack North, Sergeant Tracy Ramirez and Mike Willis, CSI. You know why we're here?"

I wouldn't put it past the man to have been lurking around the corner when we spoke to Salazar. He nodded and asked us to "Follow me to Miss Indigo's room."

"Have you worked for Mr. Salazar long?" I asked conversationally as we were led through the foyer to the staircase.

Willard didn't even glance over his shoulder as he answered. "I have worked for *Doctor* Salazar for twenty-two years this past May."

"So you knew Indigo well, then," I said, sharing a glance with Tracy. Mike was already scanning the home despite the fact that we weren't in Indigo's room yet. He had a sharp, ever-roaming eye.

"As well as one can ever know a teenager," Willard

answered evenly. It sounded like a riddle to me, but Tracy's brows rose in acknowledgment.

"And what, exactly, is your title?" I asked.

"Manager."

Manager could mean a lot of things, but I assumed he meant for it to be all-encompassing. Manager of the house, of the property, of whatever personal tasks Salazar needed done... A manager would see the private, raw slices of their employer's lives.

"Willard, I understand how you might be uncomfortable with us asking you this when Mr. Salazar isn't here, but would you by any chance know if Indigo had a boyfriend, maybe someone she didn't want her father to know about?"

Tracy gave a small snort, one only I could hear. I made a mental note to ask her about it later and tried to focus on the small man's reaction.

His expression was bland, almost empty as he looked back at me. "Miss Indigo *never* had any male or female friends over," he answered diplomatically. "Nor was I aware of any... romantic involvement."

Indigo's room was at the end of a long hallway on the second floor. The door was painted white and looked... quite normal. Boring, in fact.

"Thank you," I told Willard as he opened the door and stood to one side. He tilted his head, then retreated back downstairs.

What were the chances we were actually alone? Would there be more of Salazar's domestic staff lingering nearby, listening to see if we found anything? I wouldn't have been surprised.

"Would you like to do the honors?" I said to Mike, who carefully stepped into the room.

We all peered inside. I couldn't help a low whistle. Indigo Salazar's bedroom was at least four times the size of mine when I'd been a kid.

It was a large open space with three windows—two on one wall, one on another, all pouring light into the room. A soft, champagne-colored carpet covered most of the floor. The queen-size bed was set against the far wall. A serviceable desk that looked so minimalist it was probably insanely expensive was set under the single window, and there were the usual chests of drawers, bedside tables, a huge chest at the foot of the bed and so on and so on; and when I say usual, I should have said expensive.

"Suit up," Willis ordered, holding out a box containing Tyvec coveralls, booties, head covers and latex gloves. And we did, out in the hallway.

"All right, team," I instructed, double-checking that my hair was in a secure bun before I slipped on the Tyvec and put the gloves on, "every inch. We only have one shot at this so let's make the best of it."

"A girl with secrets has to let them out somewhere," Tracy said grimly.

Remembering her earlier snort, I waited as Jack and Mike stepped into the room before asking her about it. She shrugged.

"From how perfect everyone says Indigo was, I can guarantee you that 'unsavory' is exactly the word to describe whoever she was seeing," Tracy said, shaking her head. "My girls have always been safe, and I let them have their little secrets. But let me tell you, they know how to push the boundaries, and they do. It's a constant battle... The first boy Naomi brought home looked like she'd picked him up from under the overpass. Her father about had a conniption fit."

A small smile flitted across my lips. I recognized the truth in what she was saying; as a teen I'd found such rebellious guys attractive, too, and I was strictly controlled until I reached the age of eighteen, but I always found a way to push back.

But the difference between Indigo and I, and all the other teens who experimented with forbidden love, was that mine hadn't led to murder. Whoever Indigo had gotten tangled up with was looking more and more like the person who'd cut her throat and put her in the trunk of the car. *If not,* I thought, *wouldn't we have heard from or about a devastated boyfriend, or girlfriend?*

I stepped into the bedroom and the soft carpet gave under my feet. The expression on Mike's face told me exactly how he felt about the carpet, and I knew he was happy we weren't looking for DNA evidence. Even so, we had to be precise, meticulous.

"Jack," I said, nodding toward the desk, upon which was a slim silver laptop, its lid closed.

"Tracy, you take the bed. I'll take the closet. Mike, you okay to get the rest of the room?"

I regretted my decision as soon as I grasped the double door handles of the closet. It was no regular closet but a walk-in, a small room. And while Indigo hadn't struck me as a vain or superficial girl, I was surprised by how full it was.

A handful of purses were tossed onto a shelf along

with twelve pairs of shoes. Converse, regular sneakers, some flats, but no heels. *Nothing out of the ordinary so far as I can see.*

I started at the top and rummaged through the hangers, checking the pockets on every shirt, jacket or pair of pants. In one, I found a slip of paper and a phone number. A note scrawled across the top, in cramped handwriting, read: *new #.*

Part of me wanted to try dialing it immediately, but I had to focus on the task at hand. There'd be time for that later so I put it in an evidence bag and sealed, dated and signed it.

"Hey, Captain," Jack called, and I popped my head out. Tracy and Willis also paused. "Guess what the password was." He shook his head, and I noted the thumb drive he used to circumvent passwords plugged into the side of the laptop.

"Tell me," I said.

"It's 'Labyrinth.'"

"Not looking too good for the Jakobs, I think," Tracy commented dryly as Willis put his head down and got back to work.

The purses didn't give me a lot of hope. None appeared to be newer, older, or more used, so I started at the first forest-green clutch and worked my way down. In the second to last purse, a deep, shiny purple color, I unzipped a small hidden pocket inside and found a wad of cash.

A large wad of cash.

It was secured with a hair tie and appeared to be

mostly singles, fives, and tens. But there was a hundred-dollar bill at the end—seven hundred dollars in all.

"Looks like she was doing quite well for herself," I muttered as I slipped it and the clutch into an evidence bag. Did I know for sure that's where the money had come from? No. But by the color of the clutch and the diversity of the bills, all signs pointed to Labyrinth.

"Anything, Trace?" I called out and got a grunt in reply.

Then Tracy said so everyone could hear, "I'm going to need a bigger evidence bag."

Popping out of the closet, I found Tracy with the mattress shifted to the side to expose the box spring. In front of her, wedged between the mattress and box spring, was an impressive pile of exotic lingerie. Jack's cheeks turned red as he returned his focus to the laptop, leaning in closer. Willis, unphased, sorted around in his duffle and brought out a larger evidence bag.

"Make sure to count each piece," he instructed, handing it over.

At Tracy's side, I gazed down at the pile. Mostly black, but there were a few gold and dark purple pieces. All lace, some leather, and some fishnets, just like those we'd seen the dancers wearing.

"There seems to be a theme going on here." Tracy held up a delicate garter belt with one gloved finger. I shivered, unable to imagine being entrapped in the thing.

"Hey, Kate," Jack said softly, drawing my attention. The frown on his face told me he'd found something.

I looked over his shoulder and said, "Whatcha got, Jack?"

He looked sideways at me. "Um, I would say... intimate photos. Likely meant for someone else."

He averted his gaze politely as I leaned in closer to look.

As I flipped from one photo to the next, I could tell all were of Indigo, though not all of them included her face.

I pursed my lips and said, "It's a good thing her father didn't stick around. I wouldn't want him to have to see what we'd found hidden away in..."

"An encrypted folder," Jack said. "Twenty-six photos," he continued. "Some with her wearing the stuff Tracy found under the mattress. But look."

He pulled up one photo in particular, in which Indigo was topless. She was wearing skimpy, lace panties and had a tanned arm wrapped over her breasts, propping them up, while her other hand supported her chin resting on her knuckles, her fingernails painted a dark pink. In the background, her school uniform hung from a coat hanger, but it was the small purple mark on her wrist that caught my eye.

"Labyrinth again," I said. "Alana and Robert better be ready. Because we're coming for them."

I ground my teeth, angry that I hadn't gone in on them harder. But now, at least, we had support for the claim that Indigo had been dancing there. Illegally, underage and underpaid.

How the heck did she find her way there, of all places? I wondered as I stared at the photograph.

"Any clues who she was taking these photos for?" I asked.

"Just this, but I'm not sure it'll be much help," Jack replied.

He pulled up another photo, this one with Indigo turned away from the mirror coquettishly. She wore dark lace underwear and no top, freckles scattered across her shoulders.

"Look, here."

On the back of the underwear, along the waist, was a gold-threaded phrase: *Pan's Girl.*

Quickly, I moved back toward the bed and, taking Tracy by surprise, I flicked through the pile of lingerie and found it. I held the panties up on two fingers.

"Here it is. Pan's girl," I said.

Willis, next to the nightstand, spoke up. "Like the stamp on her wrist, right?"

I turned to look at him, confused, and he continued, "Pan. The satyr, or faun. God of music, I think, and sheep?"

"I didn't know you were keen on mythology, Willis," Tracy drawled, smirking at him.

His thick eyebrows twitched, but I cut in and thanked him. "This seems to be yet another connection to Labyrinth," I said, feeling a little frustrated. We were there to find out who Indigo had been seeing, but all we'd found so far was strong evidence of her connection to the nightclub.

She hadn't told any of her friends at Electric Blue about him, other than Rat. Why not? Was she ashamed of him? Was he abusive?

Rat Nelson knew exactly who he was, and he'd told her the guy was dangerous, so who the hell was he?

For the first time, I felt a little annoyed at the prickly little guy getting himself killed. If he'd just kept it together for another day or two, we could have circled back to him and pried it out of him.

But he was gone, and Indigo's secret had gone with him.

Now it was up to me to connect these dots, even though it seemed like an impossible task. I knew, deep in my gut, there had to be another player involved and... all roads appeared to lead back to Labyrinth.

"Let's keep looking," I said, my mood darkening as the hours passed. "There's a missing piece here somewhere. I just know there is."

18

Thursday Afternoon 12:05 pm

I WASN'T FEELING TOO CHIPPER AS I WALKED SOUTH on Wyatt that afternoon, more than a little miffed that we hadn't found anything other than the raunchy photos that morning. True, we had Indigo's laptop and Jack was back in the lab working on it, but it was the lack of a phone that bothered me more than anything. I mean, what kind of father doesn't allow his teenage kid to have her own phone, especially in these troubling times? You've no idea how helpful a phone can be to an investigation; its history, texts, calls, the possibilities are endless.

Yes, we had the lingerie, the photos and the money. Everything we needed to prove that Indigo had been working at Labyrinth as a stripper. Everything we needed to shut down Alana and Robert Jakob. But still no hint as to who it was she'd been seeing.

The Whitlow building looked slightly less empty than before. A couple of women dressed in casual business attire walked ahead of me through the front doors, talking animatedly to one another one with a lunchbox in hand. In the main foyer, a janitor was watering a small jungle of large, live plants.

And Carolyn was seated at the front desk with Jeff Sullivan.

"Good afternoon," I said. "You got a minute, Carolyn? I have some questions."

They shared a look and Sullivan glanced at the clock. "You're due for a break soon anyway. Go ahead. I'll cover for you."

Carolyn thanked him and stood, her ponytail brushing the tops of her shoulders as she maneuvered around the desk. She wore a dark navy uniform with a radio on her hip.

"Lunch?" I offered, turning back toward the front doors. "I'll buy."

Carolyn looked resigned as she replied, "Sure. There's a decent cafe just up the street at the top of the hill. They're quick." She nodded to a man in a suit walking by, who was eyeing us suspiciously.

Not five minutes later, we stepped into the café, creatively named Charlie's. It was Jamaican, and the aroma was almost intoxicating.

I ordered a flaky beef patty with peas and rice and a cup of black coffee. Carolyn ordered the same but with a cream soda to drink. We sat at an off-balance table and opened the foil of our patties, and I took a bite; it was delicious.

"So, Carolyn," I began. "Indigo was seeing someone

and I need to know who it was. Who was it?" I asked as if I knew she knew the answer.

Carolyn paused in mid-chew, her eyes darting to me and staring at me. "Why? Did you find something?"

Answering a question with a question was the classic dodge. "D'you know who it was?"

She shook her head. "I've no idea."

"You know she spent a lot of time at Electric Blue?" I said.

"Yeah, but... I never... I didn't stop her from going there because it seemed safe. They let her do her homework there." She put her food down; her expression had turned both serious and sad. "Do you remember I told you I hadn't seen Indigo in a while? And that's why I was worried?"

I nodded.

"Well, it had been almost a month since I'd seen her. And that was before she was reported missing. So, I don't know what she was doing. Well, I wouldn't, would I?"

It wasn't hard to grasp what she was getting at.

"You think she was avoiding you?"

"We were fine... I thought we were fine, anyway. And then she started coming up with all these excuses not to hang out. I thought she was cutting me out, but maybe she started dating someone and didn't want me to meet them."

Maybe you didn't really know her at all, I thought.

"Look, Carolyn," I said. "We know that Indigo was stripping at one of the clubs. Did you know that?"

Carolyn sucked in a breath, her face hardening as she shook her head. "Labyrinth?" she asked tightly.

"Why d'you say that?"

She laughed bitterly. "Oh, it's the club with the worst reputation. For a little while Indigo kept asking me to go there, but I wouldn't. They... there are a lot of reasons not to go there."

"Aside from the dancing?" I asked, though I already knew what she was getting at. Corbin had mentioned they had a bad reputation.

"Drugs?" I asked.

She hesitated for a moment, then nodded and said, "I don't think Indigo ever touched drugs, but... in my experience, even being around that stuff can get you in trouble, no matter how careful you are." She frowned, obviously thinking, then continued. "If Indigo was working there, it must be where she met... whoever killed her."

That was exactly what I'd been thinking.

We both sat in silence, our food forgotten for the moment, trying to fit the pieces together.

"What can you tell me about that club?" I asked.

Carolyn shook her head. "I really have never gone there. Some people who used to work at Whitlow, a bunch of guys, they'd go for... the dancers. I didn't like the way they talked about it. About the girls." She made a face, seemingly disgusted.

Me? I tried to fight off the thought that Indigo had been *one of those girls*.

"They'd laugh about it, a lot," she continued, "and say they wished they had the money to... I don't know. Sex, I guess, I think, though I can't tell you that, not for sure."

It was something I'd considered. I knew the nightlife in and around the city. What she was suggesting wasn't unheard of, not by a long shot. It made sense. *What if they'd pushed Indigo too far? Wanted her to do more than dance?*

But I had an itch I couldn't quite scratch. I had a feeling it was more than that. The missing beau... Lara was convinced she was seeing someone. So was Rat, and there were the texts on his phone.

"You're absolutely sure you can't think of who she might have been seeing?" I asked.

Carolyn shook her head, apologizing. "I really don't know. Like I said, that last month, we didn't even talk much. If she was going to Labyrinth..." Her eyes lit up. "Hey. Maybe you should ask Lewis."

"Lewis? You mean Lewis Massey?"

I'd meant to ask Lara more about him after seeing his photo among those of people banned from Electric Blue.

"Yes, him. He went to Labyrinth a few times with those guys. He's the last one of that group left. I'm sorry. I've got to get back."

I nodded absently, then told her I'd walk with her. My car was parked just a short walk from the Whitlow building.

Once I was back in the driver's seat, I called Danielle to make sure Samson was okay and not getting on the chief's nerves.

She laughed, then said, "Hardly. He's been in there with him most of the morning. They seem to be great pals."

I smiled and told her I'd be a while, then hung up and caught up on my messages, including one from Corbin, so I called him.

"Hey, I was thinking," he said. "I know it's a long shot, but maybe we should check with her school. Jack said they wouldn't talk to him... well, they did, but he said they were difficult, unwilling to let him talk to the students without a parent present. But I'm thinking if she was seeing a guy there, someone would know something, right?"

It wasn't a bad idea, and I told him so. But as I buckled in and headed back to the PD to pick him up, I was doubtful it would be a student. A teacher, perhaps, but that was an even longer shot. Indigo seemed to have led two very different lives. I didn't think we'd find her secret lover at her high school. No, that was too tame for her. She'd gotten herself into something toxic.

19

Thursday Afternoon 1:30 pm

THE GREEN AND GOLD COLORING OF SILVER PINES High School brought my mind back to the gold lettering on the lingerie we'd found earlier in Indigo's room.

It wasn't the first time I'd visited Silver Pines and it brought back memories from long ago, of a time when I was just a rookie, newly promoted to detective and partnered with Harry Starke for the first time. The murder of Alexandra Mayer was my first case and one I'd never forget, for more reasons than I care to relate. Suffice it to say it was a difficult time in my life, and not just because of the case.

The campus hadn't changed during the seventeen years since those days. Back then it was an exclusive, and very expensive, private school, Silver Pines Academy. They'd dropped the word academy and replaced it with "high school," but it was still private, still exclusive and still expensive.

The grounds were beautifully landscaped and meticulously kept. The drive was almost a quarter-mile long and bordered by old-growth pine trees and lawns that even an exclusive golf club would have been proud of.

The thing is, it wasn't impossible to see it. The photo on her missing person's flyer, now retired, showed a vibrant young girl, a high school student who should have been graduating next year. But almost immediately, that vision was overridden by the image of Indigo in the trunk: her pale body clad in a shimmering dress. Her hair matted with blood.

How had she gone from here to there? I shook my head. It was a question only God could answer, and he wasn't talking, at least not to me.

"Ready?" Corbin asked, waiting patiently at my side. I nodded and we started up the steps to the main entrance doors.

A male member of the administration staff was waiting for us and he showed us through to the principal's office, and again the memories came flooding back. The office had hardly changed at all. Principal Heenan was long gone, of course, replaced by a Dr. Edna Finster, a hawkish woman of about fifty. She greeted us warmly enough and promised to help if she could, but reiterated what she'd told Jack; that we couldn't interview the students without their parents being present.

"Indigo was a good student," she said after asking us to sit down. "Honestly, I rarely saw her. I only knew of her because she was one of our top students. Her grades were through the roof, and, well, her father..."

And she twittered on about how Ivan Salazar regularly donated to the school and was oh so supportive.

Eventually, she ran out of good things to say about him and we moved on. No, she didn't think Indigo had a boyfriend among the students, and she was known for keeping to herself.

I asked if we could talk to Indigo's homeroom teacher and perhaps her guidance counselor.

"Of course," Finster replied. "If you'll follow me to the conference room, I'll have Kenny call them for you," Kenny being Finster's boy Friday.

Mrs. Unger, Indigo's homeroom teacher, and her guidance counselor, Ms. Wright, duly arrived in the small conference room and sat down next to each other at a small conference table only slightly larger than the one I had in my office.

Unger was obviously uncomfortable and began immediately to pick nervously at her fingernail. Ms. Wright, on the other hand, seemed oddly unconcerned about talking to the police; but then again, she also looked as if she was barely out of college.

"I'm sorry," Finster said. "I do have a prior engagement, but my secretary Liz Sweeney will be sitting in. Please feel free to call on me if you need anything else."

I waited until she closed the door, then I introduced myself and Corbin.

Sweeney, a woman in her late fifties with hair dyed a faux-red, gave us a curt nod. She was short and stocky but seemed industrious as she whipped out a notepad and pencil, then adjusted the glasses that hung on a beaded string around her neck. She popped them on, blinked several times, then sat there, her back straight, poised.

"Mrs. Unger, Ms. Wright," I began, "I'm sure you're aware of what happened to Indigo Salazar. We're here to talk to you about her social life."

Wright, her arms crossed, turned the corner of her mouth down and raised an eyebrow. "I don't think we have much to contribute. Indigo was a loner."

Mrs. Unger glanced at the guidance counselor anxiously, but Corbin broke in, asking, "Didn't you meet with her regularly? Bi-weekly, as I understand."

Wright nodded. "Yes. At her father's request, we had regularly scheduled meetings to make sure she was on track. He wanted her to attend Johns Hopkins."

"So if you met with Indigo bi-weekly, why don't you think you'll be helpful?" I asked.

"She was very... self-contained and focused. I can tell you that she never spoke about her private life or social life. Nor did she have any close friends, not as far as I know."

At that, Unger leaned forward, her brow furrowed.

"Would you like to add something, Mrs. Unger?" I asked.

She nodded and looked somewhat relieved. "Yes. I'm sorry to interrupt, but I can't quite agree with my colleague. In homeroom, Indigo often spoke to Rachel Combs and Derek Schmidt."

The guidance counselor practically rolled her eyes, and I found myself losing patience with her. Luckily, Corbin stepped in.

"Do you have a problem, Ms. Wright?"

"No, not exactly. I just wouldn't say those two were Indigo's 'friends.' They're honors students, too. Actually, Rachel had been giving Indigo a run for her money this year."

Mrs. Unger looked disapproving at her but remained silent. Sweeney continued scratching away at her notepad. *Impressive*, I thought. *She takes more notes than Corbin.*

Catching me looking at her, Sweeney nodded and said, "That's true," she said. "Indigo has always been a wonderful student, but this year she slipped a little. Mostly in math, but who can blame her."

I could imagine this woman using a big, chunky calculator to do her taxes, but it was an endearing vision. I liked her. Definitely much more than I liked Wright, who scoffed loud enough for us to hear.

I ignored her. Instead, I focused my attention on the secretary.

"Ms. Sweeney, did you see or interact with Indigo often?"

"Yes, actually. This year she took a study hall for her last period. For our honors students, that means they have the option of leaving the school early if their parents sign off on it."

Corbin and I exchanged a look. Ivan Salazar didn't seem like the type to let his daughter leave school early and have a good time. I could practically hear him insisting that she stay and study.

"Did she take advantage of that?" Corbin asked. When she nodded, he added, "Can we see the paper Mr. Salazar signed, when you have a moment?"

Sweeney pushed her chair back and disappeared out into the hallway.

While she was gone, Corbin asked them if Indigo had a boyfriend.

Unger shook her head. "I'm assigned hall watch in between classes. I would have noticed if Indigo was walking with or talking to a boy."

"What about Derek Schmidt?" I asked. "You said they talked regularly."

"Derek's gay," Wright snapped, glancing at her watch. "He's dating a senior this year, one of the cross-country boys."

Okay, so her teachers didn't think she was seeing anyone, and she had no friends. I wasn't entirely surprised.

Sweeney returned and must have caught part of our conversation because she said, "I've heard some of the girls talking about Indigo this year."

"What were they saying about her?" I asked.

Sweeney adjusted her glasses, which now rested atop her nose, and looked at me as if she was surprised I wanted her to continue.

"That she *was* indeed seeing someone, but not anyone at the school. It's a name I've heard before, but I don't know what to make of it; the girls call him 'Peter Pan.'" I perked up. There was another reference to Pan again.

"As in?"

"As in the book *Peter Pan*?" Unger asked.

Sweeney shrugged. "I suppose. He's been a hot topic for the last few years, so I assumed it was a boy who graduated recently. You know, sometimes the ones who can't seem to move on stick around." She shook her head disapprovingly.

"But you have no idea who this Peter Pan could be?"

"No. I'm sorry. But whoever it is, he knows Silver Pines. Some of the times Indigo signed out early, she was picked up by someone other than Willard, Dr. Salazar's... butler, I think he is."

"Can you describe the car?" Corbin asked, a step ahead of me.

But we both knew what was coming. Sweeney whipped a paper out of the stack she'd set on the table and pushed it toward us. A permission slip to leave early with Ivan Salazar's signature, most likely a fake, scrawled at the bottom.

"A black Honda," she said, taking the slip back and closing the thick manilla folder with a thump.

Pan's girl—Peter Pan.

20

Thursday Night 9:15 pm

Sammy and I didn't get home until after seven that night. He was bored, and I was dog tired—pardon the pun.

I dined on three-day-old pizza from the fridge and a half bottle of red wine, also from the fridge. Samson? He dined on chicken leftovers and three cups of kibble, then lay down beside me on the sofa to watch something on Netflix. What it was, I can't remember.

What I do remember is that around nine-fifteen, my cell phone rang and the screen lit up with dispatch's number.

This can't be good. "Gazzara," I answered, unsure what to expect.

"Hi, Captain. Sorry to bother you at home. I have Ivan Salazar on the phone and he'd like to speak with you."

"Geez, at this time of night? Okay, patch him through. Thanks."

There was a moment of silence, a click. "Mr. Salazar? Captain Gazzara here."

"Captain Gazzara. I was notified by my daughter's school that you spoke with some of their staff today. And I also received an update from your department on what you took from my daughter's room."

Great. This was going to be a tough way to end the night, having to tell him that his honor student daughter was a stripper with a secret lover.

"Mr. Salazar, I need you to understand that we—"

"I'm not calling to argue, Captain," he said, interrupting me. "I simply wanted to make you aware of an incident that happened last fall."

My mouth snapped shut. Sammy, startled, lifted his head and stared at me.

"There was a substitute teacher at the school—some young hotshot from New York who took a liking to several of the sophomore girls. Indigo told me he made her feel uncomfortable, so I reported it immediately to the school board. Some things came out... Well, the upshot is that they had to let him go. Did they mention him to you?"

"No! They didn't," I said. "What was his name, d'you know?" I asked, putting him on speaker and opening a text message to Corbin.

"Andrew Mora. He was a social studies sub, I believe, for one of the teachers out on maternity leave."

Tapping the send button, I took the phone off speaker and brought the phone back to my ear.

Chapter 20

"He took an interest in Indigo?"

"She didn't say that exactly, but from what she described and what they found out later, I think she was one of the girls he was trying to get close to. She tested out of his classes, luckily, so he didn't have the opportunity. But I'd like you to look into it."

"Of course, Mr. Salazar. Thank you for telling me. I'm reaching out to my partner as we speak."

Ivan Salazar sounded tired as he thanked me and hung up. I should have been tired, too; Samson definitely was. He put his big, chunky head in my lap and sighed.

I waited ten minutes, then called Corbin.

"You get my text?" I asked. "Did you get a chance to look up his record?"

"Yeah, Cap. And I get why he was concerned. Andrew Mora is a registered sex offender. He made the list last December. Listed with offenses against more than one minor, and his court documents say he fixated on two different girls. One he had a relationship with while she was a junior. She was seventeen. It doesn't name the girls, of course."

Seventeen. Indigo's age. Was Ivan Salazar right? Had this guy snagged Indigo?

"They have his current address listed?" I asked.

"Yeah. First thing tomorrow?"

"First thing. I'm going to bring Sammy along."

"Fine by me. Get some sleep, Captain."

But I knew I wouldn't be getting much sleep. Corbin had already emailed me a pdf of Andrew Mora's file, and I'd be going through it line by line until I'd finished it.

I looked at Samson and said, "Here we go again, Sammy. Maybe this is what we've been waiting for."

Sam tilted his head to one side and looked up at me, as if waiting for more. Then, when more wasn't forthcoming, he lowered his head between his front paws and went to sleep.

Me? I opened my laptop and went to work.

"Why the hell didn't anybody at Silver Pines mention him?" I muttered.

Samson's eyes opened, his ears twitched, and then he closed his eyes once more.

21

Friday Morning 8:30 am

I WAS UP EARLY THE FOLLOWING MORNING BUT decided to forgo my usual early morning run in favor of a long hot shower, a proper breakfast of eggs, country ham, toast and two huge cups of black coffee. I fed Samson, reminding myself that I needed to stop by PetSmart for another bag of food, and then settled down with Mora's file. I'd handed off the "new #" paper scrap I'd found in Indigo's closet to Jack and asked him to make the call. I would have done it myself, but I wanted to go through Mora's file one more time to make sure I was thoroughly familiar with it.

I remember I was dressed to kill that Friday morning in a brand-new pair of dark blue skinny jeans, a white turtle neck sweater and a tan leather jacket, and my hair was tied back in a ponytail.

By the time eight o'clock rolled around I was feeling pretty damn good; wired, but good.

I loaded Sam into the back seat of my car, grabbed a third coffee to go, locked my apartment door and set off to find and interview the man I hoped would soon become my prime suspect.

ANDREW MORA LIVED ON THE CUSP OF A FAIRLY decent residential section of North Chattanooga. By eight-thirty, Corbin and I were standing on the street beside my car, with Sammy panting and secured on the back seat with the windows down. It was early, and the temperature was in the low fifties, so I figured he would be fine with the windows down for a bit.

I was... antsy, not knowing how long I could stand being around a guy like Mora without wanting to punch him in the face. From reading his file, I knew what he'd done to those girls, and it was disgusting.

"Rein it in, Kate," Corbin said. "You're practically steaming."

I worked my jaw, knowing he was right. I'd always found it hard to be around this kind of predator criminal, but if there was any chance at all he had something to do with Indigo's death, I knew I needed to play it cool until we could prove it.

The sidewalk was cracked and buckling under my boots as we approached the gray front door. The house looked like a triplex, though the top floor's windows were busted out. The "9" of 39, Mora's address, was hanging upside down.

Corbin knocked and stepped back. After a few

moments with no sign of life from the inside, he knocked again, louder this time.

It took a minute or two, but the door scraped open and before us stood a man I judged to be in his mid-to-late twenties. His dirty blond hair was lank and untidy, and he had at least two days of growth on his jaws. Worse, he wore what was once a plush bathrobe but was now matted down around the armpits and stained. Not surprising since it was so early in the morning, but I couldn't help my lip curling in distaste.

"Mr. Mora?" Corbin asked, and the guy cursed.

"Yeah. What do you want? Why are you here? I haven't done anything."

Well, I wasn't too sure about that. But, as always, I had to assume him innocent, no matter what he'd previously been found guilty of.

"We're here to talk to you about Indigo Salazar," I said coldly, hooking a thumb in my belt.

Andrew Mora suddenly looked much, much more awake.

"Who?"

"You heard me," I said. "Indigo Salazar. She's dead. Murdered. You want to talk out here or can we come in?"

"You can't think I... check with my APO," he stuttered, half-turning and fumbling in the dark of the foyer.

I tensed and put my hand on my weapon. *Surely, he can't be that stupid.*

He turned around and handed me a worn-thin business card. Minimalist, plain, the name Sasha Ochoa on it followed by a phone number and APO designation.

"She knows exactly where I've been. I'm kept on a

tight leash, all right? I have a job at a car wash. I'm there every day from eight to four-thirty."

That didn't exactly take him off my radar since Indigo's autopsy indicated she'd been taken at night. I glanced at the driveway and saw a beat-up Oldsmobile. Corbin held his hand out for the business card, and I handed it to him as Mora pressed on.

"And look! Look. My landlord lives on the second floor. He keeps security cameras up, two out here and one at the back of the house, off the garage."

I turned around and looked. He was right. There were, in fact, two security cameras on the front of the building. Whether or not the owner kept the footage for what was now almost five weeks out was questionable, but if this interview went anywhere, I'd certainly ask for the footage. But, even at that early stage, I had the disappointing feeling, as Mora continued to chatter, that he probably wasn't involved in Indigo's death after all.

Finally, after he invited us in and we all sat down, I asked him, "When you were at Silver Pines, do you remember Indigo Salazar?" I watched his every twitch and eye movement. He tightened up under the grimy bathrobe but nodded.

"Yeah. I knew her," he replied. "I only saw her around. She took advanced classes. Out of my league."

That tracked, but I felt the need to push him. "Come on, Andrew. We've spoken to several witnesses who said you had a... special interest in her."

The blood drained from his face and he held up both hands, palms out and stuttered, "Uh, uh. I... I... I did, b...

but I never touched her, I swear. Indigo was mature for her age. She looked much older than sixteen."

As he rambled on, my gut curdled. How a grown man could look at a sixteen-year-old girl and think she was mature enough to pursue, I'll never understand.

"I swear, I haven't had anything to do with any girls since..."

Girls. Not women? Was Andrew Mora Peter Pan? A man who wanted to be young forever and stole girls out of their bedrooms?

"Where were you the night of Saturday, the ninth of this month, and between nine and six the following morning?" I asked.

"Nowhere. I was nowhere. I was here. I'm always here. I don't go out. Ever. I was here. Watching TV. I swear."

"Can anyone corroborate that?" I asked.

He slowly shook his head, then said, "No. But you can check the footage. Please. I told you. I never go out."

And the thing about it was, I believed him. And Corbin must have believed him too because he stood up, thanked Mora curtly for his time, handed him a business card and told the bathrobe-clad sex offender that we'd be checking in with his APO and with him.

"I believe him," Corbin said as we walked slowly back to my car.

"Yes, so do I," I said, "but I wouldn't trust him anywhere near any kid of mine."

Back in the car, Samson happily slobbered Corbin's ear and I couldn't help but smile. Samson had a way of easing the tension. Corbin took it like a champ.

"So what do you think?" Corbin asked as I pulled away from the curb.

"I'm not sure," I replied. "It's a... possibility, but a slim one. And I'm sure he's right when he says he's being watched closely. And not just by the law, either. I'm sure everyone in the neighborhood knows who he is and what he's done. It probably wouldn't take much to earn him a visit from a lynch mob. We'll check with his parole officer anyway. And you might as well check with the owner of the building to see if there's any footage, though I doubt it, not unless his system records it. Those cheap systems are usually on a loop, and anything longer than a couple of weeks is recorded over."

22

Friday Morning 10:30 am

When we arrived in my office, we found Hawk, Anne and Cooper hunched over the small, round conference table, either filling out reports or going over them.

Jack North was busy in the computer lab working his way through Indigo's laptop, and Mike Willis had finished checking the few items he'd pulled from Indigo's room, and unfortunately none had DNA on them. Obviously, Indigo hadn't been rebellious—or stupid—enough to try and sneak whoever her guy was into her room at night.

But I was still hung up on several things: Labyrinth, for one, and the fact that Indigo was stripping there. I fully intended to go back there that day to interview the dancers. I figured Alana and Robert Jakob would try to make it hard for us, but I needed more information and to know what Indigo actually did there. Was she there of her own volition, or had she been coerced into dancing? Had she tried to leave?

"Want some company?" Cooper offered when I'd voiced my intentions. "Tracy should be free by then. Her kid's basketball game ends around two."

"Yeah, I think that's probably a good idea. And while you're at it, we're going to need a warrant. Fill it out for me, would you, and I'll get Judge Strange to sign it. Has anyone talked to Jack? Seen him?"

"Me," Anne said, looking up briefly from her work. "Caught him earlier today. So far he hasn't found anything else on her laptop, but he's still working on it."

With a sigh, I walked back behind my desk and sat down. It still seemed to me that we were solving the case inch by inch, and it just wasn't fast enough for me, *or for the chief*.

As if in answer to my prayers, my desk phone lit up, showing a call coming in from Willis' room. "Hey, what's up, Mike?"

"Good news. You know how we took all the purses from the closet? Well, I found a paystub in one of them."

"A paystub? From where?"

"From Labyrinth. It's a direct tie to them, but guess what? It says 'cleaning staff' on it."

I highly doubted Indigo was actually a member of the cleaning staff at Labyrinth, and from Willis' tone, so did he.

"I've got it set aside with the other evidence for you. Let me know when you want it. I'm assuming you're going back out there?"

Chapter 22

"You'd be right about that, Mike. I'm taking Ramirez and Cooper with me."

"Well, I'm about done with it, I guess. I just hope it's enough to get what you need from them."

"Me too, Mike. Thanks."

Hanging up the phone, I quickly updated the team, all of whom looked relieved. "Tell Tracy we're out of here after lunch and you're both to be here in my office at one-thirty. Got it?"

He looked down at Samson. "You bringing him with us, Captain?"

I shook my head. "No. That's a little too iffy. There's a lot going on at Labyrinth and we'll need to stay focused. He can stay here." I turned to look at Robar. "You mind watching him for me, Anne?"

"Sure," she said. "I have reports to finish up so I can be here most of the afternoon."

Then, out of nowhere, Hawk scoffed. One glance told me which report he was holding up.

"Seriously?" he said. "This pervert is describing teenage girls as 'mature for their age'?"

It still made me sick to even think of Andrew Mora. I wanted to be able to cut him out of my mind completely, but unfortunately there was still a remote chance he might somehow be tied to the case. I mean, what if Mora was indeed Peter Pan? What if he had somehow snagged Indigo and had been picking her up after school?

"I know," I said, picking the report up with two fingers as if it was trash. "I don't know how Corbin played it so cool during that conversation. I was ready to deck him."

Hawk shook his head. "Makes me want to get home and see my girls. All of them. I don't think they'd ever get snared in something like that, but..."

All of us in the room were thinking it. No one wanted to believe that a girl as bright as Indigo, guaranteed to get into any college she wanted to attend, would fall for someone like Mora. But it was impossible to know for sure since she wasn't here to tell us. We would be her voice; speak up for her.

"Anne, can you do me a favor and reach out to Ivan Salazar? Let him know we talked to Mora. But nothing else. I don't want him thinking this guy is involved and hunting him down."

Anne nodded, stepping out of the room and heading to her own desk to make the call. I told everyone else I'd be back soon and headed out with Sammy to grab a quick lunch and find Judge Strange.

Hawk's words echoed in my mind: "Makes me want to get home and see my girls."

What would I be going home to? Samson. Well, that was something. I was lucky to have found him, even under the sad circumstances that had led me to him.

But beyond Samson... maybe I would have been better off alone, because with my current canine companion, I found myself suddenly aware of other empty areas of my life. Not just my love life, but the hole where a family could—should?—be. Did I want that for myself? I didn't know. Maybe I did.

Shaking my head, I focused on the drive and the big lump of love I had sitting beside me on the front seat.

23

Friday Afternoon 2:45 pm

Tracy and Cooper flanked me as Corbin had a surprisingly heated—for him—discussion with Labyrinth's manager, who didn't want to let us in until Alana or Robert arrived.

"You do understand how a warrant works, don't you?" Tracy asked sarcastically.

The manager, a thin, fragile-looking man, glared at her. But he couldn't deny the warrant and what it called for: access to all employees and records from the last three years, including payroll information.

In the daylight, Labyrinth didn't look so good. The cleaning crew—of which I was sure Indigo hadn't been a part—was busy cleaning, scrubbing the cracked floor tiles, wiping down tables and... well, you know how it works.

A bartender, who was busy behind the bar setting up for the night, looked half-dead and surprisingly old, given the vibe Labyrinth was trying to go for. Her face was wrinkled, almost concave, and when we finally forced our way in, she stared at us with dead eyes.

Outside, parked on the street in front of the entrance, four uniformed officers in two blue and white cruisers were standing by in case of trouble, not that we were anticipating any; but from the jittery actions of the manager, I had an idea we were going to find something the Jakobs wouldn't want exposed.

"Be on the lookout for illegal substances," I murmured to Tracy, who was watching the manager with a disgusted sneer. She nodded.

We were led back through the purple room, where I glanced again at the pedestals, and into the hallway that led to Alana and Robert's office. But that's not where he took us. Instead, he scuttled along the hallway to a small room all the way in the back, opened the door and stood aside. I stepped inside.

At one point, it must've been a closet because it was small, really small, about eight feet by eight, and it was packed with three oversized file cabinets, a medium size box safe, and a steel desk and chair.

He shot another glare over his shoulder, unlocked the cabinets and, riffling through the top drawer of one of them, extracted a thick manilla folder which he tossed onto the desk.

"Payroll," he snapped.

"Thanks," Cooper said dryly, reaching for it. "Now the safe, and we still need a list of all of your employees, including their employment paperwork."

The request seemed to aggravate the little guy, but he opened another drawer and started digging around in it. I motioned for Tracy and Corbin to wait in the hallway and for Cooper to keep his eyes on the manager, and then I headed back to the purple room.

I stood for a moment, letting my eyes adjust to the dim light, and looked around. The walls were painted deep purple and hung with purple sheers. The five pedestals were elevated... about two feet. The room contained eight tables, each big enough to seat four people, and were arranged strategically around the pedestals.

I shook my head. It was a cattle show. I sucked on my bottom lip, trying to picture a typical night with the tables full and the girls gyrating... and it sickened me, especially when I knew at least one of them had been underage.

I didn't think there was any point in calling in Mike Willis and his team, not with the constant ebb and flow of patrons and dancers. And I knew the only way we were going to connect Indigo to a stripping job was the paystub, the stripper's stamp on her wrist, or the testimony of one or more of the dancers.

I couldn't have been in the purple room more than five minutes when Cooper appeared with the manager, who looked more than a little disgruntled.

"Mr. and Mrs. Jakob are on their way," he said with a superior sniff.

"Good. I need you to call in all of your dancing staff, too. And I do mean all of them. Do it now, please... Oh, and I need that list."

His eyes widened and he opened his mouth to protest, but before he could, Corbin said, "It's in the warrant. You can either do it, or we can put you in a car for obstruction. It's up to you."

The manager's mouth snapped shut. He pulled out a cell phone, eyes red and irritated looking, and started texting. "I'll try to have them here within the hour, but I can't guarantee it. Some of them have other jobs."

"Check them off the list as they come in," I said.

They were going to need those other jobs if Labyrinth was shut down as a result of the investigation. I had nothing against strippers, or dancers as they're more commonly called these days. In fact, I applauded their resilience and ability to read a room. These women almost always had sharp instincts and a talent for identifying creeps and criminals.

"We've got an hour to kill," I told Tracy and Corbin back in the hallway. Corbin now had the list of employees and their folders. "So let's take it out to the club room and go through the files."

***

It was just after three-thirty that afternoon when the Jakobs stormed in, teeth bared and ready for a fight.

"You have no right to do this," Alana snapped. "You have no proof that girl was here."

"Actually, we do. We have this," I said, holding up a two-month series of biweekly paychecks made out to Indigo Salazar. All marked her as cleaning staff, and she'd been getting paid minimum wage to work two hours a week on Saturdays. Unlikely.

Alana Jakob's face contorted into an ugly expression. The lighting in the club room was harsh, exposing the makeup gathering in her wrinkles and the gray roots in her hair. Yet she'd turned up wearing a stylish miniskirt, knee-high boots, and a suede top.

I glanced toward the back of the room where Corbin was talking with one of the cleaning crew, a short woman with close-cropped hair. We'd caught the manager trying to rush her out of the building no less than fifteen minutes prior.

"Mrs. Jakob, you told Sergeants Russell and Ramirez that you'd never seen Indigo Salazar before. You told me that you had no interest in 'wayward girls.' So can you explain to me why she's on your payroll?"

Alana's eyes flashed, but she couldn't deny the paperwork. It was a clear link.

"My husband and I aren't directly involved with hiring. If the girl was a part of our staff, we were unaware."

"Mmm. I could almost believe that—except, you lied to us about the stamps, too, didn't you?"

For a moment, that flash in her eyes turned to one of fear. I did a small victory lap in my head. But now wasn't the time to celebrate. It was the time to play it very, very carefully. Alana and Robert Jakob—the latter of whom Tracy was questioning and making him sweat, by the look of it—were a slippery duo.

"I did not lie about the stamps."

"Let me make this very clear to you, Mrs. Jakob. We have it from a reliable source that the purple stamps are used only for the dancers and have nothing to do with what day of the week it might be. We have your dancers here, right now. *All* of them. And we'll begin questioning them shortly."

Cooper had texted me only moments earlier confirming that the last of them had arrived.

"You and your husband are going to stay out here with Officers Shelton and Knapp while I interview them, and if I find either of you have been lying further, it's going to be an issue for you. Do you understand?"

Over her shoulder, I saw Robert Jakob deflate. At least he understood the situation they were in.

"Yes," Alana Jakob answered tightly, crossing her arms over her suede top.

"Good. Feel free to ask the officers if you need anything."

I glanced at Shelton and Knapp. They were fairly new on the force, having graduated from the academy the year before. They both nodded, their expressions stoic, their arms folded, feet apart. They knew not to let the Jakobs move even an inch.

I turned on my heel and headed back to the staff room, which I hadn't seen yet. But Cooper had said it was across from the tiny closet-office. The door was pretty banged up, scratched, discolored. I pushed it open and was faced with twelve women propped on various seats around the small room. A television in the corner playing some kind of soap, though the volume was turned down. Cooper was standing behind the women and watching them carefully.

"Hello, everyone," I said, my eyes taking them all in. Most of them appeared to range in age from maybe twenty to the mid-thirties, though it was hard to tell with the ones who wore makeup. I recognized the young woman we'd seen in the alley. She looked slightly tense. And no wonder. The Jakobs were a scary couple.

"I'm Captain Gazzara. I think you all know why you're here, but to clarify just in case: I'm heading the investigation into the disappearance and murder of Indigo Salazar. We know that she worked here. We also know that she was a dancer. Now, I have three officers with me so we are going to interview each of you individually. Who wants to go first?"

There were a few tense moments of silence; looks shared. But no one spoke.

One of the older women with short black hair and a plain face rolled her eyes, raised her hand and said, "I really don't have time for this. I need to get back to work, so I'll go first and get it over with, okay?"

I nodded, then picked out a couple more, including the young woman I'd met in the alley outside the club and told them to come with me, and then I left it to Corbin, Ramirez and Cooper to interview the other nine.

I took my little group to Alana Jakob's office, grabbed a couple of chairs, put them outside the door and asked the two girls to sit down and wait while I talked to the one who'd volunteered first.

I closed the door and sat Mary Livage—stage name Scarlett—down in front of the desk, perched myself on the edge of the desk, took out my phone and turned on the recording app. Then I dictated the time, date, place and all the other relevant information, and began.

"As I said, Mary, we know that Indigo worked here as

a dancer. And we know she was on the company payroll as a cleaner. What can you tell me about that?"

"That's true," she said. "Indigo was a dancer. She was never on the cleaning crew, but she did get on her knees, if you get my drift." She smirked at the pun.

I raised an eyebrow. "Would you care to explain that?"

She just stared up at me, said nothing. The silence was deafening.

"Look," I said, finally. "We're all well aware of what goes on here. And if we wanted to book anyone for drug use, drug distribution, or prostitution, we would have already done so. All I want are answers. I have no interest in pursuing anything else. So talk to me."

She nodded slowly, thoughtfully, then said, "Okay. Yeah, they expect us to provide sexual favors. You know, hand jobs, blow jobs, nothing more," she said. "Can't say they force us to; not exactly, but... if we turn a customer down, they cut our hours."

I shook my head as I stared down at her, angry at the thought of Alana and Robert Jakob coercing these women into performing sex acts. "And you're saying Indigo was part of that?" I asked.

"Yes. She was. But she didn't want to, though. Hell, none of us really want to."

"Are you paid to perform these acts?" I asked.

She shook her head. "No, but we get tips. And some of the girls make dates outside of the club and hook up, for money, you know, but don't ask me who, 'cause I ain't tellin'."

I nodded, smiling at her. "I told you, that's not what I'm here for. Did Indigo 'hook up,' as you call it?"

"No! Not to my knowledge. She rarely did more than the occasional hand job, if she could avoid it. She was popular, though. Probably because she was so young."

"So you knew she was underage?" I said.

She turned her mouth down at the corner, then said, "We all did, including the Jakobs. I guess she was good for business. I wasn't too fond of it myself. I have a good husband at home and... if ever he finds out..." She didn't finish the thought, but I knew what she meant.

"So why stay?" I asked.

"This crowd pays well. Better than the other clubs, probably because they can get more... services here."

"Did she have friends here?" I asked. "Did you or anyone else talk to her, go out around town with her?"

"No, Indigo didn't have any friends here. To be honest, none of us do. Most of us are not proud of what we do, and we have a life outside these walls." Her lip curled at the last comment.

My brow furrowed. "So tell me, how did she come to be hired?"

"Hah! She was young, fresh and unspoiled. They like to start them off young."

"Alana and Robert, you mean?"

"It's actually harder to get a foot in this place than you might think, especially when you're older, which is kind of ironic, don't you think, considering Alana's age? Most of the girls are hand-picked."

"What do you mean by that? 'Hand-picked'?"

Mary shrugged. "Just that. I guess you could call it a

talent show. We were recruited. Most of the girls were... recruited."

"But not you?" I said.

"Nope. I got in on luck. They were short a girl about a year ago. She rolled her ankle playing frisbee with her kid, and I was a regular behind the bar. I offered to take her spot temporarily and it turned into a full-time gig."

"How often was Indigo here?"

"Saturdays every week, and sometimes Fridays."

"You said most of you were recruited. Who did the recruiting?"

"Pan," she replied.

The hairs on the back of my neck stood up. *Peter Pan*.

I grabbed my phone from the desktop and quickly pulled up Andrew Mora's photo.

"Is this him?" I asked, showing it to her.

Mary shook her head decisively. "No. That's definitely not him. And no, I don't know his name. We just call him Pan. No one knows his real name."

Her lids had lowered, and the way she said the name wasn't affectionate or careless. It was careful, calculated.

"How many of the girls did this... Pan recruit?"

She made a face, then said, "Probably half of them. Teresa I know for sure and... Connie, I think."

"Teresa?" The name rang a bell. "Which one is she?"

"She's outside," she said. "Waiting to talk to you.

She's the kid from the alley, I thought. *Okay then.*

I slid off the desk and went to the door, opened it and said, "Teresa?"

They both looked up at me. The girl from the alley said, "Yes?"

"Come on in. Bring your chair. What's your full name?"

"Teresa Davidson."

"Teresa Davidson is entering the room at," and I gave the time for the record.

I had her sit down and showed her the photograph of Andrew Mora. "Do you know this man?" I asked.

She looked at the photo, then at Mary, then at me and said, "No. I've never seen him before."

"Are you sure? Please look again."

She did, then shook her head and said,

"No. I don't know who he is."

"So this is not Pan?"

"What? No. That's nothing like him."

"I'm told that it was Pan that recruited you. Is that correct, Teresa?"

There was only a moment of hesitation before she nodded and said, "Yeah."

"How long ago?" I asked.

"I don't know. A few years ago... Four?"

Four years ago. I knew it.

"How old are you, Teresa?"

She looked down at the floor, then said, "Twenty. I'll be twenty-one in March."

"So... you were sixteen when you started here?" I asked. "It's okay. You're not going to get into trouble. Just tell me the truth."

She nodded, then said, "Yes. Sixteen."

Oh, I was pissed. This was much bigger than I'd expected, and I'd have to go see the chief immediately after I was done interviewing.

"Was it Pan who brought Indigo in?" I asked.

"Yes," Mary said firmly. She seemed resolute, and I wondered just how tenuous the loyalty of these women was to the Jakobs. If what I just learned was true, they were looking at some serious time behind bars.

"How often does this guy Pan come around?" I asked.

"We don't see him much," Teresa said. "He never comes back to the purple room. He brings new girls every three or four months, maybe, and Alana and Robert decide if they stay or not. I've heard he's out at the bar some nights."

"But he never wants your... services?" I asked. That seemed weird. Why not take advantage of the perks of the job? Why not test out the talent?

"I saw him with Indigo sometimes," Teresa said.

"Did you, now?" I said.

She looked scared and nodded. Mary reached over and clutched her hand tightly. Despite her comment about not being friends, it seemed there was an element of camaraderie between them. I hoped when all of this was over, they'd be able to find a way out of this hellhole.

"Out loud. For the record, please, Teresa," I said.

"Yes," she said. "She met him sometimes out in the alleyway. I think maybe he was giving her rides or something. They'd walk down the street."

"In what direction?"

The way she pointed was toward the Whitlow building and the parking garage.

I texted Corbin and asked him to find out if there was a camera in the alley or across the street. Thinking that maybe we'd get lucky and get some footage of the pair. Then I pressed on.

"Do either of you know what kind of car he drives?"

"I never saw the car," Mary replied.

"Me neither," Teresa said.

"So what makes you think he was driving her somewhere?"

Teresa shrugged. "Well, Indigo didn't have a car, did she? I figured she had to be getting home somehow, and it was too late for the buses to run down this way."

"One last question," I said, "then you can go. Do either of you know if Indigo had a boyfriend, other than Pan?"

"No," Teresa said, shaking her head. "Not that I ever saw."

I looked at Mary.

She smiled at me, pursed her lips and said, "No."

"Okay. Thank you. You've both been really helpful. You can go now."

They had no idea how helpful they'd been. We could now tie not only Indigo but this Peter Pan to Labyrinth. And we could take Andrew Mora off the list of suspects.

The interview with the other girl went quickly. She was reluctant to talk at all, and when she did it was mostly in monosyllables. So, as I had more than enough to justify the warrant, I closed it down, leaving Corbin, Ramirez and Cooper to finish up with the rest of the women.

I closed the office door and called the chief.

"Hey, Chief. It's me. Will you be in your office for the next couple of hours? I need to talk to you."

"Yes," he replied. "I'll be here late tonight finalizing some paperwork. What have you got? Good news, I hope."

"Thanks," I said, ignoring the question. "I'll be there as soon as I can." And I hung up.

I went back to the staff room, intending to thank Mary again for her transparency. She was talking to Cooper. As I began to walk across the room toward them, I saw something that stopped me dead in my tracks. Several of the women had their lockers open, preparing to go to work, I presumed. But one of them happened to be holding a pair of black lace panties upon which, embroidered in gold letters, were the words, *Pan's Girl*.

"Excuse me," I said as she pulled a hand back hurriedly. "Where did you get that?"

Like Teresa, she was young. And she looked at me like a deer caught in the headlights.

"Um... he gives them to us," she squeaked, clutching a duffle bag to her chest.

"He? Do you mean the guy they call Pan?"

She nodded, shrinking away from me, and I realized I was coming across as a hard ass.

"I'm sorry," I said. "D'you, by any chance, know his real name?"

"Umm... No. I Just... He just... he got me the job. That's all. I only seen him a couple of times. He seemed really nice... He asked me out a couple of times, just for a drink, you know?"

"How about the other girls?" I asked. "Did he ask any of them out; Indigo, for instance?"

She shrugged. "I dunno. I did see them out in the

alley one time, but they were just talking, you know? That's all I know."

I would have liked to have talked further with her, but I didn't have time, and I really didn't think she had anything more to offer than I already had, so I gave her my card and said, "If any of you think of anything..."

"Well, that was... something," Cooper said as I joined him out in the hall.

"Yeah," I said, feeling a headache starting in just behind my eyes. And it wasn't even five o'clock yet. "Did you learn anything?"

"Yes. There's this guy they all call—"

"Pan. Yes, I know," I said, cutting him off. "Sounds like we've gotten some answers. I think maybe we're on solid ground at last."

"You think?" he asked.

I smiled wryly and shook my head, not wanting to answer, thinking of how many times I'd thought I was about to crack a case only to find out at the last moment that I was wrong.

Still, we did have some answers and maybe a couple of new leads, but the big questions remained.

Who was Pan? Did he murder Indigo? And if he did, why?

24

***

Friday Evening 5:15 pm

"Any luck?" I asked Jack, who was waiting for me at the rear entrance when I arrived back at the PD.

He shook his head. "Sorry, Kate. There aren't any cameras in the alleyway, which I'm thinking isn't a coincidence. There's a bank down the street, but it'll take me a while to go through all that footage, and we can't be sure that's the direction this 'Pan' guy took Indigo, if he picked her up."

I could tell that Jack was skeptical, but it was the best chance we had.

"Gazzara." Chief Johnston was leaning out of his office, gesturing impatiently. "You wanted to see me?"

I gave Jack a tight smile, then followed Johnston into his office.

"Sit down, Kate. You and the team were at Labyrinth this afternoon? Did you talk to Detective Robar by any chance?"

"No," I replied. "What did I miss?"

"Not much. It looks like Salazar's on the warpath again. We need to get this thing figured out, and quickly. What happened this afternoon that's so important? Are we any closer to a solution?"

"I think so," I replied and proceeded to fill him in on what we'd learned at Labyrinth.

He listened patiently without interrupting until I'd finished, then he leaned forward, clasped his hands together on top of his desk and said, "You're telling me they're employing underage dancers and coercing them into prostitution?"

"I am, including Indigo. And the recruiter, this guy, Peter Pan, is my prime suspect. I think she was seeing him outside of work, and she either saw or found out something she shouldn't and he had to shut her up."

Johnston sat back in his chair, brows creased as he considered. "That makes sense," he said, "but can you prove it?"

I blew air out through my lips, shook my head and said, "Not yet. We don't even have his name. No one seems to know what it is, or if they do, they're not telling."

"You ruled out Mora?"

I nodded, "Yes. We did. Several employees at the club confirmed he wasn't Pan. And his PO reached out to Hawk earlier today. They're confident it wasn't him. They have him on a tight leash."

He opened his mouth, but we were interrupted by his desk phone ringing. "Johnston."

He was silent for a moment, then looked at me and said, "Yes, she's with me. Send them in."

I frowned and raised my eyebrows in question. He hung up. There was a knock on the door. It opened and Cooper stepped inside with one of the dancers from Labyrinth.

He stood to the side, held the door open for her and she strutted in with her chin held high, as if in defiance. She was wearing loose sweatpants and a t-shirt.

"Chief, Captain," Cooper said. "This is—"

"Holly," she said, her eyes locking on mine. "Holly Friedman. I work at Labyrinth. I asked Detective Cooper if I could speak with you, but you'd already left."

"Please, sit down, Ms. Friedman," Johnston said. "You too, Cooper."

She sat down on the chair next to me. Cooper sat down at the back of the room.

"How long have you worked at the nightclub, Holly?" I asked.

"For almost four years, but it seems like forever," she said with a no-nonsense attitude. "Pan recruited me from another club."

"What do you want to talk to me about, Holly?" I asked.

"When Khadija was telling you about seeing Indigo and Pan in the alley, I remembered something."

"Khadija? Which one is she?"

"The blonde with... by the lockers."

Then I remembered. She was talking about the girl with the Pan lingerie.

"Ah, yes. I remember. Go on."

"Well, I saw Indigo and Pan talking together sometimes, but I never thought anything of it. But I did see his car once, I think."

She glanced sideways at the chief.

"What kind of car?" I asked.

"It was a black Honda. I saw it a couple months back when he dropped Indigo off at the club." She shrugged.

I smiled and asked the question to which I already knew the answer. "You didn't happen to get the license number, I suppose?"

"No, but I recognized the make and model. My mom has one exactly like it. It was a Honda Accord."

Exactly the same make and model as the stolen car in which we'd found Indigo's body.

"Thank you for that information, Holly," I said. "By the way, when Indigo started at Labyrinth, do you remember who interviewed her for the job?" I was hoping it was Alana or Robert Jakob, and I could catch them in their lie about not knowing Indigo.

"It would have been Roy, the manager," Holly said. "He always talks to the new girls first, and then if he thinks they're okay, Robert meets with them." Her mouth puckered in distaste.

I was tempted to pursue that line of questioning. *What, exactly, was* he *interviewing them for?* I wondered. *As if I couldn't guess.*

Holly looked nervous, then blurted out, "They took it too far this time." She shut her mouth, then bit her lip and continued, "They never treat us girls well. The money is pretty good. We make more than we would at any of the other clubs, trust me. But if..." She shook her head. "I'm putting in my notice. D'you think the Jakobs..."

Ignoring the chief's warning look, I told her, "I can't talk about the investigation, Holly, but you do need to be careful. Don't go anywhere alone... Do you carry a weapon?"

She hesitated, then shook her head. "No. D'you think I should? Whatever happened to Indigo happened because she worked at the club. I'm right, aren't I?"

She was right. Indigo's fate had been sealed the moment she stepped foot through those doors, but I didn't tell Holly that. Instead, I stood up and said, "Come on, Holly. I'll have someone drive you home."

25

Friday Evening 11:35 pm

IT WAS FRIDAY NIGHT, ALMOST A WEEK SINCE INDIGO Salazar's body had been discovered and, while we were making progress, the investigation wasn't going quickly enough for me and most certainly not for the chief. That being so, I went to bed early that night—early for me, that is—at around ten o'clock. But sleep wouldn't come. My mind was in a whirl.

At around eleven-thirty, I finally gave it up. I sighed, rolled over, glanced at the clock, then slipped out of bed. Samson huffed, stretched, shook himself and then dropped heavily into my spot, his paws alongside his head, and stared soulfully up at me.

I half-staggered to the bathroom, then from there to the kitchen where I made myself a cup of hot chocolate. Holding it in both hands, I went to the living room and flopped down on the couch to be joined only seconds later by Samson, who promptly jumped up beside me and parked his huge head in my lap.

I smiled down at him, took a sip of my chocolate, tilted my head to one side and said, "What are we going to do, Sam?"

He perked up, lifted his head and looked sideways at me, his tongue hanging out of his mouth.

"You know," I said, "I feel like we're chasing ghosts. No, just one ghost. What d'you think?"

He panted.

"Yeah, that's exactly how I feel... What I want to know is, how did Indigo and Rat manage to run into a man who left no trace? Well, almost no trace," I said as I stared vacantly at the empty vase on the sideboard under the window. "We do have his DNA." Images of a shadowy individual in a black hooded sweatshirt, a stolen car, and two stubbed-out joints swam through my mind.

I scratched behind his ears and he sighed and lowered his head back to my lap.

"You know—"

He perked up again, almost knocking the cup and its contents all over me.

"Sammy!" I scolded, then immediately relented.

"You know, Corbin called me just after Holly left the office this afternoon, and you know what he told me? You don't? Well, he told me... Now look, Sammy, you're not to tell anyone I told you—" *Oh hell, what am I doing? I must be losing it. I'm talking to a dog.*

And then I thought, *so what? I don't have anyone else to talk to! Right, so you need to get a life, Kate.*

Chapter 25

But I couldn't help thinking about what Corbin had told me.

Alana and Robert Jakob had both insisted they didn't know Pan's real name, but they admitted they did business with him... well, Robert did, though his wife, by all accounts, wasn't happy about it. On further questioning by Corbin, they admitted they had an ongoing deal with him. Pan brought them girls, and the Jakobs paid him in cash. A fifteen percent cut of whatever the girls made their first month. But it was the manager, Roy, who paid him. He said they met down by the old, empty bank building, where he handed over the cash.

"The bank... Hmm. That's not much more than a block away from the Whitlow building."

Again, Samson perked up, but this time he sat up and breathed in my face.

"Phew! Doggy breath," I said, pushing his nose to one side with my free hand. Actually, his breath was quite sweet.

"Hmm. I'm thinking that maybe he parks there regularly, whenever he has business in the area. I wonder if he... Nah, not the night he dumped Indigo. Not if he was driving that car. It doesn't feel like it was planned," I murmured. "I mean," I continued, ruffling Samson's ears, "the guy must be pretty smart, right? He's covered his tracks really well... but something about it feels... rushed. Him leaving the car up there, out in the open, slitting her throat... one quick slash. Rushed. And he must have been covered in blood."

I turned my head and looked at Sam. He was staring

back at me, his eyes level with mine, and I couldn't help it. I burst out laughing. He looked so bewildered.

"Kate, have you considered that he might be watching the high school?" Corbin had asked me. "He could be recruiting his girls there? During one of the interviews we conducted after you left, the girl mentioned she'd graduated Silver Springs, and we know someone was picking Indigo up there."

That was an interesting connection. And no, I didn't know that, but it made sense... especially given that Ms. Sweeney, the secretary, had mentioned someone lingering around.

HOLLY SAID SHE SAW INDIGO IN THE BLACK HONDA, I thought. *And Carolyn stopped hearing from Indigo, which she said made her think she was seeing someone. If so, who was it? What had Indigo gotten herself into?* I figured it must have been Pan. And it was that that was keeping me up at night. I was being haunted by a faceless figure walking my dreams.

Who the hell is he?

26

Saturday Evening 8:45 pm

"Sure you're ready for this?" I asked Anne and Tracy, both of whom were waiting just inside Labyrinth on the main floor. Inside, the club was already pulsing, dark and sultry, filled to the brim with gyrating young people. *Not for much frickin' longer, I hope.*

We, all three of us, were dressed for the evening. Anne was wearing a conservative, black, shin-length dress that showed off her curves. Tracy was decked out in a slinky top that made her shoulders look amazing and some kind of jegging-type pants. Me? I'd struggled to find anything to suit the occasion. Clubbing wasn't exactly one of my pastimes. And I felt I couldn't wear what I'd worn before. Or... maybe I could have, but the society-trained female in me wouldn't let me.

So, I chose a red square-necked top and a black skirt that zipped all the way up the back. The latter had been a misguided gift from a friend. It wasn't something I'd ever wear in the office, but it worked okay for that night.

Somewhere deep in the bowels of the club, Jack North was staked out watching security screens, and Corbin and Hawk were with Alana and Robert. I could just see Cooper out of the corner of my eye, stationed at the bar in a floral button-down that made me grin. He looked good. Maybe too good, since a woman nearby was chatting him up and distracting him.

"Do we have an ETA?" Anne asked casually, sipping what looked like a cocktail but was actually just cranberry juice and seltzer.

"Not exactly," I replied. "They said he usually showed early... early for a night club, that is."

At that point in the case, I felt as if I was running on fumes. I eyed the bar, wondering what the chances were that they served energy drinks.

"So fill me in," Anne said, leaning casually against the high-top table we were gathered around close to the entrance. "What are you hoping will happen tonight?"

"We grab Peter Pan," Tracy said, adjusting her strap to show a little less cleavage. "Corbin worked out some kind of deal with the Jakobs. We know there's been some real off-the-wall shit going on here, so he told them if they cooperate tonight, things might go smoother for them in the future."

"That kind of shit?" Anne asked, her brows raised as she nodded toward a bartender doing a bad job of surreptitiously passing a small baggie to a long-haired ape of a man.

"Yes, that kind," I said dryly. "We're going to wait

until this mess is over, and then the chief is going to send Finkle and his team in."

Tracy snorted. "Let's see if he can manage to mishandle this one, too."

"Some of the dancers quit last night. Three, I think. We knew it was going to happen so Corbin was able to cut the deal. They agreed to have Pan bring in a couple of new girls tonight."

Anne nodded slowly. "You're thinking this 'Peter Pan' is the guy who murdered Indigo?"

"At this point," I replied, "I don't know, but it's the best lead we've got. What we do know is that we can get him for trafficking underage girls. So, whether or not he killed Indigo, he needs to be stopped."

"Where's Sammy?" Tracy asked, brows knit.

He was back with Corbin, keeping an eye on the Jakobs. I'd gotten a text from Corbin not ten minutes earlier: *Turns out Alana Jakob isn't fond of dogs. Who would've guessed?*

I'd smirked at that, and I'd have given anything to be in that room. Hopefully my boy had her backed into a corner, shaking in her fancy boots.

"Danielle couldn't watch him tonight and my other dogsitter is out of the country, so he's stuck with us."

"We'll probably all need a little pet therapy when this is over," she said morosely. "Good call, Cap."

"What about this guy?" Cooper's voice was quiet in my earpiece, and I saw Anne roll her shoulders in reaction to his words.

At the doorway was a short, dark man whose profile, just for a moment, reminded me of Rat Nelson. But it obviously wasn't him. When he stepped further into the light, he grinned, revealing a set of yellowed teeth. *Gross!*

Roy, the manager, greeted him with a smile and led him toward the back of the club. *Ah, another sleazeball for the purple room. I wonder how it's going back there.*

"A customer," I said quietly, touching my earpiece to transmit. Tracy and Anne nodded in agreement. Between the three of us, I figured we'd be able to spot our target the minute he walked through the door with his merchandise.

Twenty more minutes went by, and I was just beginning to wonder if he was going to show when I saw Anne stiffen. I turned my head to look toward the entrance and saw a male figure of average height in a dark-colored hoodie talking to the manager. The room was too dark to see any distinguishing features.

"Damn it," I muttered. "He's going to give it away." Even in the dim lighting I could see he was talking animatedly to the man. Roy was obviously nervous, but Pan, if that's who it was, didn't seem to notice.

I put my finger to my earpiece and said, "Heads up, everybody. He's here." I *knew* it was him. I could feel it in my bones. And just a step behind him was a young girl with almond-shaped eyes and dark skin. She was pretty, and she looked confident. And I had to wonder if she had any idea what she was getting into.

"Jack. You watching?" I whispered.

"Yes, Captain. Eyes on him."

We were all on the alert but playing it cool. Anne laughed at something Tracy said that I knew couldn't have been a joke. Me? I had both hands on the table jigging and shaking my hair to the beat of the music.

"Don't do anything until I tell you," I said. "Let Roy go through his routine. He told me he usually takes them to the bar for a drink and then takes them back to the office. The idea is to put the girls at ease before the interview."

Pan, wearing a dark baseball cap that shadowed his face, was smiling as he followed Roy into the club. He beckoned to the girl, who walked confidently in and tossed her ombré hair over a shoulder.

"I need confirmation it's him, Jack," I said quietly.

It was Corbin who answered almost immediately. "Confirmed. It's him."

"The Jakobs. They're secure?" I asked.

"Yes. Sammy is... keeping an eye on them."

I smirked. *That's my boy*.

Roy took Pan to the bar, put his mouth close to his ear and tried to speak over the music pumping out from the overhead speakers. Pan nodded and gestured to the girl, who leaned in close to his other ear and said something. He nodded again and said something to the bartender, who handed him an El Presidente cocktail, which I could tell by the type of glass, the color of the liquid, and the twist of orange peel, and that caught my attention. There was something... familiar about that. What it was, I couldn't fathom; not then, anyway.

Inwardly, I shrugged and continued to watch as the girl was handed what looked like a rum and cola, or something similar.

"If she's underage, we can add that to the list of charges," Anne's voice spoke softly in my ear.

"You good, Cap?" Tracy asked, frowning at me.

I nodded, but I couldn't let it go. *An El Presidente... Why? What did that remind me of?*

Pan adjusted his cap and turned to grin at the girl. He leaned in close to her and said something. She laughed, almost choking on her drink. She put her glass down, grabbed a tissue from her clutch and wiped her mouth.

I tried to get a good look at him, but the top half of his face was shadowed by the cap. It was impossible to tell his age or anything else about him.

Tracy shifted restlessly at my side.

"How long do you want to wait?" she asked.

I opened my mouth to reply, but then Roy looked across at me over Pan's shoulder. His eyes flicked and he gave the slightest nod, but it was enough.

"Now!" I shouted. Pan must have heard me because he tensed and looked around.

Anne and Tracy rounded the table and started toward the bar.

Cooper stood up. He was only feet away along the bar. He made it in two steps, but Pan ducked down and barreled into him, head first into his stomach. I, too, was on the move toward the bar, but from where I was, I couldn't hear anything but did see Cooper double up and slump and stagger back against the bar top.

Pan ran, heading toward the back of the building.

"Corbin, Jack, Hawk," I yelled. "He's running, coming your way!"

I cursed the heels and kicked them off, feeling the

grimy floor under my bare feet, and I ran, sprinting through the crowd. I could feel the zipper of my skirt opening as I tore across the dance floor, knocking people out of the way, ignoring their shouts.

"Get the girl!" I shouted, hoping someone on the team would hear me. I didn't have time to look over my shoulder as I lunged toward the heavy door into the purple room, shoving it open, charging into another world.

The music was slower, lower, sensual. Teresa, on her pedestal, froze; her eyes met mine.

Khadija went into a half crouch, clutching her bare breasts. "That's him!" she shouted.

I barely had time to glance at the outraged patrons lounging in front of her before I was through the room and out into the hallway.

But Pan was fast, and I had to skid to a stop. North was on his back on the floor in the middle of the hall, clutching his bleeding nose. "Go, go, go," he yelped.

I didn't hesitate. Pan was already at the door, wrenching it open. If I didn't catch him, he'd be gone, and all would have been for nothing.

He put his shoulder to the door, his hands on the emergency bar and started to shove. But just as he was about to exit, a dark shape streaked out of the hallway from the side where Alana and Robert were holed up in their office.

I was taken completely by surprise: "Corbin?"

No. It wasn't Corbin. It was smaller, too compact to be a grown man, and then I heard a low growl as it streaked past.

In the blink of an eye, Samson had Pan by the arm, dragging him down as he shouted in pain and fear.

A second later, I tackled him, the zipper on my skirt finally giving way. Samson, his jaws clamped on Pan's forearm, his muscles rippling under his coat, growled as he hunkered down and jerked Pan's arm, tearing at the sleeve of the hooded sweatshirt.

"Good boy," I said firmly. "Drop it."

Sammy dropped Pan's arm but stood close, head down, front paws wide apart, teeth bared, panting as Pan scrambled backward. I hauled my body over to his and planted a knee on his chest.

Corbin and Hawk rushed to my side, both reaching for their cuffs. Corbin secured him as Samson, head down, watched from behind, between his legs.

And I stared down into the face of Pan, whose hat had been knocked off in the fray. Looking back up at me was the face of Carolyn's friend Oskar Pope, the security guard from the Whitlow Building.

27

Saturday Night 10:35 pm

OSKAR POPE SAT SLUMPED IN A CHAIR IN ONE OF THE interview rooms, the left arm of his sweatshirt cut off at the bicep and a gauze wrapped around his forearm.

Sammy hadn't banged him up too badly; it was mostly bruises, plus a superficial scrape that had barely bled. But when we'd brought Oskar in, he'd spent the first twenty minutes threatening to have Samson put down and demanding to know why he was being arrested.

"All right," Cooper said, cracking his neck and rubbing his hands together. "The seventy-two hours starts now. Not including tomorrow." He shot me a wink, and I raised an eyebrow.

While I appreciated his enthusiasm, we had to proceed carefully. Oskar didn't seem to be holding together too well. His moods were swinging wildly. I knew we had to ease into it, because the second he decided to shut up and refuse to speak to us was the second we ran out of luck.

I stood watching him muttering to himself. My backside was covered by a sweater someone had lent me. The waistband of my skirt was still intact; the zipper wasn't.

"Corbin." I jerked my head toward the door, and my partner nodded, finishing off a much-needed bottle of water.

It was late, and it had been a long day, for all of us, including Samson, who lay flat out under the table after being lauded by just about everyone in the situation room; those that were left anyway.

I was just about to reach out to the handle of the interview room when the door behind me opened and Chief Johnston stepped in. His face was grave, made even graver by the Hulk Hogan mustache.

"I want an update before you start, please," he said.

I glanced at Corbin. We'd sent the rest of the team home, all except Jack. They'd all be back in the morning to tidy up. Jack? He was filing the footage and outlining the bones of the report. He'd looked dead tired, but I needed someone tech-savvy to handle that part of the job.

"Oskar Pope entered Labyrinth in the company of a young girl at nine-fourteen," I began, crossing my arms. "Tracy caught her running toward the door when we attempted to arrest Pope. Her name's Taylor Lind. She said she had just moved here from Michigan. She's seventeen and she knew what she was getting into... sort of. She knew she'd be stripping."

Johnston nodded. "You're sure it's Pan?"

"I am. He was identified by the manager, Robert

Jakob and several of the girls; two of them he introduced to the club within the last year."

Johnston's eyes moved between us. "But you two, you already knew him?"

I nodded. "Yes. We interviewed him the day Indigo's body was discovered. He's a security guard at the Whitlow building."

"So he looks good for it so far," Johnston grunted. "But can you tie him to the girl?"

"Well, there's this," I said, picking up a copy of a photograph and handing it to him. "We got that from Urban One when we were initially canvassing the area. That's Pope. That's Lewis Massey—he's also a security guard at Whitlow—and that's Indigo. The club owner told us that Indigo had been there with these two several times, sometimes with Carolyn Brown, Indigo's friend.

"When we interviewed Pope and Massey, their story was that all four of them hung out that night before they walked her back to Electric Blue. She caught an Uber from there. We can confirm that from the security footage."

"So what's your game plan?" he asked.

"Aside from getting him to confess?" I said a little saucily, loosening up now that it seemed like we might be ahead of the game. "We have DNA from the two crime scenes. If we can match it to him, we have him."

Johnston considered that for a moment, stroking his mustache, but for some reason, he didn't look entirely convinced. And to be truthful, I had a gut feeling he was right.

"Good luck," he said as he turned to leave. *Thank you for that, oh exalted one!*

It was cold in the interview room. Pope was lounging back in his chair, his arms crossed over his chest. I could see goose bumps on his bare bicep, just above the bandage, and inwardly I smiled, thinking Sammy might not be a trained detective but, in his way, he was just as good a partner as Corbin.

"Oskar Pope," I said slowly, moving toward the table and leaning against it, both hands flat on the tabletop.

Corbin took a seat opposite him, his expression calm and attentive. He stated the preamble for the record, and I began.

"How about we start by you telling us why you ran tonight?" I said quietly.

He opened his mouth but only scoffed and stuttered for a moment. Then he said, "You-you were *chasing* me!"

"True, but why run if you hadn't done anything wrong? We weren't in uniform."

"Obviously that doesn't matter." He muttered it, but his face was sickly-pale, hinting at his nerves.

"Do you know why we brought you here, Oskar?"

He looked up at me. "No."

"We brought you here to talk about the work you do for the Jakobs."

"Oh-kay?"

A pause. This is where he figured out we were on to him. He had that caught hare look, like he'd been snagged in a trap by his toes and was looking for a way out. Considering gnawing off his own foot.

"You're Peter Pan," Corbin said mildly. "Isn't that a name you use?"

He looked back and forth between us. And I wondered if I should call for a bucket. He looked as if he was about to puke.

"For business purposes, yeah."

"And what kind of business are you in, Oskar?" I asked, fighting to keep the sarcasm out of my voice.

For a moment, a hardness flickered across his features, catching me by surprise. It was as if Oskar Pope was two different men. And from the look on Corbin's face, I knew he'd seen it too.

But there was a hollow knock on the door and Jack North stuck his head in, his eyes wide. My gut sank. Whatever it was, it wouldn't be good.

"Captain. There's someone here to see you."

———

IVAN SALAZAR LOOKED DISHEVELED. HIS SILVER HAIR glinted under the fluorescent lights of my office and the neck of his t-shirt was pulled loose, his shirt wrinkled. He was wearing jogger pants with tight cuffs around the ankles. They were in style but looked oddly out of place on a man his age.

"You've arrested someone," he stated as I walked in.

"Who told you that?" I said, neither confirming nor denying it. I deadpanned it, trying to keep my cool. In truth, I was royally pissed off. We'd barely begun to interview Pope, and I'd been dragged out for this.

Salazar glared at me, his eyes flashing and... desperate.

"That doesn't matter. Have you arrested someone or not?"

Did I really want to go through the whole due process with him? No. Especially since, given his "in" at the department, he likely already knew. There was no other way he could have caught on that we had a suspect so quickly. I had to tell Johnston we had ourselves a mole, well-meaning or not.

"Mr. Salazar, you know I can't discuss an ongoing investigation with you—"

"I know you're questioning someone, detective, and I also know that you think he killed my Indigo. He should be in a secure facility. He should be under arrest."

"Again, I'm not at liberty—"

The surgeon, playing Jekyll and Hyde, scoffed, spun on his heel and paced from one end of the office to the other and then back again.

"And you think he'll tell the truth, Miss Gazzara? You think he'll admit that he slit Indigo's throat—"

"Doctor Salazar, I cannot and will not keep repeating myself. I must ask you to leave. Right now. If not, I'll have you escorted from the premises. I promise I'll call you as soon as we know more."

He stood for a moment staring at me.

I locked eyes with him and said, "Are we done now?"

Sammy, who'd been sleeping peacefully on his bed, rose to his feet and stretched.

Salazar glanced at him, stared at my large companion,

then looked me in the eye and said, "I'll be waiting for your call, Captain Gazzara."

I didn't bother to respond. He turned on his heel and stalked out of my office, and I watched as he crossed the situation room to the officer waiting to escort him out of the building.

I took out my phone and texted Johnston: *We need to talk about Ivan Salazar.*

Within seconds I heard the tone indicating the message had been delivered, but he didn't respond.

Sighing, I crouched down to ruffle Samson's ears. "Stay here boy, okay? I promise we'll be home soon, sleeping in our bed."

Samson huffed out a sigh, licked my nose and dropped back down between his paws, his big brown eyes looking up at me.

Me? I clenched my fists and headed back to the interview room and Oskar Pope, more determined than ever to get through to him. That thanks to indignation as much as adrenaline.

It was almost midnight in the garden of good and evil.

28

Sunday Morning 12:01 am

Pope's demeanor had changed a bit in the half-hour I'd been gone. Corbin gave me a sidelong glance and shrugged. The man known as "Pan" didn't look boyish at all, though he was probably in his mid-to-late twenties. He had dark hair, an olive complexion, and his eyes were no longer wide and innocent. They were narrowed at me as I sat across from him.

"Listen, Oskar. We know what you do. We know you traffic girls to Labyrinth—"

He scoffed. "I don't traffic them. I just hook them up with job opportunities."

"Jobs you lie about," Corbin said nastily. "You tell these girls they're getting an under-the-table job, which in itself is illegal; and most of them are underage. They think they're just going to be dancing, but we both know that isn't quite true, that they're expected to perform sex acts for the club patrons."

Oskar's jaw worked sideways, back and forth, then he said, "Look, what happens once they pass through those doors isn't on me. If Alana asks them to do a few favors for her guests—"

"Oskar," I said gently. "You knowingly introduced female minors into prostitution. That's sex trafficking and it carries a stiff penalty. Okay, enough of that for now. Let's talk about Indigo Salazar. How well did you know her?"

I watched him closely as he considered his options. He took a deep breath.

"I had nothing to do with that girl. With Indigo," he said, choosing his words carefully.

I stood and circled the table slowly. He was tense, his face pale.

"The problem is, Oskar," I said, "several of the women at Labyrinth and a solid witness at Indigo's high school will testify that Peter Pan—that's you, isn't it, Oskar?—was seen picking her up and driving her around. Not just once, but many times."

His brow creased in concentration. I glanced at Corbin. He looked back at me and raised his eyebrows. Not a good sign.

"Okay, I go to Labyrinth now and then, and yeah, for a drink. And sometimes I end up seeing the girls I introduced there. But I'm not friendly with any of them."

"So you weren't friendly with Indigo?" I asked, standing behind him.

He shrugged. "No, and I ain't never driven her anywhere neither."

I could tell by the expression on his face that I wasn't

going to get anywhere with that line of questioning, so I changed tactics.

"Oskar," I said thoughtfully, "you do know that if the trafficking charges go through, you're looking at eight years in jail, minimum. You might want to start talking. Tell us how you got involved with Indigo."

"I wasn't involved with her," he said in a flash of anger that piqued my curiosity. I recalled his interview with Anne and Hawk, and the way he'd seemed uncomfortable talking about Indigo. What were we missing?

"So how did you meet her?"

"Through a mutual friend," he replied through gritted teeth.

"And you decided she'd be a good fit for Labyrinth?"

Oskar laughed. "No, not at first. She looked like a good kid in that school uniform. Uptight, yeah. But see, I was wrong about that." He shook his head, sighed, shifted in his chair and crossed his legs at the ankles.

"Most of the girls I find for them just need the money. Or a fix. Both of which Alana is happy to supply," he added dryly. "And I get a commission. So what?"

"You said that at first you didn't think Indigo would be a good fit for Labyrinth," Corbin said. "So why did you take her there?"

"Because she insisted," he snapped.

I couldn't help laughing. "You're telling me a seventeen-year-old girl cornered you into *making* her become a stripper?"

His eyes dropped to the left; he was leaving something out.

"I told you, I didn't want to involve her. I wish I'd

never met her. But I... owed a friend a favor." He shrugged as if it was no big deal.

Now that got my attention, and Corbin's. *So there's someone else involved? Is that what I've been missing?*

"This friend brought Indigo to you?"

Oskar nodded. Corbin and I locked eyes again.

"We're going to need a name," Corbin said, shifting restlessly in his seat.

Oskar shook his head, "Oh no. We're not going there."

"Eight years," I reminded him. "And I can tack on a couple more for obstructing a criminal investigation. So let's cooperate, shall we?"

He glared up at me, then his face softened and his shoulders slumped.

"Lewis. It was Lewis," he all but whispered the name.

We'd had a Lewis Massey, who was a guard with Whitlow, in for questioning on Tuesday.

"You're talking about Lewis Massey?" I said. "He's the friend?"

He nodded.

"You said you owed him a favor," Corbin said. "What favor was that?"

With a sigh, Oskar reluctantly explained. "Lewis and Indigo were not... like... together. Know what I mean? I don't know. They met up a lot. She showed up that night at Urban One when it was just supposed to be me and him. I was scouting." His lips had twisted into an angry pout.

"So they hung out?" I asked, "and you didn't like it, and that's what put you off her?"

He shook his head. "No! Lewis was... a little too into her. You know?" He sneered, his dark eyes flashing up at me. "She was only seventeen years old," he continued. "Yeah, I bring them to Labyrinth, but I'm not stupid enough to touch them."

"But Lewis, he did... touch her?" I asked.

Again, he shrugged, looked down at the tabletop and said, "I don't know."

He looked up at me, then at Corbin and, seeing the skepticism on our faces, he repeated angrily, "I don't know, okay? But I didn't like her hanging around. I didn't want to send her to Labyrinth. I knew something about her was off but—"

He caught himself and stopped going further. Corbin and I waited, on edge, but Oskar had shut down.

"Oskar," I said gently, "there's something we haven't told you. We have DNA from both crime scenes: Indigo's and Rat Nelson's. And guess what?" I stared down at him. He didn't answer, so I told him. "They match, and I'm betting it will lead us straight to the killer."

"Yeah? Well, I didn't kill her, see?" he burst out, angrily slamming a fist on the table.

I sat back down. I was angry.

"So you're willing to give us a DNA sample?" I asked.

"Yeah. Absolutely," he snapped, spreading his arms wide. Another unexpected surprise. "Yeah," he said again, "And now I'm done talking until I have a lawyer present. But I'll give you a DNA sample. I didn't kill nobody."

I sat there staring at him, my mind in a whirl. If

Oskar Pope was so sure his DNA wouldn't match that at the crime scenes, he couldn't be the murderer.

I felt defeated—like the case was back to square one.

29

Sunday Morning 8:30 am

AS YOU CAN IMAGINE, IT WAS LATE, OR SHOULD I SAY early morning, when Sammy and I finally got home that Sunday morning. I set the alarm for six, stripped off my clothes and fell into bed a few minutes after two o'clock and went out like a light with Sam's backside jammed tight against my right hip.

The alarm woke me up two minutes later—well, that's what it felt like—and I literally fell out of bed and staggered to the bathroom. *Oh... God help me,* I remember thinking. *I'm too old for this shit.* And I stood under the shower hanging onto the grab rail for dear life. It was a long moment of self-examination, and right there and then, I made up my mind that I wasn't going to play the game anymore. Never again would I spend half the night interviewing a suspect. *No,* I thought. *They can rot in a holding cell until the following day.* But even as I thought it, I knew it was a fallacy and that I was kidding myself. It just wasn't who I was.

I arrived at work that morning at eight-thirty feeling as if the Empire State Building had fallen on me to find Anne at her desk staring at the screen, shaking her head as she watched the video of our interview with Oskar Pope.

"I just... he's like an entirely different person," she said.

Hawk, who was standing behind her, nodded and said, "Yeah, we didn't see this side of him when we interviewed him. He seemed skittish, nervous. But not like this."

"So," Hawk said, turning to look at me, "if he's so willing to provide a DNA sample, he's not our killer. Not unless he's playing it smart and hoping that because he's so willing, we'll give him a pass. We've got him for trafficking, though."

"I agree," I said. "He's not that smart. The trafficking? Sure... But... I think we need to talk to Lewis Massey. There's a connection between him and Indigo. Anne, see if he has a record, and then both of you come to my office. Oh, and has anyone seen Jack this morning?"

"Yeah," Hawk said, "he's in the lab, I think."

"Okay. Good," I said. "Soon as you can, guys." And with that I went to my office, turned Samson loose, and called Jack.

"Hey," I said when he picked up. "Did you ever do anything with that number I gave you? The one I found in Indigo's closet."

"Yeah. I meant to tell you about that, but with all the

rushing around yesterday, I forgot. Sorry. It was out of service. It was a burner. Untraceable, but I'm still working on it."

"Damn!" I said. "Okay. Later."

I hung up, stared at the whiteboard for a minute, then opened the box that contained copies of the Whitlow company's employee files just as Hawk and Anne entered my office.

According to Lewis' employment file, he was twenty-eight, turning twenty-nine in two months. He'd grown up in Cleveland, Tennessee, just twenty miles north of Chattanooga, graduated from Bradley Central in 2009 and had lived in the city for the last seven years.

"Hmm," I said, passing the file to Hawk. "There are no blemishes on his employment record. Anne, did you find anything?"

"No. He's clean. Not even a parking ticket."

I stared up at the whiteboard, thinking... Actually, I wasn't; my mind was a complete blank, and I was pissed. When we grabbed Pope, I'd thought we had this thing all wrapped up. Now I was effectively back at square one unless we got really lucky and Pope's DNA matched that at the crime scenes. The more I stared at the whiteboard —with Indigo's face staring back at me—and revisited the interview with Pope, I realized we had one more thread to pull.

Inwardly, I heaved a sigh, then said, "Hawk, see if you can track Massey down and bring him in for a chat."

"You got it, Cap. You want me to go now?"

I nodded absently, then said, "Yep! Get him in here. Maybe he's the one we're looking for. If not, maybe he can give us a lead. God knows we need one. Where are Cooper and Ramirez, by the way?"

"Cooper's around here somewhere," Anne said. "Tracy called in and said she was going to be a little late. She should be in soon."

And then, as if I'd summoned her, Tracy popped her head into the room, looking slightly frazzled, and clinging onto the edge of the door, and said, "Kate, there's someone here to see you."

"I swear, if it's Ivan Salazar—"

But it wasn't. A quick glance out through the glass walls surprised me. It was Lara, the bartender from Electric Blue. She was standing nervously with her hands balled together in the middle of the situation room.

"Bring her in," I said. "Hawk. You stay for a minute."

Anne shifted from the chair in front of my desk to one at the table. Hawk sat down beside her. Tracy ushered Lara in.

"Lara," I said, giving her a bright smile. "Please. Sit down. What brings you here this morning?"

She gave me a nervous smile and sat down in the chair Anne had just vacated. Tracy joined Hawk and Anne at the table.

Lara took a breath, swallowed, and said, "I heard you arrested Pan last night, but I think I found something."

"And what was that?" I asked encouragingly.

By then, Lara had her cell phone in her hands. She tapped the screen several times, then turned it around to show me.

The video wasn't that good. It was dark, dim, of a woman dancing. It took a few seconds before I realized it had been shot in the purple room at Labyrinth, but I was unable to tell who the dancer was. I glanced up at Lara.

"This is?" I asked.

"It's on Labyrinth's social media account," Lara said as the video started to replay. "I haven't been able to stop thinking about everything, about Indigo and Rat, and I've been kind of stalking them."

Still unsure what the point of the video was, I squinted and looked closer.

"In the back corner," Lara said. "See? It's hard to make out, but..."

The area she referred to was tiny on the phone and only dimly lit by a wall sconce, but I could just make out two figures. I squinted and watched as one of the figures leaned in close to the other. The swing of the hair as the other person moved away told me it was a female. A hand shot out, grabbed her by the upper arm and jerked her closer.

No! I thought. *There's no way I could get that lucky.*

I grabbed the phone from her, scrabbled through my desk drawer for a USB cord and plugged the phone into my iMac and brought up the video, full screen, and turned it so everyone could see.

As it replayed again, my mouth dropped open. In the first few seconds, the two individuals seemed to be arguing. Then the one to the left moves in close; the other, the female, moves away, and then the first individual grabs the female, his features twisted in a malicious smile as she winces, and pulls her back.

We were looking at Indigo Salazar and Lewis Massey.

"When was this posted?" I said, dumbfounded.

"Two days ago," Lara replied. "I've been watching their account. I can't help it. And I noticed this. Obviously they didn't, or they wouldn't have posted it."

"It's an old video?" Anne asked.

Lara nodded. "Yeah. We all do it. We save up videos and photos for our social presence. Rat used to have them scheduled to post automatically. I'm guessing that's what Labyrinth does, too, and they just didn't notice."

We now had video footage of Lewis Massey being aggressive with Indigo Salazar, sometime before she'd disappeared.

Anne and I made eye contact, but we couldn't discuss our thoughts in front of Lara. Tracy looked grave.

"I'll be back," Hawk said, standing up.

I nodded. "Take Cooper with you."

"Thank you, Lara," I said. "You've been a great help."

The young woman nodded, swallowing thickly. "This guy... we banned him from Electric Blue months ago. Well, Rat did. Do you think..."

I knew where she was going with it. She was wondering if Rat had found out that Lewis Massey was obsessed with Indigo and had tried to do something about it. We already knew from his texts that he'd tried to warn someone off.

"You said you thought Indigo was seeing someone," I said. "What made you think that?"

"Huh, it wasn't difficult. She started being secretive, getting rides, you know. From the same person. Same car. I saw her. And I knew they were going to other clubs after she left Electric Blue, when she was supposed to be going home. And she'd be putting on makeup before she left. I mean, nobody does that; do they?"

"Did she ever actually tell you she had a boyfriend or was dating someone?" Anne asked.

Lara shook her head slowly. "No. I thought... we thought maybe she was just embarrassed. Or knew it was someone we wouldn't like."

Which was obviously true, because when Rat had caught him pursuing Indigo, he'd banned Lewis from the club. Despite my initial bad feelings about Rat, I was slowly beginning to understand he was one of the good guys, with good instincts and good intentions.

"Was he... Is he... Is this guy someone dangerous?" Lara asked, looking from me to Anne.

I pursed my lips, looked her in the eye and said, "Lara, I don't know, and if I did, I couldn't tell you anything more than what the public already knows. Now." I stood up, unhooked the phone after saving it to a file on my computer, walked around my desk, stood in front of her, handed it to her and held out my hand. "Again, I can't thank you enough," I said as she stood up. "You've been a great help. I'll have someone see you out." I looked at Tracy. She nodded and stood up.

Lara nodded and sniffed, her eyes red-rimmed and watery. Tracy gently took her arm and guided her out into the situation room and from there to the elevators.

The door closed and Anne let out a big breath.

"That was strangely good timing," she said. "We just got lucky."

"Yes. You can say that again," I muttered.

I returned to my seat behind my desk and played the

video again. It really wasn't that big of a deal, but what it did was provide us with a second solid link between Massey and Indigo. Massey had some explaining to do.

"Anne, reach out to that guy Roy—whatever his name is—the manager at Labyrinth and see if you can find out when that video was shot. I'll bet they have a social media manager who has it on their phone."

Anne nodded and stood up, looked at me as if she was about to say something, then left the office.

Me? I headed for the lab to find Jack.

"How're we doing, Jack?" I said as I walked in. I wanted to make sure every audio or visual file from the night before had been checked, logged and properly filed. Because I didn't trust him? No, absolutely not. I'd have trusted him with my life. I wanted to check because it was my job to do so, but more than that, I wanted him to look at the video file Lara had brought us.

He swung around in his chair, and from the bright look in his eyes, I knew I was in for something good.

"Just the captain I was looking for," he quipped. "I was about to come find you."

"Oh? What for?"

He rolled back a bit and gestured to the computer screen.

"What am I looking at?"

"It's an app. The phone number you gave me. I finally broke it."

"Broke it? What are you talking about, Jack?"

He barely held back from rolling his eyes. I was happy he was on my team, but sometimes he pushed the boundaries and the limits of my patience. This was one of those times.

"As I told you. The number's out of service, and the phone it's logged to is a burner. Bad news, right? Yep, but the good news is, I was able to tag it because of Rat Nelson's phone. It was the phone used to send those text messages. And..." He paused for emphasis. "And... I was able to find where it was purchased."

"You little... darlin'," I said, smiling down at him. "It was the one Rat was texting to? You're sure about that?" I needed confirmation.

"Yup. It was," he replied.

"Grab your gear and let's go... Oh, and I came to tell you I sent you a video file. There are two people in it. When we get back, I need you to enhance it for me ASAP. Come on. We're going to need a warrant to get the receipt."

Luckily, my old friend Judge Strange was in a good mood when I called him and told him what I wanted, and he wasn't in court that morning—another piece of good luck.

"We're about two minutes out," Jack said, glancing at the GPS. We were in my unmarked cruiser, which meant it would stick out like a sore thumb.

Citico is a quiet, residential street bounded on both sides mostly by rental properties. It was around ten-forty-five on Sunday morning and, as most folks were in church, it was pretty deserted except for a few young kids kicking a soccer ball around.

As we drove past an empty, overgrown lot, I saw our destination coming up on my right—a standalone brick building with a gated double-front door. No windows. Weathered beer and lotto signs were tacked to the outside and an ice machine that looked older than I was stood forlornly to the left of the door.

The sign over the door read: Deluxe Mini Mart.

I parked out front and rolled down the rear windows, stepped out and scanned the street, then made sure Samson was secured in the back seat, and then nodded at Jack.

A bell over the inside of the door tinkled as we stepped into the store and headed to the right, away from the cash register. I wanted to get my bearings first, and there were two customers already inside. One was an older woman, sweating noticeably in her muumuu, who was staring at the dairy section unseeingly. The other was an older, bald man. He gave us a knowing glance as he pocketed his change, a pack of cigarettes, a lotto ticket, and what looked to be a Goo Goo cluster. I hadn't seen those for years and my mouth watered, and it was then I realized I hadn't had breakfast. Any other time, I would have bought one... but I had other things to focus on.

When it was clear the old woman wasn't going to make a decision anytime soon, Jack walked casually to the front of the store and stepped up to the counter, where I joined him.

The clerk, a young Indian guy who looked a little

high-maintenance, eyed first Jack, then me. He had a hand resting on the counter. His beautifully manicured nails put mine to shame.

"Hello, Ajay," I said after glancing at his nametag. "My name is Captain Gazzara and this is Detective Jack North. We're here to ask for the details on a phone purchased from this store back in September; September seven, to be precise. And I do have a warrant if it's needed."

I held my ID close to my chest, and Ajay's eyes met mine before staring at it.

He looked up at me, swallowed visibly, his Adam's apple bobbing up and down, and then said, "I... this is my dad's store. I'm just filling in for today, but... what do you need?"

"I need a copy of the receipt, and I want to look at your security camera footage."

He looked back and forth between the two of us. "I... I don't know how I can help with that."

Jack gave him a crooked grin, leaned against the counter and said, "Well, Ajay, it's as easy as looking up a receipt and taking us back to see the system recorder. As the Captain said, we have a warrant. You have to cooperate."

He looked unsure but nodded, and I pulled the warrant from an inside pocket. Ajay read it over quickly, still looking nervous, but quickly became more agreeable.

"Okay, yeah. Just tell me what you need. I... I've never done this before."

Jack told him the phone number and the date the phone had been activated, and Ajay clunked around on the register, squinting at the screen. He'd been telling the truth. He really wasn't familiar with the equipment. But he managed.

"I think this is it?" he said, finally.

He turned the screen so we could see it if we both leaned over the counter. A digital receipt showed a purchase of a prepaid phone, a minutes card and... chocolate-cherry cigarette wraps. *YES! Another huge chunk of luck. Now all we need is an image.*

Jack looked satisfied, but it was obvious that he hadn't put it together yet. He asked Ajay to print a copy of the receipt and stared down at it in his hands, frowning.

"Paid in cash, then?"

I smiled. A credit card would have been too much to ask. But it didn't matter. I could feel the pull of the tidal wave coming. We were about to get some of the many answers we'd been looking for, but I wasn't sure I was going to like them.

"The video footage?" I asked, but Ajay's gaze had strayed over my shoulder. I half-turned to find the old woman standing there holding a stick of butter and a pair of sunglasses, and she wasn't smiling. I smiled at her and shuffled to the side and waited as Ajay checked her out, bagging the butter and glasses, which she commented were for her granddaughter.

"I'm sure she'll like them," Ajay said awkwardly with a tight smile. The woman shuffled out of the store.

"The machine. It's in back," Ajay said. "Let me lock the door and put the sign up. I can't leave the register alone."

The security system was located in a cramped office

that doubled as a cleaning and storage room. A damp mop leaned up against the wall and boxes of single-serve chips were stacked on shelves.

He tinkered with an old video system, a small box television that Jack looked at with an impressed expression.

"Here. This must be him, I think." Ajay moved aside as Jack and I crowded in, watching the black and gray screen busy with pixelation.

A man wearing a hooded sweatshirt—dark-colored, like Oskar's—had his back to the camera as he looked back into the store. A cell phone and a minutes card were on the counter. The cashier wasn't Ajay. It was an older man, his father, I assumed. He shifted restlessly until the customer turned around, tossing a sleeve of wrapping papers on the counter.

The suspect glanced up at the security camera over the counter, and there he was. We were looking at Lewis Massey.

Part of me was surprised but, for some reason, the other part was... deflated. And then, moments later, my phone buzzed, indicating I had a text. I flipped the screen and... didn't I know it: *No match on the DNA from the two crime scenes and Oskar Pope.*

I nudged Jack and showed him the text. He grunted, then said, "Well, at least we know for sure who we're looking for now."

30

Sunday Afternoon 1 pm

SAMSON TROTTED ALONG THE HALLWAY AT MY SIDE as I headed for Chief Johnston's office. He, the chief, had been trying to take Sundays off but found himself stuck at the PD that day awaiting updates on several sensitive cases, mine included.

The last time we'd spoken it hadn't gone well. We both were short with one another, and he told me not to worry about whoever was feeding Salazar information. But that was the point, wasn't it? It was my case, and it was my job to worry. Needless to say, I lost that argument and left his office hoping that the next time I saw him, I'd have apprehended Indigo's murderer.

Now I was about to face him again, and I'd already worked myself up for another confrontation. I tilted my head, set my jaw and took a deep breath.

"Here we go, Sammy," I said as I stood for a moment outside his outer door. "Wish me luck."

I felt him lick my hand and looked down at him and said, "You really are something else, Sammy. Thank you." And with that I opened the door and stepped inside, crossed the empty outer office to the open door of the chief's office and knocked on the doorframe.

Johnston looked up at my knock and gestured for me to come in. I did, shutting the door behind me.

"I saw North in the hall," he said, "and he mentioned that the convenience store was a hit."

"It was," I said, perching on the edge of a chair. Samson went around Johnston's desk, his tail wagging slowly, and bopped the chief's thigh with his nose.

I had to hide a smile. Even Johnston, maintaining a serious face, couldn't resist him. He lowered a big hand and ruffled the dog's ears.

"All right, let's hear it then," he said.

"Oskar Pope, the man ID'd as Peter Pan, admitted to introducing Indigo to Labyrinth, but he didn't kill her. The DNA found at the scene tends to prove it was someone else. He didn't kill Rat Nelson either."

Johnston sighed. "I was hoping this would be a one-and-done."

"Me, too," I said. "The good news is, North was able to trace the burner to the convenience store. We have the receipt and video footage of the guy who purchased it. It was also the phone that produced the number Rat was texting."

Johnston leaned back in his seat, rested his elbows on the armrests, steepled his fingers, narrowed his eyes, stared at me and said, "So all signs point to..."

"Lewis Massey," I said. "He was the guy who purchased the burner. No doubt about that. We have the footage. But there's more. Just before we went to the convenience store, Lara Crump, the barkeep at Electric Blue, came in with a video Labyrinth posted on social media a few days ago, on which Massey can be seen arguing with Indigo. We also know Oskar Pope never had anything else to do with the girls he worked with, those he introduced to Labyrinth."

"So you think he's good for the murder of Indigo and Rat Nelson?" Johnston asked.

"I think, but I'm not sure yet," I admitted. "But I do have a few ideas. Indigo's father wouldn't allow her to have a phone. Massey bought a phone that day, so I'm wondering if Indigo persuaded Massey to buy one for her. Indigo was a smart girl. She probably wanted something secure to keep in touch with him. If I'm right, he must have gotten rid of it, because we never found it. And Massey's is disconnected. So he's either not using it or he's gotten rid of it too."

He nodded. "So, what's your plan?"

If I'd been truthful, I'd have told him I didn't have one, but instead, I told him:

"Corbin and I are waiting for the convenience store owner to arrive at the PD at our request. I want to talk to him, cover all the bases. Hawk's out trying to track Massey down. When he finds him, he'll bring him in for questioning and a DNA swab. I also want to talk to Pope again. There's something there I'm not quite getting. We're close, Chief, but what we have is all circumstantial. I need more."

"Good. Stay with it and keep *me* updated, understood?"

I almost rolled my eyes. Of course I'd keep him updated.

Johnston's desk phone rang and he picked it up. After a few curt words, he hung up and said, "Your convenience store owner is here, in reception, with Sergeant Russell down at the interview rooms."

I nodded my thanks and headed out, clicking my tongue for Samson to follow along.

Mr. Patel, Ajay's father, wasn't the first nervous person I'd seen in the police department. He had no reason to be, of course, but people do tend to get that way when confronted with an official investigation, and Patel was no exception.

"Mr. Patel," I began after we'd gotten him seated in the interview room and Corbin had done the preamble for the record, "there's nothing to worry about, okay? We just need to ask you a few questions."

The older man nodded, dark circles under his eyes.

"It's just you and Ajay at the store, correct?"

"Yes. He helps me when he can."

"That must be exhausting," I said.

"Yes, but it works well for us."

It worked well for me too, because it meant he'd had eyes on Lewis Massey.

I took a print copy of the screenshot we'd taken from

his own surveillance system and laid it on the table in front of him.

"Do you remember this man? He came into your store on September seven at four-twenty in the afternoon."

Mr. Patel's immediate nod took me by surprise. We were hoping he'd remember something, anything, but given how long ago the phone had been purchased, I was expecting him to at least have to think about it.

"He bought a phone and a minutes card, I think."

Nailed it. Every item but the wrapping papers.

"Did he buy anything else?" Corbin asked.

"Perhaps. I can't remember."

"Did you notice anything strange about him?" Corbin asked, leaning forward. "How come you remembered him so readily?"

Patel looked up at us across the table; his eyes were the color of caramel. "He caused a bit of a disturbance. Nothing aggressive or violent, you understand, but I remember it."

"What kind of disturbance?" I asked.

"He was arguing with someone, a woman."

Jack and I hadn't seen a woman in the video.

"Can you describe her, please?" I asked.

He thought for a moment. "She was young. I thought maybe they were siblings, but... the girl bought a phone just a few minutes before he did. He didn't want to buy his—that's what they were arguing about—but she insisted. She had kind of bushy hair, a little frizzy, and she was wearing a school uniform."

"I need that security footage, Mr. Patel," I said. "And

a copy of her receipt. Can you get them for me and have someone drop them off? Better yet, I'll have someone follow you back to the store and get them from you."

"If you wish," he replied.

"Did they argue about anything else? Or say anything else that you remember?" Corbin asked.

Patel shook his head slowly. "No. They weren't in the store for more than ten minutes. She bought a phone. He bought his phone, and they left together."

"Where was the girl when this was happening?" Corbin asked, pointing to the photo.

"This way. Near the door."

There wasn't much else we could ask for, so we thanked him and sent him on his way, promising to have what we needed right away.

Corbin called Traffic and asked for a uniformed officer to go by and pick it up.

Outside the interview room, Corbin stared down the hall after the older man and his escort.

"Pope's still in custody?" he asked.

"Oh, yes," I replied. "We're following through on the trafficking charges. What are you thinking?"

"I'm thinking we need to talk to him again about Massey. He was too closed-mouthed for a guy who had an opinion about his buddy's love for little girls."

I agreed. We didn't have the whole story yet. It was obvious now that Massey had been obsessed with Indigo, but how did that lead to her murder? Had she refused his advances, or was there something deeper going on?

"I'll stop by Anne and Hawk's desks," I promised.

"I've got to grab Samson, anyway. Can you touch base with Tracy and Cooper?"

"No need," Corbin said grimly, looking down at his phone. "They're at Massey's apartment, but it doesn't sound good. Want to head over there with me when you're done?"

I did.

31

Sunday Afternoon 3 pm

WHEN WE ARRIVED, WE FOUND TRACY AND COOPER waiting outside of a long L-shaped apartment building called Sutton Place. It was built on a rise of grass with identical Chinese elm trees planted every twenty or so feet and identical apartments. Blinded windows stared out into the parking lot.

I let Samson out and joined them, staring up at the building. I can't say I was too impressed.

"What's going on?" I asked, squinting against the bright sunlight.

Tracy sighed, scuffed her boots, and said, "No one is answering at his apartment. We're waiting for the land-lord to get here."

"Which one?" I asked, gesturing toward the building.

"3H," Cooper replied.

Gazing up at the building, I could see the route we'd

have to take: a staircase that climbed all four levels, the last of which had beige siding instead of dark red brick.

"Let's take a look," I said.

Cooper took the lead, shifting two bikes out of the way as he went.

We reached the third floor to find ourselves faced with a glass door with a keypad that gave way to a long hall.

"Do we have a code?" I asked, looking over my shoulder at Tracy and Cooper.

"Landlord said to use the code 4-4-5-8," Tracy said. "He said he'll be here soon, but I don't think he wants to let us into Massey's apartment."

I punched in the code. The door clicked loudly and I pulled it open.

Apartment 3H was on the left side and had a dark wood door with scratches and chips around the edge. The hallway was long with a dark red rug and relatively clean. It smelled of concrete and damp.

"You knocked, right?" I asked.

"Several times," Cooper replied. "No answer. No sounds inside either."

Two doors down, a door creaked open and an eye peered out around the frame.

"Hello?" Corbin said, stepping forward.

The door didn't open further, but a shaky voice asked, "Can I help you?"

"Police," Corbin said, showing her his ID.

The door opened further to reveal a short woman I estimated to be in her late sixties. She was hunched over and wearing a house coat. She glanced at 3H.

"Is he in trouble?" she asked.

"Have you seen the occupant lately?" I asked, dodging the question. "A Mr. Massey, right?"

The woman hesitated but nodded. "I never met him, but I seen him and his mail."

"When did you last see him?" I asked.

She shook her head, glancing again at the door. "He hasn't been here in three or four weeks; not that I seen. The landlord can maybe let you in."

Corbin thanked her, and she shuffled back inside the apartment and closed the door.

It was almost ten minutes before the landlord, a man named Otto Gaines, arrived, huffing and puffing. The shirt he wore barely covered his paunch, and his hair stuck out around his ears like a halo. He looked concerned, serious, and nodded briefly as we all flashed our IDs.

"Can one of you tell me why exactly you need to see my tenant?" he said, squinting at me and then down at Samson.

"We're conducting a murder investigation and we need to talk to him," I replied. "That's all I can tell you. The tenant in 3G said she hasn't seen him in almost a month. I need you to let us in, please."

"Lewis Massey?" he asked.

"Yes."

Otto pursed his lips. "Normally, I wouldn't do this, but if he hasn't been seen, I guess there's a concern for his wellbeing."

Gaines took out a set of master keys from his belt, unlocked the door, pushed it open, and then backed away, seemingly reluctant to go inside, and I can't say I blamed him.

"Ready?" I asked Corbin, shortening Samson's leash in my left hand and putting my right on my weapon. Gaines saw me do it and shifted further back down the hall.

Corbin nodded.

"Lewis Massey?" I called out. "Police!"

No answer. All was quiet. I stepped inside, Samson leading. The apartment smelled... musty, the air thick and heavy.

"Mr. Massey?" I shouted as I walked slowly into the apartment, past a closet and then a small bathroom on the right.

No answer.

Corbin peeled off to the left to check a bedroom and another closet.

"Clear!" he shouted, then joined me in the living room. "I checked the closet, under the bed and behind the door. Nothing."

I checked the small kitchenette. The refrigerator was working, but there was nothing in it except a half-gallon of spoiled milk, two beers and the remains of pizza. The old girl was right. Massey hadn't lived in the apartment for at least a month.

Cooper and Ramirez had remained outside with Gaines. But he stepped cautiously inside, peering this way and that.

He looked at me and said, "He's not here?"

"No," I replied, "and by the looks of things, he hasn't

been in quite a while. I'd like to take a look around, if you don't mind."

He nodded and backed out into the hall, muttering something I couldn't understand, a garbled mess of words. I beckoned Cooper and Ramirez and they joined us in the apartment.

"Tracy. You take the bathroom and the kitchen," I said. "Coop, you do the bedroom. Corbin and I will do the living room."

Twenty minutes later, after a thorough search, we'd found absolutely nothing, nada, squat. There was no sign, other than the contents of the refrigerator, that Massey had ever been there, though we knew from the neighbor that he had.

I stepped out into the hall to talk to the landlord. Gaines glanced nervously down at Samson, backed away a step, and looked up at me.

Samson parked his backside on the floor and stared up at him, mouth open, tongue lolling out, panting.

"How long has Massey been your tenant?" I asked.

"Three years, come January," he replied.

"Is he a good tenant?"

He shrugged, then said, "As far as it goes, yes. He always pays his rent on time. Better than most."

"Any complaints about him from the other tenants?"

He shook his head. "Not that I can remember. He's a quiet one. Pays his rent by direct deposit. I wish I had more like him... Are you done in there? If so, I need to lock up and get out of here. I have an appointment at the dentist."

I nodded, thinking hard. *If he hasn't been here...*

"If he hasn't been here," Corbin said, echoing my thought. "Where's he been?"

"Search me," I said. "I think we need to pay another visit to the Whitlow building." Turning to Cooper and Tracy, I said, "You two meet us there in... say, thirty minutes."

WYATT STREET WAS QUIET, WHICH WAS NOT surprising, given it was late Sunday afternoon and an industrial/business district. We parked out front of the Whitlow building behind Cooper and watched as he and Ramirez got out.

I stared up at the building through my window, wondering what the chances were that Massey was inside.

My gut was telling me he wasn't, and I was beginning to worry that something bad might have happened to him. I mean... why would he abandon his apartment but still clock in to work every day? No. I figured either something had happened to him or he was in the wind—disappeared down a rabbit hole.

Tracy and Cooper waited for us at the front doors while I got Sammy out of the car and climbed the three steps to the entrance, and together, the five of us stepped inside.

Other than the two people seated behind the security desk, the foyer was deserted.

I stepped up to the desk, creds in hand, and a young

woman with a blonde ponytail bounced up out of her seat. I was surprised to see it was none other than Carolyn Brown, and her companion in security was Jeff Sullivan.

"Captain," he greeted me. "How can we help you?"

"Hi," I said. "We're looking for Lewis Massey. Is he on duty today?"

Carolyn's eyes opened wide. Jeff said, "Lewis quit four days ago. I haven't seen him since. He cleared out his locker and disappeared."

"Indigo," Carolyn asked abruptly, her palms flat on the desk. "This is about her, isn't it? Does he have something to do with her death?"

"Why would you think that?" Tracy asked quietly, watching her reaction.

"Why else would you be here?" she said. The color had drained from her face. She looked as if she was about to throw up.

She took a half step back, put one hand on her stomach and the other on her forehead.

"He... I knew he had something to do with it," she said. "He was always asking me if we were going out or if Indigo was meeting me. And she was... always a little weird when he was around."

"Weird how?" I asked, wishing she'd told me this days ago.

Carolyn shook her head. "I don't think... She didn't like him. Well, I thought she didn't anyway. She never said either way if she wanted to hang out with him or not, but... sometimes it was like... like they had something going on."

Jeff looked at me and said, "You really think Lewis is involved in this?"

"Have you any idea where he might be?" Corbin asked, ignoring the question. "Is there anyone you think that he might be staying with?"

Jeff shook his head.

"You should check with Oskar," Carolyn said. "He might know where he is. I can get his address for you." She half-turned, but I stopped her.

"Thank you, Carolyn, but there's no need. We know where he is."

I glanced at Corbin and could tell he was trying hard not to smirk.

"Well," I said, "if there's nothing else you can think of, we'll leave you to it. But if by any chance you do see him, call me or Detective Russell immediately, but don't tell him we're looking for him. Do you understand?"

They both nodded, looking at us, awed.

Corbin and I gave them each one of our cards, and we left them staring after us.

"Tracy, Coop," I said. "You can call it a day. Go home and get some rest. I'll see you both bright and early in the morning. Corbin, you and I are going to go talk to Oskar Pope. Call it in and have him placed in a room."

32

Sunday Evening 7 pm

I can't say Oskar Pope was thrilled to be seated across from me once again, but there we were. He was well aware of the trafficking charges filed against him. We'd pulled him from temporary holding. His arraignment was at 8:30 the following morning, Monday. I'd handed Samson off to Danielle, much to her delight.

Pope was already seated with his arms folded and a belligerent look on his face when we arrived. Corbin and I sat down at the table opposite him and spoke the preamble for the record, and reminded him he was still under oath.

"So," he said. "What kind of deal are you offering?" His tone was terse. All signs of the unsure, nervous guy Anne and Hawk had interviewed just six days ago were gone.

"That, Oskar, depends entirely on what you tell us."

His lawyer, a severe-looking woman, was sitting

ramrod straight next to him. She looked at him and said, "You should consider helping them if you can, Mr. Pope."

Luckily, we'd worked with her before and she knew we generally kept our promises. Of course, there was no way we were going to let him off completely. But, if he helped us catch a murderer... Well, we'd put in a good word with the prosecutor, and who knows? One thing was for sure; he'd be very carefully watched when he got out in five to eight years.

Pope was silent for several moments, then he said, "I already told you I didn't like how Lewis was with Indigo."

"Right," I confirmed. "You also told us that he was the one who brought Indigo to you." Oskar nodded. "Tell me how that happened."

With a sigh, he began from the beginning, what I'd wanted the whole time: "He met her when she and Carolyn were out clubbing. He was obsessed with her."

"Did he know how old she was?" Corbin asked.

"Hell, yeah. He was tickled to death by it. She was only sixteen then. I don't know how he knew. I think maybe Carolyn... warned him off or something."

"So Massey met Indigo when she was on a night out with Carolyn," I said. "What happened then?"

"I don't know." He shrugged, his lawyer watching him like a hawk, ready to interrupt if he said something he shouldn't.

"He talked about her a lot... you know? But I didn't think they were hanging out, not for sure. And then one night she showed up at Urban One. I told Lewis then it was a bad idea. But he took no damn notice."

"And you walked her back to the other club, Electric Blue?"

His expression shifted immediately, blanking at the memory. "Y...es."

There followed a long moment of silence, waiting for him to say something, but he remained silent so, following my instincts, I said, "Did you have a problem with Electric Blue?"

His eyes met mine, then he said coldly, "I don't go there."

I thought for a moment, remembering that his face hadn't been on Rat's wall of shame.

"Why not?"

He shrugged. "I've had run-ins with the owner before. He's... territorial."

Territorial? Rat Nelson? Yes, I suppose he was, if it meant keeping the likes of Pope and Massey from defiling his club. There was a lot I could have said in reply to that, but it wasn't the time.

"But Lewis had no problem going there?"

"No," he replied, looking down at the tabletop. "He used to go there until he got himself banned. We didn't go in with her that night. We just walked her to the door, is all."

And she took an Uber home, I thought. *So that much is the truth. Where did things go wrong that night?*

"Okay," I said. "So how did it go for you with Massey when you offered her up to Labyrinth?"

Oskar chose to ignore my sarcasm and settled back in his chair, folded his arms and grinned at me. "That was on him. He kept bringing her around when I was working. And the girl... see, she was pushy about it. It was clear she was the one controlling the conversation."

"But you must have talked her into it," Corbin said.

"Talk her into it? Me? Are you kidding? I did my best to talk her out of it. Hell, I tried to scare her off, but she was having none of it... she was persistent. And, unfortunately, she was good at the work."

Of course she was. Indigo was, by everyone's account, smart, a good learner, focused.

"Anyway," he continued, "I was into it with Alana and Robert. I took them a couple of bad girls they rejected, and they said I owed them, so... I got her an interview. Roy liked her. And that was enough. They hired her."

It wasn't exactly like pulling teeth to keep him talking, but he had a habit of lapsing into silence. It seemed like he was sunk in his memories and reluctant to talk about them.

"So the Jakobs hired her, and Indigo went to work dancing there and providing sexual favors. So where did things go wrong?"

Oskar stared at me, seemingly weighing the question as if he knew the seriousness of the moment. His lawyer shifted restlessly in her seat.

"Things got kind of complicated with Indigo. She was having some... issues at work. So I told Lewis he needed to handle his girl."

"His girl? But I thought they weren't involved?"

Oskar scoffed. "They weren't. He wanted to be; that was obvious. But I wasn't about to get into that mess with her. I washed my hands of her the moment Alana decided to hire her."

"What kind of problems was she causing?"

"She was stirring things up with the girls. She reckoned that they should all be getting paid more, and she was... resistant."

"Resistant? To what?" I asked.

"To other types of work," he said dryly.

"Sex work, you mean?" Corbin said caustically.

Oskar nodded and said, "Yeah, that. She didn't want any part of it, and she was trying to... organize some of the girls. Alana got wind of it. She knew things could go sideways pretty quick if Indigo kept on pushing."

Now that in itself was surprising, and yet it really wasn't. Indigo was a bright girl, and obviously had at least some principles and lines she wasn't prepared to cross. It was also interesting that the more we talked about the Jakobs, the less and less Robert Jakob's name cropped up. It was now clear who was really running Labyrinth.

"Oskar," I said gently. "We're trying to find Massey. He hasn't been seen at his Sutton Place apartment in weeks, and he quit his job at the Whitlow company four days ago. Do you have any idea where he might be?"

Pope's eyebrows furrowed in a frown, and for a minute, he looked confused. Then just as quickly as it appeared, his confusion dissipated.

"Oh yeah," he said. "Sutton Place. I forgot he even had that place. Lewis has a place off Wyatt Street, only a few blocks away. We walked there some nights after partying a little too hard, and I know he brought girls there."

"Where is it, Oskar?" Corbin asked, his voice uncharacteristically harsh. "We need an address."

Oskar glanced at him, seemingly unconcerned.

"Trinity Ave. I don't know the name of the building. There's a pizza place and a laundromat on the first floor. Lewis lives on the fourth floor, I think."

Corbin, who'd been leaning against the wall with his arms folded, pushed himself off as if he was ready to go, but I wasn't finished. It seemed to me that every time a question was answered, two more popped up. I leaned over the table, meeting Pope's gaze.

"Oskar, do you think Lewis could have killed Indigo?"

He stared at me, his eyes narrowed almost to slits, and I suddenly felt exhausted but knew I couldn't quit until I had the answers we needed. I had an idea it was going to be a long night.

"Lewis was weak when it came to Indigo," Pope replied, "but only when it came to her. He's ruthless. I wasn't shocked when she went missing, and I wasn't shocked when you told me he'd quit his job at Whitlow. If you can find him, and I do mean if, I think he'll end up in the cell right next to mine."

"You weren't shocked she went missing?" I asked. "Why not?"

"Because when the girl became a problem, I made sure he understood. I told him he could either end the problem or I'd end it for him."

His lawyer stiffened, and I knew what she was thinking. It almost, almost sounded like Oskar had ordered a hit on a seventeen-year-old girl who, for some reason known only to her, was pushing the wrong buttons at her illegal job.

"What do you mean by that?" I asked. "That you'd end it for him?"

"I'd have beaten the shit out of him, is what."

"So, you think he killed her?" I said.

"I didn't say that." He smirked at me and said, "You did."

I looked at him and shook my head. He was indeed a nasty little SOB, but I wasn't sure it was worth pursuing that line of questioning any further. My main concern was finding Lewis Massey. Because no matter what Pope might think, he was looking more and more like Indigo's killer.

I stood. The chair scraped loudly on the concrete floor. Corbin already had the door open. But then, as I turned to leave, I had a sudden thought.

"Oskar," I said. "How long have you been Peter Pan?"

"About a year. Why?"

"I was just wondering. How did you get the job in the first place?"

He grinned at me and said, "I thought you'd never ask. I got it from Lewis Massey. He was Peter Pan before me."

And that, my friends, was the ultimate eye-opener.

"How exactly do you intend to handle it?" Chief Johnston asked when I called him and gave him the update.

"We're going to need a warrant. I have officers out looking for the apartment building on Trinity. When they find it, we'll keep it under observation. We get the warrant, then we'll do a knock and enter."

I had no intention of enduring another episode like what we'd had with Otto Gaines, that was for sure. This time, I needed guarantees.

"What kind of turnaround are you expecting?" Johnston asked.

"Not tonight," I said. "My team's exhausted, as am I. We'll go home and get some sleep. Hopefully, we can get the warrant signed first thing tomorrow morning. I'd like to be on Massey's doorstep by nine, catch him off guard. I'm betting he's the kind of guy who sleeps in."

"Good enough, Kate. Go home. Get some sleep. Good luck tomorrow. Keep me updated." And he hung up.

33

.

Monday Morning 9:15 am

GETTING THE WARRANT SIGNED ON A MONDAY morning was... difficult. The courthouse was a hive of activity, and though Judge Strange was in chambers, he'd put it out that he wasn't receiving visitors. So I had to go to my second source, Judge Andrew Harper.

Harper was... crusty, and meticulous, and he demanded an explanation for every nuance on the document. But, in the end, he signed it, somewhat reluctantly, I thought. By then it was almost nine o'clock and I had to rush through the early morning traffic, and I can tell you, that's never fun in Chattanooga, especially when you have to negotiate the I-24/I-75 split. It was nine-fifteen when I finally arrived to find my entire team and what seemed like half the department waiting for me. There were blue and whites parked on the street and round back. If Massey was in there, he was going nowhere but the PD on Amnicola.

The apartment building Oskar Pope pointed us to was Hawthorn Hills, which was ironic since there wasn't a hawthorn tree anywhere in the area. There was, once, but they had all been completely wiped out to build what only could be called a concrete jungle. Non-native trees and bushes lined the street, but most were dying. What really populated this area were beat-up garbage bins, cars missing hubcaps and the occasional stray dog. I watched one dart down an alley and was happy Samson was home and safe.

There was, in fact, a laundromat on the first floor. It had once been a pizza place but had been shut down for repeated health violations. Classy joint.

Corbin and I waited out on the street, about two blocks down from the building. My thinking was that Massey, having quit his job in a hurry, knew something was up and was probably on high alert, and I didn't want him running.

Jack had arrived first, sometime around five o'clock, and was stationed across the street, chatting with Tracy and Cooper. Anne and Hawk, who pulled up moments before me, walked over and joined Corbin and me.

"You two ready?" I asked, adjusting my earpiece.

"I need a minute, Cap—" Anne began. I could see she was holding a slim manila file folder, but whatever it was would have to wait.

"Can it wait?" I snapped, interrupting her.

She looked... chastened, and I immediately regretted my impatience.

"Sorry, Anne," I said. "Let's get this out of the way first. Then we'll talk."

She nodded. Hawk crossed his arms over his barrel chest and shook his head. He looked tired, and I wondered when Jenny would push him to retire, if she wasn't already doing so. The day we lost Arthur Hawkins would be tough for me, and it was something I didn't even want to think about. I'd come to rely on his solid disposition and soft heart.

"Tracy, Cooper and North are going to head around back and cover the exits. The four of us will head right up."

"We've been in touch with the landlord and he said Massey is in 421," Tracy said.

I nodded and said, "Anne, Hawk, you two take the elevator up and scope it out. Corbin and I will take the stairs."

It only took a few minutes to walk to the building, where the landlord silently pushed the front door open for us. Not knowing what to expect from Massey, we were all wearing ballistic vests, just in case. I wasn't taking any chances.

"You don't need to be here," I told the landlord curtly, and he turned on his heels and walked quickly away. *Perfect!* I thought as he ducked back out onto the street.

And, together with four heavily armed officers leading, one with a door ram in hand, we started up the stairs.

Four flights of concrete stairs can really get the adrenaline pumping, and you have time to think on the way up. I was in decent shape and not struggling, but my mind was doing somersaults. What were we going to find? Would he be asleep, or would he be waiting for us?

Would he have a girl with him? Would he put up a fight? Would—

"I'm on the ground floor, back stairway," Jack's voice said in my ear, interrupting my thoughts.

"Copy," I said. "Tracy?"

"Third-floor stairway entrance."

"This is Cooper. I'm at the back of the building, maintenance entrance and exit, I think."

"Copy."

Hawk and Anne would be on the fourth floor by now. We reached the heavy fire door and I looked back at Corbin for his "ready" nod. I tapped the uniformed sergeant on the shoulder and he pushed the door open.

To the right, the numbers went up from 401; even-numbered units were on the left. We headed north to 421.

Hawthorn Hills was more beat up than Sutton Place. The hallway smelled of mold. Somewhere, something was damp. The ugly, beige-yellow plastic tiles on the hallway floor were cracked and some were missing corners.

We passed the single elevator where we were joined by Hawk and Anne, and both hunkered in behind Corbin and me.

We paused outside 421 and gathered ourselves, mentally and physically. Then the sergeant hammered the door with his fist and shouted, "Lewis Massey, this is the police. Open the door. *NOW!*"

There was a moment of silence, and then he hammered again and shouted, "Police. Open the door *NOW!* If you don't, we'll enter forcibly."

We waited one beat, two beats. No response.

"Mr. Massey, I'm going to repeat one more time: you need to open this door. We have a search warrant and a warrant for your arrest."

Again, silence.

The sergeant looked at me. I nodded. He tapped the officer with the ram on the shoulder and nodded. The officer readied himself and, feet apart, swung the ram at the door lock. The doorframe split apart. The door slammed inward and the four armed officers entered the apartment, weapons at the point.

Thirty seconds later, after four shouts of "clear," the four officers came trooping out again.

"Nobody home. Sorry," the sergeant said as the four of them stepped aside. "We'll be downstairs if you need us."

The apartment was a studio with just a half-wall dividing the kitchen from the living/sleeping area and a small bathroom in the back left corner.

It was, as the sergeant said, empty, but at least it looked lived in. It was cluttered—too little space for too much stuff. A small coffee table almost touching the over-size couch. A dining table with two computer monitors, a keyboard, a mess of wires, a mouse and an overturned babycam.

"The couch is a pull-out," Anne said.

The entire apartment couldn't have been more than seven hundred square feet. With the four of us in there, there wasn't room to swing the proverbial cat.

"Willis?" I asked.

"On his way up right now," Corbin replied.

Mike Willis slipped into the apartment a couple of moments later, and I could see two more techs outside in the hall.

"Give me a minute, will you, Mike?" I said. "I'd like to take a quick look around before you get started."

"Sure. Just don't move anything," he replied.

I told Corbin and the others to wait outside, snapped on a pair of latex gloves, and then I walked around the studio, opening cabinets in the tiny kitchen to find they held nothing but canned food and boxes of cereal. The sink had a couple of plates, a mug, a couple of glasses and some standing water in it. I was quickly coming to the conclusion that Mr. Massey hadn't been in the apartment for at least a couple of days.

"He was maybe here a day or two ago," I said aloud as Cooper poked his head in and told me he'd checked the second set of stairs and that Ramirez and North were checking the roof.

"Check in with neighbors, too," I said. "See if anyone's seen him or knows where he might be."

"Kate." Willis motioned me toward a small stand with a flatscreen TV on it. A pair of socks were on the floor next to it.

"There," Willis said, pointing toward a small ashtray with the word *Arizona* in script.

Tipped against the side of the ashtray were two joints. Willis picked one up gingerly, and I leaned in to get a whiff.

"Cherry," I said. "He's our guy. If we get a DNA match, it ties him to the car and Rat Nelson's crime scene.

I need you to put a rush on it. What about the computer? Can North have it?"

"Let me get it dusted first," Willis said as he bagged the two joints.

"Okay. I'll get out of your way, then. Please keep me updated." And, feeling more than a little claustrophobic, I stepped out into the hallway where the rest of my team were waiting for me, including North and Ramirez.

"You can have the computer when Mike's finished with it," I told Jack.

He looked pensive, then said, "I'll check in with Willis later and start going through it."

"Perfect," I replied.

"Captain," Anne said. "Can we talk now?"

I looked at her, smiled and said, "Yes, of course. What is it?"

"I think I have something," she replied. "We've been so busy we didn't have time to go through these. But something had been bugging me, and, well..."

She paused, opened the file, turned it around so I could see it and said, "I know why Massey's been wiping his prints." She pointed to the preamble at the top of the page. It read:

Agreement between the Whitlow Company (the employer) and Warrior Security Services (the contractor).

Warrior Security Services employees are required to provide certified identification, proof of US citizenship, and a certified copy of fingerprint records prior to employment at the Whitlow Company. Failure to do so—

I didn't bother reading any further. I looked up at Anne.

"He signed that," she said.

"His prints are in the system!" I stated.

She nodded. "Yup. Same as a police officer. Lewis Massey was fingerprinted when he started working for Warrior Security."

I looked back into the apartment with a new perspective.

"Good work, Anne," I said. "Reach out to the security company and get a copy of those prints."

Tracy spoke up. "Most people are at work, but I found one neighbor who said she saw Massey leave late at just after six on Friday. He was carrying a backpack. Nothing else. She doesn't know him personally. Only to say hello to, and she has no idea where he might be."

"He's gone to ground, somewhere," Corbin said.

"Yeah, that," I said thoughtfully. And then I had an idea.

I looked at Anne and said, "Are you still fielding Ivan Salazar's calls?"

She pursed her lips and nodded. "Hah! Yes, unfortunately. As many as three a day. The man never gives up. He's always polite, but he's pushy. He wants results. I'm keeping him updated, minimally."

"Give him a call and ask him if he can see us," I said. "Tell him it's urgent. Maybe he can help us draw Massey out."

34

Monday Afternoon 2 pm

Like many healthcare providers, Ivan Salazar's office wasn't actually in the hospital. It was in a Victorian-style house a block away down the street.

"Hello," the receptionist said as we walked into the foyer. "Can I help you?"

"I'm Captain Gazzara. Doctor Salazar's expecting us," I replied, showing her my credentials.

She smiled up at me and said, "Yes. Of course." Then she stood and said, "If you'll follow me, please."

She led us back to an ornate, wooden staircase, chunky and beautiful, that curved up to the second floor. "His office is on the second floor. First door on the left."

I thanked her. She left, and we started up the stairs.

Ivan Salazar's office was large, comfortable and airy. Two large windows overlooking the street flooded the room with natural light. A maple tree blocked half of the view, and I could imagine his patients must have felt at ease during their consultations.

But Salazar was not at ease. He was agitated, pacing back and forth behind his desk. Two and a half steps each way.

"Dr. Salazar," I said, tapping lightly on the doorframe.

He stopped and motioned us in anxiously.

"Captain Gazzara, Sergeant..." He searched uselessly for Corbin's surname, which my partner supplied.

"Russell."

Salazar nodded and motioned for us to sit down.

"Please, sit. Can I get you something to drink?"

"Not for me, thank you," I replied. Corbin simply shook his head.

"Detective Robar said you wanted to talk to me. Did you find..." He trailed off, the question that all parents and loved ones always asked unfinished.

"Not yet," I said, feeling sad as I watched his face fall.

He sighed and sat down behind his desk. The white coat draped over the chair looked rumpled, and his hair was less than carefully groomed.

I couldn't help but feel sorry for the man. I couldn't imagine the strain of losing a child, knowing the world was watching you with pity, and having to go to work each day and perform complex surgeries on top of it all. It was a miracle Ivan Salazar hadn't lost his mind.

"We can't tell you much," I said, choosing my words carefully, wanting to make sure he understood. "And what I do tell you needs to be held in the strictest confidence. Do you understand, Doctor?"

He nodded. "Yes, yes. Of course. You have my word."

"Our team has identified a man we think is responsible for Indigo's murder." I said the words quietly, aware that the door was still open. Salazar stared at me, listening intently.

"I thought you already had someone," he said.

I shook my head. "The man you're talking about had nothing to do with Indigo's death. He is, however, being charged with other offenses. During the course of our interviews with him, he was able to provide some information about what really happened to your daughter."

He looked confused, upset. "Are you sure? You were able to rule him out—"

"DNA," Corbin interrupted gently.

"Very well," he said bleakly. "So why are you here?"

"We're here to ask you if you'd be willing to help us," I said. "Our suspect has disappeared. I'd like to draw him out."

Salazar's tanned face creased in confusion. "That makes sense, but I'm not sure how I can help."

"We understand you're holding a memorial for Indigo tomorrow evening. We've consulted with a police profiler and we think there's a good chance he'll show up. That being so, we'd like to post plain-clothed officers in the crowd."

I actually flinched at his reaction. Salazar jumped to his feet, livid with anger. His face flushed and he looked as if he was about to explode. But his anger wasn't directed at us.

"He wouldn't dare!" He almost choked on the words.

"It's a possibility," I said. "But you have to understand, Dr. Salazar, if we do this, on no account must you interfere. You need to run the memorial just as you planned it, and let us do our job. My team knows exactly who we're looking for, and we're prepared to take him down the moment we spot him."

Salazar's jaw worked as he tried to get his head around what we'd just said. It took him a second or two, but he finally came around to it and said, "I understand."

He looked at me, then at Corbin. "I do," he snapped. "I understand. I'll stay out of your way. Can I... Can I know what he looks like?"

I shook my head. "I'm sorry," I said. *I can't have you going off half-cocked and doing something crazy,* I thought to myself. Although I wouldn't have blamed him if he did. If it was me... I didn't know what I would have done in his situation, but I did know I would have done something. Put him on crutches for the rest of his life, probably.

He took a deep breath in through his nose, rolled his shoulders, seemed to compose himself, and nodded. "Here," he said, digging through one of the top drawers of the desk and taking out a flyer. "Take this. My sister has been putting them up around town. All the information you need is there."

He handed it to me and I quickly read it through.

Coolidge Park, Tuesday, 7:30 p.m. A candlelight memorial for Indigo Suarez Salazar.

"I used to take her there when she was a child," Salazar said, almost choking on the words. "She loved it there..." He drifted off into silence, lost in the memory.

I glanced at Corbin and stood up. Corbin did the same. Salazar looked at us, his eyes red-rimmed.

"Dr. Salazar," I said gently. "Thank you. I promise you; now that we know who he is, we're going to catch him. No matter what it takes. And if this works, you'll have played a part in catching Indigo's killer."

Ivan Salazar nodded, swallowing tightly. "Anything. I'll do anything, of course. Just give me a call if you need anything."

"We'll see you there, then," I said. "In the meantime, Detective Robar will be in touch with instructions."

And we left that old Victorian building feeling both subdued and optimistic—at least I was— and that we were perhaps one step closer to catching a double murderer.

"Let's go get some coffee," I said as we stood at the top of Salazar's porch steps enjoying the late afternoon sunshine. "My treat."

Corbin smiled at me and said, "Sure you can afford it?"

35

Tuesday Night 7 pm

I WENT HOME EARLY THAT AFTERNOON, AND FOR THE first time in more than a week, since Indigo's body had been discovered, I slept well.

I woke early the next morning, Tuesday, and was up by six. I took Samson for a four-mile run, showered, dressed, fed us both, loaded him into the car, and we were at work by eight o'clock, ready to face the day and whatever it might throw at us.

At nine o'clock, I contacted the district attorney's office and talked to my old friend, Larry Spruce.

Oskar Pope had been arraigned the day before on a litany of charges; Larry was the prosecutor.

I told Larry that I'd promised to put in a good word for Pope and, seeing as how the information he'd provided was good and helpful, I was keeping my word, and would he please take my request into consideration.

He laughed and said, "That's a first, Kate. You never

ask for such favors. You do know this guy Pope is a predator? I should throw the book at him, but seeing as you asked..."

"Oh, don't get me wrong," I said. "I'm not asking for a favor. I'm just keeping my word. I told Pope I'd let you know that he gave us a lot of valuable information. What he shared has led us to who we believe is the perp in an active homicide case."

"Well, okay. That's helpful to know," Larry said. "No promises, but I'll see how he behaves in court. I'll let the judge know about his cooperation when we get to sentencing."

And so the day went on. I had a meeting with the chief and brought him up to speed. I had a meeting with my team and set the rules and the strategy for the evening. I even added Danielle to the team, temporarily of course, my excuse being that I intended to take Samson with me.

Coolidge Park at twilight was beautiful, with lights along the pathway providing amber pools and the surface of the river reflecting the light of an almost-full moon. It was quiet but for the hushed murmuring of the crowd. At a guess, several hundred people had shown up for Indigo's memorial, and not just family, friends, Dr. Salazar's coworkers, or schoolmates, but the people of the community; all had been rocked by her murder.

They gathered in groups and couples, talking quietly together, holding hands. A light breeze blew my hair across my face and the moment was ruined as I spluttered.

"All right there, Captain?" Cooper asked in my earpiece. He sounded amused.

I didn't know exactly where he was, but I rolled my eyes and said, "I'm just not used to having my hair down like this. That's all."

Hell, all I wanted to do was blend in—a woman and her dog. Massey had already seen me a couple of times, as well as some of the members of my team, but not the four extra detectives from the serious crimes squad I managed to commandeer for the night. If he was here, I wanted to be sure he wouldn't recognize any of us. So I was wearing a long coat that came all the way down to my calves and a floppy hat that I hoped would shadow my face.

I shifted a bit closer to a group of four women. It was hard not to stand out when you were alone with a dog that would have rivaled the hound of the Baskervilles. Especially if it looked like I was talking to myself. I hoped I didn't look like a crazy person trying to listen in on their conversation, so I smiled and talked to Sam, just knowing I stuck out from the rest of the crowd.

It was Anne who chimed in next. "You sure you're okay, Cap?"

Dropping the smile, I put my cell up to my ear as if I was talking to someone and said, "Listen, you guys, don't you dare make me laugh. I already look like a crazy kook. The memorial is set to begin in half an hour. Is everyone good?"

"Good," Corbin sounded off, followed by four more repetitions from Anne, Hawk, Tracy, and Cooper. Jack had stayed at the station to work on the computer with Willis. He, Willis, had found several empty wrapping paper packets, all chocolate-cherry. And somewhere—only God knew where—Chief Johnston was waiting for a call.

Toward the front of the crowd, Ivan Salazar was conversing quietly with a woman I assumed was his sister. She had the same striking silver-gray hair, but she was shorter and a little on the heavy side. She appeared to be with a man who I assumed was her husband. He was standing beside her with his hand on her back.

Boxes of candles were set at intervals around the area, along with tea lights, tapers, and boxes of matches. I watched as Anne and Hawk, pretending to be a couple, went to retrieve tea lights.

Ivan and his family and friends had also set up a table with photos of Indigo on it. There were posterboards here and there with blown-up versions of the same picture we had in her missing person's file. Two times life-size and smiling widely, she was even more beautiful.

Time passed slowly and I was beginning to do those "what ifs?" What if he didn't turn up? What if we missed him? What if he caught onto us?

A dog barked somewhere off to one side and was immediately hushed by its owner. It was a German Pinscher and Samson was instantly on the alert, posing like a show dog, his ears pricked.

I stroked his huge head and whispered, "Easy, Sammy. It's nothing to worry about." He seemed to understand because he looked up at me and sat down. When this was over, I promised myself I'd take him home and cuddle up to him, bury my face in his hair and ask Johnston for at least a week off to recuperate, knowing damn well that if he agreed, I'd probably spend the week running the trails until I was sore to the bone and half-dead. Rest and relaxation wasn't my thing.

"Captain, I've got a guy in a dark gray hoodie to my left, toward the water." Cooper's voice was low and grave. I perked up, turned and casually looked in that direction. Behind Cooper, the water glittered in the lights of the Market Street and Walnut Street bridges that bounded the park to the east and west. The crowd was thin over there and I easily spotted Cooper. As well as the person he was talking about.

A slightly hunched figure, hood pulled up over his head and hands in his pockets, was standing silhouetted against the light.

It was a tense few moments. I was sure the rest of the team was watching him, too. Cooper shifted restlessly as the figure turned, scanning the park as if looking for something...

And then two girls ran up to him, seemingly full of nervous energy, and then another guy joined them and they all began talking animatedly and laughing. They were obviously all teens. The hooded figure yanked the hood down to reveal him as a thin-faced youngster.

"High schoolers, I think," I said into my comms unit. "See the girl's t-shirt? Silver Springs. They're just Indigo's classmates."

The group soon quieted down under the stern gaze of several nearby groups of adults.

A quick glance at my cell told me Ivan Salazar would soon be getting things started. And, as if sensing the moment was nigh, the crowd began to shift forward toward the small, homemade riser.

He took the stand and I saw him cough, though I couldn't hear it. He raised a wireless mic to his chin and began to speak. His voice sounded... strained.

"Good evening, everyone. I want to thank you for coming tonight. It's beautiful out here, isn't it, and a beautiful night. Indigo loved Coolidge Park. I used to bring her here when she was young. She loved the walkway, the lights, the riv—" He choked up, and the woman stepped closer to him, rubbing his back in support. It was a few moments before he was able to go on.

"I know everyone says this, but Indigo had a bright future ahead of her. She was a hard worker, smart, and always offering to help others by tutoring at school. I didn't get the chance to meet many of her friends, and for that I apologize, but..." He looked out at the crowd, his eyes shining with unshed tears. "I wish she could be here to see you all."

He sounded pitiful, and my heart ached for him, especially when I realized that many of these people probably weren't what Indigo had considered "friends." More like acquaintances. Many of them she wouldn't have known at all. Carolyn seemed to be the only true friend she had. As far as I could tell, Indigo had led a sheltered life, almost isolated, always working hard to do better, and I wondered if Ivan Salazar even knew the pressure he'd put on his daughter. I was pretty sure that he did, but more to the point, did he regret it? *Probably not.*

"My Indigo was a smart kid. Even so, she still

managed to find trouble. And I want all the parents here tonight to hear this: No matter how you raise your kids, how safe you think they are..." His voice broke again, and this time, the woman took the microphone from him.

For once, we were getting a look at Ivan Salazar's vulnerability. Not the harsh, professional man demanding answers, but the father who'd lost a child.

"Hello, everyone. I'm Naomi, Indigo's aunt. I want to reiterate Ivan's thanks for you all showing up here tonight. Shortly, when everyone has a candle, we'll light them and our pastor will lead us through a prayer of remembrance and peace. Please keep in mind that while Indigo's death was a tragedy, that's what we're here for: peace on earth."

"There won't be peace until her killer's caught," I heard someone nearby murmur. I turned slowly to see who it was. Standing no more than ten feet away from me were Carolyn Brown and Jeff Sullivan, along with a handful of others from the security company. They stood together in a tight group, mostly silent, all serious, with their eyes glued to Ivan Salazar. As always, Carolyn's hair was pulled back into a ponytail, her bare face looked raw, her eyes red-rimmed with grief.

"Perimeter check," I murmured into the radio. The team sounded off, one by one. Nothing was happening.

Frowning and shortening Samson's leash, I followed the crowd toward one of the boxes of candles. I took a taper, knowing I'd fumble a tealight or accidentally light my jacket on fire. The last thing we needed was a call to the fire department, although I knew a handful of volunteers were there that night to keep an eye on things.

Ivan Salazar finally took the mic back from his sister and quietly introduced the pastor. A hush fell over the crowd. Even the Pinscher seemed to settle down.

Just as I was focused on lighting the taper while holding Sam's leash and trying to make sure the flame didn't catch my split ends, I heard a shout.

"It's him!"

I looked up wildly, fully expecting my team to be chasing Lewis Massey down, but also confused by the shout. It was unprofessional and...

I saw Carolyn and the group of security guards tackling a man to the ground near the eastern edge of the crowd. They were piled on top of him, seething and rolling and screaming. Carolyn's ponytail was flying wildly as she delivered punch after punch.

"Get over there, *now!*" I shouted, and my team and the four officers converged on the scene, pulling the security guards off him.

At the bottom of the pile, face already bruising and lip busted, lay a somewhat crumpled Lewis Massey.

Samson lunged forward, but I had him on a short leash and told him to stay, and he did, his nose barely inches from Massey's. I pulled him away. Massey squinted up at us, panting, his sandy-colored hair cropped short. He tried to kick away from us, but Hawk caught him by the scruff of his neck and hauled him to his feet. Then Cooper slapped the cuffs on him. Barely able to stand upright, he glared at us, all of us, but especially hard at Carolyn.

"You piece of—" Carolyn started and lunged at him with hands curled into talons. But Sullivan and another guard I didn't recognize grabbed her by the arms and pulled her back. She was crying, angry, and struggling wildly, and the crowd around backed away.

It was at that moment that Ivan Salazar broke through the crowd like a man on a mission. Mouth open and eyes wide, he stared at Lewis Massey, who looked at him seemingly unconcerned.

"The hat," Corbin said quietly. Massey had been wearing a Titans cap that had fallen off in the melee.

"Grab it," I said as Hawk dragged him away, Tracy and Cooper close by on either side, protecting him from the crowd.

Corbin scooped up the cap, and Anne and I blocked Salazar from following.

"Dr. Salazar, I know you want to come with us, but you need to trust us—"

"Is that him?" he snapped, interrupting me. "Is that the man you're looking for?"

Of course it was; who else would it be? But I stuck to my guns.

"I'm sorry, Doctor, but I can't allow anything, *anything* that might taint our case. You need to let us handle it. We'll call you as soon as we know something."

Salazar was breathing heavily, but his sister, Naomi, appeared at his side and held tightly to his shirt. "Ivan, come on. Let them do their jobs. All these people..."

Ivan Salazar wouldn't be satisfied until he saw Massey go down for his daughter's murder, but for now he backed off, giving me a meaningful look as he did so.

"As soon as you know," he said, letting Naomi pull

him back toward the makeshift stage. "As soon as you know," he shouted over his shoulder.

I grabbed Corbin by the arm.

"Let's go," I said. "I want to get him in a room and, if possible, I want him charged *tonight!*"

36

Tuesday Night 8:45 pm

IT WAS ALMOST TOO EASY. FOR WHATEVER REASON, Lewis Massey barely put up a fight. He was grinning when I walked into the interview room and Anne glanced at me over her shoulder, her expression grave. She hadn't gotten further than having Massey confirm his identity. She'd asked why he was at Indigo Salazar's memorial, and he'd told her he was "supporting the community."

I sat down next to her, opposite Massey, dropped the manila folder I was carrying on the table, opened it and looked up at him.

"D'you know why you're here?" I asked him.

He simply stared at me and shrugged but said nothing.

I nodded and said, "Lewis Massey. We're holding you on suspicion of the murder of Indigo Salazar on Saturday evening, November the ninth. You have the right to remain silent. Anything you say can and will be used against you in a court of law. You have a right to an attorney. If you cannot afford an attorney, one will be appointed for you. Do you understand your rights?"

He made a face and said, "Yeah, I understand."

Perhaps I should have asked him if he wanted an attorney present, but I didn't. One, I didn't want to lose the opportunity to question him. Two, I figured he was smart enough to ask for one if he thought he needed it, and three, I figured he thought he was smart enough to outsmart me. So I put my head down and got on with it.

The folder was full of photos. All of them were from Indigo's social media page; all of them showing that Lewis Massey had liked the photos. And I had printouts of the final few pages of her direct messaging.

"What happened that night, Lewis?" I said. "Why did you kill her?"

"I didn't," he replied. "I don't know what you're talking about."

"We already know you two were close," I said flatly, "and we know how you met her. So we can skip that part, Lewis. You were obsessed with her. We also know you had several run-ins with her and that you were banned from Electric Blue because of her. We know you persuaded Oskar Pope to introduce her to Labyrinth as a dancer. What we don't know is why you slit her throat and left her in the trunk of a car." I pushed a photo of her body in the car across the table toward him.

Lewis' grin remained unchanged. He didn't even look down at the photo, and I was reminded of the last time we'd interviewed him. His confidence, self-assurance. He thought he was smarter than we were. I'd run across his kind too many times to count; they always stepped over the line and trapped themselves.

"I don't know what you're talking about," he said mildly, glancing at the folder.

"Lewis," Anne said, "we have quite a bit more than that. We know you two were communicating on private cell phones. We also know you and Indigo were arguing about the phones when you purchased them. Why were you angry with Indigo? Was it because she didn't want anyone to know about you?"

His grin remained, but now there was no humor in it. His eyes narrowed. He folded his arms and stared sullenly at us across the table.

"It wasn't like that," he said coldly. "The phones were her idea. She insisted."

"Maybe she did," I said. "But that doesn't change the fact she was ashamed to be seen with you, that she didn't want anyone to know about her relationship with you. She didn't even tell her best friend, Carolyn Brown, about you. Or her friends at Electric Blue. That must have hurt, right?"

His jaw muscles tightened. "Those assholes at Electric Blue!" he said in a low growl. "Especially Nelson. He was filth."

"Yes, we know you and Rat Nelson didn't get along," I said. "We have his text messages to your burner phone. He warned you off Indigo, didn't he?" I pushed the sheet of paper with the printout toward him.

Massey glanced at it and said, "Hah! See where that got him."

Then he went dead silent, realizing what he'd said.

Anne and I waited, and then she said, acting as if she'd missed it, "But you got your way, anyway. You and Indigo kept on hanging out, even after Rat told her to stay away from you."

He glared at her but answered, though a little reluctantly. "Indigo and I had our problems, yeah, but we were getting to know each other. We hooked up after work and I'd take her home. It was working out."

"Hooked up? As in hooked up, or just hanging out?" I asked. "Because from what we know from Carolyn and Pope, Indigo wasn't interested in you at all."

His jaw tightened again. "I told you. We were working it out. She was coming around. I had to..."

"Had to convince her?" I said. "Because Indigo was smart, right? Picky, too. You had to convince her to like you."

"No!" he snapped, frowning, his eyes narrowed almost to slits. "No, she did like me. She liked it when I came to see her at work."

"At Labyrinth?"

He nodded. I shuffled the deck of photos, found the one from Labyrinth's social media account and shoved it across the table to him.

"Like this night?" I asked. "She doesn't look happy to me. Just the opposite, in fact."

He sat back, not bothering to look at the photo. "She did like it. She danced for me, and yeah. I got her the job at Labyrinth."

"Oskar told us he got her the job," Anne said.

Lewis shook his head. "No, no. It was me who hooked Oskar up with Labyrinth. He took over when I got out of it and—"

He stopped abruptly, his brain seeming to catch up with his mouth.

I figured we needed to ease up on him, or we'd lose him; he'd lawyer up, and I wasn't ready for that. Not yet.

"Right," I said. "We know Indigo asked you to get her a job there, Lewis. She was looking for a little extra money, right? And excitement?"

He nodded slowly, his eyes dark and angry. "Yeah. Her dad, that guy at the memorial, he didn't know her at all. Indigo liked excitement. She liked when I drove fast, and she liked dancing. I even convinced her to try a little coke to loosen her up when she danced. She liked that."

"Oh did she?" Anne said. "And now she's dead. Good job, Lewis."

Anne's words sat heavy between the three of us. Lewis' facial muscles slackened slightly. He wouldn't meet our eyes. It was as if it had only just hit him.

"I think you know we have Oskar Pope in custody," I said, not wanting to start in with the accusations yet. I needed to pull him back in.

"Oskar had quite a lot to say about Indigo," I said. "He told us she was trouble. That she was causing problems at Labyrinth."

He shook his head. "No, not really. Indigo was smart, you know? She knew that Alana wasn't paying them enough, but she couldn't ask for more unless the other girls got more, too. She was good."

He sounded like he believed it. Like he'd been impressed with her. But apparently, he'd had no problem snuffing "good" out.

"So when Oskar told you to take care of the problem, what did you do?" I asked. "Did you talk to her? Did you two get into another argument? Did she make you angry? How'd you 'take care' of it?"

Lewis looked sideways at me. "Yeah. We talked," he said. "She was right, but I was afraid Oskar was going to..."

"To what?" Anne asked when he stopped talking. "To hurt her? Did Oskar take care of it for you?"

Lewis scoffed. "Nah! Oskar couldn't handle Indigo."

"But you could?" I said.

Lust lit his eyes, and I partly regretted asking. But I needed more; I needed a confession.

"I told you. Indigo was smart," he said. "She was perfect. Beautiful and smart, and she could dance. She put all the other dancers at Labyrinth to shame. And she could've brought Labyrinth down if she wanted to. Because she was smart, I knew she'd understand so I just talked to her about it."

"When?" I asked. I needed a date. "That last Saturday? What happened that night, Lewis? Were you and Indigo hanging out?"

Massey shook his head, then shrugged. "Kind of. She was working Labyrinth and needed a ride home."

"So she called you?"

"Well... yeah. She said she was going to call an Uber, but I needed to talk to her so I told her I'd pick her up."

"But she told you no, right? And you showed up anyway. Did she go with you?"

His face twisted up. "Well, not at first, but I needed to talk to her, so I took her in the alley."

Huh. The alley without security cameras. How convenient.

"And you talked to her about the issues at Labyrinth?" I asked. "How did she take it?"

He rolled his shoulders and made a face. "She really, really wanted to get the girls together. She told me she'd already been talking to some of them."

"And that bothered you?" Anne said.

Massey nodded. "Yeah. Well, I mean, if the girls had some kind of weird rebellion against Alana and Robert, we were all in trouble. If Indigo did what she said she was going to do and went to the Department of Labor..."

What? That's the first we'd heard about that.

"She threatened to go to the Department of Labor?" I asked.

That was a real, a very real threat and a motive for murder. Especially for Alana and Robert Jakob, and Oskar Pope, too. They were all involved in trafficking, prostitution, drugs, and God only knew what else. Indigo had stepped way over the line and was threatening to bring the whole thing tumbling down.

The look in Massey's eyes told me he knew I'd caught on. "She did," he said, "but I was going to try to talk her out of it."

"Tell me about that, Lewis," I said, leaning forward.

His face flushed slightly. "I... I talked to her in the

alley. She kept arguing with me. I tried to get her to see reason. I told her that if she did go to the Labor office, she wouldn't have the job at Labyrinth because they'd get shut down and then we couldn't be together. But she wouldn't... She..."

He rambled on a bit further, but it was the words, *We couldn't be together,* that stuck with me. It was time to play hardball.

"Here's what I think, Lewis," I said calmly as I leaned toward him. "I don't think Indigo cared about any of that. I don't think she wanted to be with you at all. In fact, I think she was disgusted by you."

His mouth dropped open. His expression was one of shock. And, for a moment, he seemed lost in thought. Then he locked eyes with me, sneered and said, "Indigo didn't know what the hell she wanted. She was only seventeen."

"We're well aware of that," Anne said, trying to keep the vitriol out of her voice. "She was only seventeen, and you wanted a relationship with her, knowing she was underage."

But Massey was shaking his head. "No!" he snapped back. "It wasn't like that. Indigo was smart, mature. She could have ended us all if she wanted to."

"But she *did* want to, Lewis," I said. "So what happened when you realized that was exactly what she was going to do?"

The measure of the conversation had changed, picked up, and the air seemed full of tension. Massey's face had turned from pink to red.

"I told her she had to shut her mouth," he said in an

unrecognizable growl of a voice. "I told her if she wouldn't, I'd shut it for her."

"What did you do to her when she told you to go to hell, Lewis?" I said calmly.

"*I frickin' killed her, didn't I?*" he shouted through clenched teeth, spittle flying. "I kept my promise and I shut her up. Is that what you want to hear? Indigo wouldn't stop pushing everyone's buttons. She was going to get everyone arrested, get Labyrinth shut down, and she told me she never wanted to see me again, so..."

"So you murdered her."

I didn't need him to confirm that. He'd already confessed.

At that point, he was halfway out of his chair, breathing heavily and eyes wide, and then he realized what he'd said and collapsed back onto his seat.

"I... I..."

"Lewis Massey," I said, "I'm charging you with the murders of Indigo Marie Salazar and..." It was at that point I realized I didn't know Nelson's real first name, but it didn't stop me. "...and the individual known as Rat Nelson." And I read him his rights again, just for good measure.

"I want a lawyer," he blurted out as I picked up the folder and stood up.

"Of course. We'll see that you get one. Detective Robar will finish up here."

I left the room, ignoring Lewis' protests that he didn't kill Rat. It made no difference. We had the DNA evidence.

Me? I was feeling drained. But we had our killer.

I stepped out into the hallway and closed the door behind me. Corbin and Johnston, who'd both been watching the interview, along with Tracy and Cooper, were waiting for me.

"Well done, Captain," Johnston said seriously.

"Thanks," I said. "It was a team effort. Everyone played their part. I couldn't be more pleased. Corbin, can you place him under arrest when Anne's done in there?"

"Of course, Captain. Nice job getting it out of him."

I nodded, but in truth, I didn't feel that I'd done that much. What I did feel was infinitely sad.

Indigo Salazar was lost to the world because of her own ambition, curiosity and her bad choice in men, and I knew all about that. But I also blamed her parents—or should I say, parent? He'd been so obsessed with making sure she'd be a success that he'd lost sight of the basics. Kids at that age need love and guidance, not the tyrannical figure Ivan Salazar was. People like Massey and Pope exist to prey on kids like Indigo. They are everywhere, all around us, hiding in plain sight, waiting to pounce on the gullible and unloved, and there's not a damn thing any of us can do about it except try to get them off the streets.

"Thanks," I said. "If you'll excuse me, I need to go call Salazar and pick up Samson." And I turned and walked away.

"Kate!" Johnston called, jogging to catch up with me. I waited a moment until he was at my side. "Get the dog and go home," he said solemnly. "I'll call Salazar myself. Take the morning off. I'll have Hawkins finish tidying up."

I nodded, too tired to argue.

The truth was, all I wanted now was to go home and sink into bed. But it wasn't quite over yet.

37

Wednesday Morning 11 am

Despite being told to take the morning off, I strolled into the PD at around eleven the following morning and headed straight up to the situation room.

Lewis Massey had already been arraigned and was in custody. And I was sure he'd never get out.

"Hey, Cap," Jack North said, catching me as I walked into my office where Corbin, Anne, and Hawk were waiting for me. Tracy and Cooper both had two days off, a long weekend.

"Good morning, all," I greeted them brightly. "What's the update on Pope?" I asked as I sat down behind my desk, linked my fingers together behind my neck, and pushed back. Samson took his place on his bed under the window.

"Pope's been shipped out to Bledsoe. He's being assessed."

"Anne, have you heard anything from Salazar?"

She nodded. "He wants to stop by today." She glanced up at the clock and added, "He should be here soon. He said he was coming by on his lunch break."

I sighed but didn't argue about it. The chief had notified him of Massey's arrest and the fact that he'd confessed to Indigo's murder.

Anne had continued the interview after I left and had obtained a full confession, including where we could find the murder weapon—in a duffle bag in a shelter where he was staying—and that he'd dumped her body in the Honda.

It was bittersweet, but we had all we needed for a conviction. The DNA eventually came back conclusive and linked Massey to both crime scenes. He tried for a plea bargain in return for telling us everything he knew about Labyrinth's many illegal activities, but he was too late. Oskar Pope grabbed that and received a reduced sentence of five to ten years, and Finkle's team took over the Labyrinth case the morning after Massey admitted what he'd done.

I didn't have much faith in Finkle, but it would have been hard for him to mess this one up. Apparently, their initial raid had uncovered a litany of illegal drugs, including PCP, ecstasy, coke, meth and worse, Fentanyl.

But someone—I didn't know or care who—had given the girls a heads up, and none of the dancers could be found except for Jesse and Holly. Both women were over twenty-five and more than happy to testify that Alana Jakob had threatened and berated them into providing sexual favors.

"Heard anything back from Isla?" Anne asked

conversationally, referring to Cooper's cousin who was a realtor. I opened my mouth to answer, but it was at that moment Danielle appeared in my doorway.

"Captain. There's someone here to see you."

Behind her, Ivan Salazar towered over her by several inches.

I gestured for him to come in and thanked Danielle. I kind of liked the girl. In some ways she reminded me of Janet Tolliver, my ex-partner. Dani was a little more by-the-book than I liked, but it never hurt to have a little balance, and if Hawk was going to retire anytime soon... well, I'd have to have a chat with her. And besides, Samson absolutely adored her.

One glance around the table from me and the office emptied pretty quickly, but Dr. Salazar made sure to thank each member of my team quietly and shake their hands as they left, which I thought was extremely nice of him.

Corbin, the last one out, closed the door behind him.

"Dr. Salazar," I said. "Good morning. Please, have a seat. You wanted to talk?" I asked as I sat down at the table with him.

He hesitated for a moment before replying, "Yes. I know that Detective Robar has been updating me, and she's been doing an excellent job. But I wanted to check with you... I want to be sure, that you're sure, this man Massey is not going to be able to get out of it."

I understood his concern. It kept me up at night, too. Every case I closed, I had the same concerns: What if something went wrong in court once it was out of my hands? What if I'd screwed something up? What if a member of my team had made a mistake and he got off on a technicality? Fortunately, it had never happened to me, but I still suffered deeply from the "what ifs."

"I'm sure," I said. "We have a full confession. We have his DNA at both scenes, and we have the murder weapon. It's going to be all right."

Salazar sighed, in relief, I assumed, and said, "Thank you, Captain." But he didn't seem to want to leave, so I waited out the silence, my instincts telling me he wanted to get something off his chest.

"Indigo," he started, eyes wandering upward, "she was always a good girl. Always, from the day she was born. And she was ambitious. I taught her to want more, to push. I think... I think that's what she was doing, wasn't it?"

Right now, all he knew was that Indigo had been standing up for something she thought was important, and it got her killed. But he'd hear all that in court. What was Indigo really fighting for? There was no way of knowing. She'd taken her reasons with her to the grave.

Me? I preferred to think she was not fighting just for herself but also for others, and against injustice.

I nodded. "Yes, that's what she was doing. You raised her to help others, Dr. Salazar. She was a good person."

He nodded in agreement, but the tears were streaming down his cheeks. The nod turned into denial as he shook his head. "It didn't matter, though," he choked in a whisper. "She was brilliant, kind, good, and I lost her."

Somehow, deep down in my psyche, I knew exactly what he was going through. I'd seen it so many times before. And the selfish side of me was happy that I wasn't a parent. I never wanted to lose someone I loved the way he'd lost Indigo. Could it have been avoided? I thought so then, and I think so now, but I won't go into that here.

"Dr. Salazar," I said firmly, reaching out and taking his hand. "It's never fair, but Indigo did more good than you'll ever know. She made a difference. And she'll be remembered for it, always. And Lewis Massey? He'll be put away for what he did. And he'll be forgotten."

He nodded again, sniffing and palming away a wet streak down one side of his face.

He stood up. So did I.

"Thank you again, Captain Gazzara," he said, gripping my hand tightly in both of his. "I'm happy she had you and your team to fight for her, and I'm sure she is, too."

I smiled tightly. "Of course. We'll see you in court, Dr. Salazar."

He departed quietly, head bent as he made his way back through the situation room toward the elevators. Danielle met him halfway to escort him out.

I closed the door and the blinds. I had to take a moment to come down from... something. I didn't quite know what: an adrenaline rush? Grief for Salazar and his daughter?

My job... it never got any easier; it never got any better. But I knew I couldn't stop. There are hundreds more Indigo Salazar's out there. If I did, who else would make things right for those who were no longer with us?

I glanced at my watch and then hurriedly picked up my bag and headed for the door.

"Come on, Sam," I said, waiting at the door for him.

Jack tipped his chin up at me in farewell as I passed his desk on my way to the elevator. Anne waved to me. So did Hawk. Corbin had gone to lunch.

Me? I had a date with my realtor. I was in the process of buying a small house on the outskirts of Chattanooga, one with a big fenced-in yard for Samson to run around in.

Thank you. If you enjoyed Indigo: Case Fifteen, and would like to start at the beginning read Jasmine: Case One.

Get Jasmine: Case One Today At Blair Howard Books

It was Lt. Kate Gazzara's first case as lead detective. For eight years she played Dr. Watson to Sergeant Harry Starke's Sherlock Holmes, and then he was gone. Jasmine changed her life.

THE PEACEMAKER

BOOK ONE

1

THIS CITY, LIKE SO MANY OTHER CITIES ACROSS THE
US of A, never sleeps, but not because of rampant partying, although if you ask around, there's fun to be had, and
for every taste and wallet. No, sir, this isn't Vegas. This
city doesn't sleep because it can't afford to, but not
because of stock trade or poverty, although if you ask
around, you'll find it has its fair share of both. No, sir, this
isn't the Big Apple, either. This city can't afford to sleep
because this is where the fates of nations are decided.
Here, the game of politics that started some two and a
half centuries ago is still being played, and with more
vigor than ever before, and sleep, even for an hour, means
falling behind.

This city's days are filled with never-ending meetings, conferences, and hearings, with business lunches
and paperwork. Oh, so much paperwork, even in 2010,
when every house has a personal computer, and every
teenager has a phone in his or her pocket. And so, the city
buzzes with phone calls and printers and copiers and fax

machines until late into the night, until there's nothing left to say, and no one left to listen. And only then do the real players of the game come out to play.

This is Washington, District of Columbia.

On one such night, just after midnight, a nondescript —even by this city's standards—black Chevrolet Suburban sped along a snow-powdered street, its tires grabbing at the asphalt with the tenacity of a wild animal, sending chunks of dirty snow flying across the sidewalks, its xenon headlights piercing the night, reaching far into the distance like a pair of silver scimitars.

The driver, a man in his late twenties wearing a freshly pressed, dark blue suit, kept both hands firmly on the steering wheel and stared resolutely ahead. He was in control of the situation, knowing full well the importance of the man in the back seat who was staring intently at his laptop, the cold blue light illuminating his face.

What he was reading, the driver had no idea, but the man's brows were furrowed, his thin lips raised slightly at the corners in what might loosely be interpreted as a smile. The man in the back seat pursed his lips, sat back, relaxed, produced a leather cigar case and extracted a Cuban.

A few minutes later, without a turn signal, the Suburban slowed and pulled over at the curb in front of a rundown antique store, its windows dark, the word *Vintage* in ugly, faded gold letters emblazoned above the entrance. A neon sign flickering tiredly in the door window declared that the store was *Closed*.

"I won't be long," the older man growled, puffing out a thick cloud of smoke. The driver nodded. His passenger stepped out. A low humming sounded as the driver rolled down the windows to clear the air.

The man crossed the sidewalk, grasped the doorknob, turned it, pushed open the door, and entered the store. He walked purposefully between the jumbled rows of old furniture, shelves full of worn-out toys, racks of used clothes and other junk, to the counter where a heavy-set woman roughly his own age was seated working on a crossword puzzle. The man introduced himself. Skeptically, she looked him over.

"But of course," she said. "You are expected. Please, go through." Her accent was soft, mid-European.

She lifted the trap in the counter for him to pass through.

The man grunted, sourly, thinking, *Don't you know who I am?* But he didn't say anything. She'd know soon enough. Everyone would.

He walked past the counter then through another heavier door into what appeared to be a small, dimly lit barroom. At the far end of the room, on either side of a door, two men in suits and dark glasses stood motionless and alert. To their left, seated alone at a small round table, a woman in a sharp gray business suit nursed a whiskey glass in a perfectly manicured hand.

"What the hell kind of place is this?" the man said as he stepped up to the bar, trailing smoke.

"Sit," the woman ordered.

The man looked around the room. They were alone, the four of them. He went behind the bar, fixed himself a drink, sat down at the table opposite her, leaned back in his chair, stared at her and sipped his drink.

"Why are we here?" she asked.

"We're ready," he said. "My people are in place. Everything is going as planned. A month from now, at long last, we'll have achieved our goal. To peace on earth." He raised his glass, then drank the toast. The woman simply continued to stare at him, her pale blue eyes fixed on his own with a stare so cold he almost shuddered.

"I'm well aware of what you say," she said. "But that is not why you requested this meeting, is it? Get to the point."

The man shook the ashes off his cigar down onto the floor, held her gaze, and said, "Four weeks from tonight, the mission will be over. I want to keep the assets for myself... The human assets, that is."

"Why?"

"Let's just say I have plans of my own."

"What plans?"

"That's none of your business."

The woman took a sip of her whiskey and, without taking her eyes off him, she nodded slowly then said, "When the mission is successfully concluded, you will be free to do whatever you want. Are we done?"

"We're done." *Bitch!*

They both took another sip, laid down their half-empty glasses, and then they left the bar, each leaving the way they'd entered. The man passed quickly through the store, ignoring the woman at the counter, crossed the sidewalk and climbed into the back seat of his Suburban.

AT AROUND THE SAME TIME—THOUGH THREE HOURS earlier due to the time zone difference—and approximately 2,000 miles away to the west, Albert Westwood loaded his groceries into the passenger seat of a pickup truck built by the same manufacturer but twenty years prior, its lines simple, the chains on its wheels ready to take on the season. He threw his hat atop the paper bags, and then circled the pickup to climb in behind the wheel of a vehicle for which he had little affection. He turned the key, flipped the gas pedal with his foot, and the truck rumbled to life. He flipped on the headlights and a minute later was driving out of the Safeway parking lot onto a freshly plowed road.

Westwood didn't really mind the truck. Despite it having a passing resemblance to the Foxhound armored trucks he'd operated in the British army, it was much more comfortable and all but floated down the winding road. *Kind of like a boat,* he thought as, one-handed, he fished a barbeque flavored Slim Jim from the bag in the passenger seat.

He turned up the radio, singing along to a 90s rock hit the words to which he remembered only every other line. Like most of his days, this one had been quiet, but now it was Friday night and the weekend had arrived, and along with it, he hoped, some fun out on the town.

Five minutes later, the truck rolled into the tiny parking lot in front of the Waystation Bar and Grill, and Westwood was surprised when he realized how eager he was to get inside. He turned off the motor and hopped out of the truck, stood for a moment, his breath steamy white in the cold night air. He took one last deep breath, then strolled into the bar.

"'Night. Nice to see ya," the bouncer at the door said, exhaling cigarette smoke.

Westwood smiled at the large man's jolly red cheeks, touched him gently on the arm, and said, "Thanks. You too, mate."

As roadside bars go, the Waystation was a decent place, brightly lit, though not uncomfortably so, with a spotless pool table, currently occupied by a group of locals Westwood sometimes saw around and had even joined for a game once in a while. One of them looked up when he entered and jerked his chin in a polite greeting. Westwood returned the greeting with a nod and stepped up to the bar.

"Al, haven't seen you in a while," the barkeep said. "Where've you been?"

Her name was Van, as in Vanessa, and she was by far the best part about the place. Dressed, as always, in a black leather jacket, a white top, and a black leather mini-skirt, Van wore her black hair up in a ponytail. Her eyes were bright and blue, laughing. The silver piercing in her nose glittering.

"Hey, Van," Albert said as he slid onto the bar stool in front of her. She was already pouring him a glass of beer. "Just doing my thing. You know how it is. Gotta keep the big bad wolf at bay."

"Yeah? So what's new?" she asked, genuinely interested, as she set the glass on a coaster in front of him.

"Thanks, love," he said as he picked it up and sipped the icy liquid, then smacked his lips in appreciation.

She smiled. Albert had long ago gotten used to the way American women loved his accent. That being so, and putting it on a little thicker, he said, "Not much new, I'm afraid... I was out in the woods earlier today, though, and I caught a glimpse of a buck, a six-pointer: cute little bugger." He looked pointedly at her. The double meaning of that last obvious to her.

Van beamed, and Albert sipped the beer with delight and licked the foam from his mustache. If he played his cards right, he might have company tonight. "What about you, then?" he asked.

"Oh, you know, same old same old, just work," she said and gestured around. "Busy night and all."

"Anyone give you any trouble?"

"Nah, all regulars tonight, except for those three over there, truckers." She nodded at a trio of men in flannel jackets and thick sweaters.

Westwood turned on his stool to look at them. They were drinking and laughing, and minding their own business, for the most part. He made a note of them and turned back to the bar.

"It's a lovely night, yeah?" he asked.

"Kinda cold," Van said with an innocent little shrug.

Albert played along. "Yeah, true. Well, may I interest you in a fireplace, then?"

"I got one of those." She tilted her head.

"I bet mine's bigger," he replied.

"Don't tell me you're one of those guys, Al! Size isn't everything, you know." She winked and switched her attention to another customer, one of the three truckers, who leaned on the bar in a way that suggested he couldn't stand upright without it.

"Shots, babe," he demanded. He was the youngest of the three men, perhaps ten years younger than Albert, and had a young man's bravado about him: he glanced at Albert as if they were old pals. Westwood offered a thin smile and turned his eyes up to the small flat screen on the wall above the bottles.

"Breaking news from Washington, DC," the newscaster was saying. "An unprecedented ruling has been reached in the Cassandra Wu case. Wu, a former CIA officer turned mercenary, has been charged with six counts of murder, as well as..." The words faded momentarily as Westwood stared at the mugshot of the woman he had fought alongside so many times in the past. Casey, a pretty Asian American woman, had been a long-time friend, and sometime lover and companion, until a few years back, when...

"Hey, turn that bullshit off!" the guy next to him yelled to Van, who was working on his shots.

"Gimme a sec here, will you?" she said.

Westwood took a deep breath and continued listening.

"Less than a year ago, Cassandra Wu, head of a private security firm, was allegedly responsible for a series of murders in Chattanooga, Tennessee. Thanks to the efforts of the local law enforcement and a former CPD Detective, Harry Starke, Wu's plans were foiled and three of her associates killed. Wu's fourth accomplice, known only as Nero, remains unaccounted for—"

"Bo-ring!" the young guy complained.

His eyes never leaving the screen, Albert said, "Well, I happen to be watching."

The trucker stared, and then laughed. "Oi happen to be watching," he said, mocking Al's accent. "This ain't jolly ol' England, buddy. Our TVs are for football and commercials. Am I right?" He turned to Van.

"Your shots are ready to go," she said.

"Don't you worry, I got them, as soon as I talk some sense into this joker you got here."

As the words left his mouth, the young man stood up straight, puffing out his chest.

Albert ignored him.

The newscaster said, "We have official confirmation of a joint operation between the FBI and British MI6. On Thursday next, Cassandra Wu will be transported to London, where she will be questioned regarding a series of murders committed in several European countries, including London and Paris. The murders, all committed during the past six years, are thought to be contract killings. We turn now to our senior intelligence corre-spondent, Emily—"

"Hey, I'm talking to you, buddy."

Westwood turned to see the young guy only a couple of feet away, his half-drunken stare fixed in front of him, squarely on Albert's neck. Both men waited.

Finally, Van said, "Hey, how about another round of shots, huh? On the house... Since it's your first time here and all."

Surprisingly, it worked. The young would-be brawler eased up, his eyes involuntarily sliding aside at the six shiny shots, until his whole body turned to the bar and both his hands reached for the shots as if he was catching a basketball, spilling half of their contents when he grabbed them.

"You got lucky this time, buddy," he said, and then left to join his buddies.

"Good thing those moppets aren't locals," Westwood said. He took out his wallet, extracted two twenty-dollar bills and handed them to Van. "For the shots."

Van hesitated, but then took the money and tucked it away in her apron. "Thanks, Al."

He smiled, slipped his wallet into his jeans pocket, and raised his glass. "To counting our blessings."

She nodded, looking up at the screen. "Those bastards, huh? They tried to kill a senator, didn't they? And one of them is still out there, can you believe it?"

"You think he's fled the country, yeah?" Albert said, sipping the beer.

"Wherever he is, he's definitely far away by now."

"Gone to ground somewhere, I shouldn't wonder," Westwood said.

She agreed, he ordered another beer, and they chatted for a while longer, but the mood had soured, and they were both leaning towards a rain check.

The truckers grew louder as they grew drunker, until one of them called it quits and urged his buddies to wrap things up. They made sure not to leave any glasses empty, and then stumbled out the door, past the bouncer, who was standing just outside enjoying a smoke.

"Well, I should probably be on my way, as well, love. Unless... you want some company?"

She smiled. "You go on. I've a long shift ahead of me."

"And when might you have a shorter shift, then?" he asked, hoping against hope.

"Beats me!"

They both chuckled. Albert patted the bar and dropped another twenty, then slipped off his stool, zipped up his coat and stepped out into the cold night, wishing the bouncer a good one as he went.

And that's when he saw the three drunken idiots shuffling in place next to his truck, clearly up to no good. He stopped and watched as one of them took out a pocketknife, flicked it open, and bent down beside the driver's side front wheel.

"I'd think twice before doing that," Westwood said quietly.

Behind him, he heard the bouncer say, "You need a hand here, Al?"

Without taking his eyes off the trio, he said, "Thanks, Thomas mate. I got this."

"Suit yourself," the large man said, and Albert heard the bar door open and close.

The truckers sized him up as he stepped closer. The one with the knife was about Albert's age and the least drunk of the three. He was a thin guy with a thick red mustache and furry eyebrows. His buddies swayed in place; fists raised.

"You may think you got me outnumbered, fellas, but that would be erroneous."

"Ero what? What did you just say?" the youngest of the three, the one that had challenged him at the bar earlier, mumbled.

Negotiations, so it seemed, weren't an option, which

didn't bother Westwood. It was, after all, a cold night, and he was feeling like he could do with a warm-up, especially so since Van would be unavailable for the task.

As he expected, the young brawler stepped up first and swung his right fist in a ridiculously wide arc, which Westwood easily avoided and then delivered two swift hard punches—one for each of his attacker's kidneys. The young man folded and stumbled to one side, throwing up. *One down.*

"Two to go," Westwood declared lightly, smiling at them, but he didn't give them time to respond, or to formulate a new strategy. He went first for the one with the knife, knocking it out of his hand with a precise slap of his left hand, and then he knocked the trucker spinning sideways with a right hook. The last guy stumbled backward, waving his fists. Westwood, almost casually, kicked his feet from under him, sending him down to the wet concrete. All three squirmed on the ground, grunting, none of them seriously injured.

"You guys have a good night, now," Westwood said as he climbed into his truck.

Years later, at a Labor Day barbeque, after too many bottles of cheap beer, all three men would swear they'd gotten their asses handed to them that night by the man known only as Nero.

2

TRUE AS IT MAY BE THAT THIS CITY NEVER SLEEPS, its loyal servants have to, at least from time to time. Not, perhaps for a full eight hours as the doctors recommend, and often not even for five, and sometimes, when those loyal servants elect to spend those nights with each other, even less than that.

"We gotta go," Ellie Millard whispered under the blanket.

The sun wasn't quite up yet, but it was bright enough outside the windows to light their motel room. The blanket was thin, the top cover thrown back in the heat of the night. Pete Donovan's face was half-covered by the thin fabric, half-hidden in shadows that enhanced the outline of his jaw and right cheekbone.

He rolled over onto his back and said, "We still have a few minutes, don't we?"

"Yes, but we'll need more than a few minutes..."

"Agent Millard!"

"I have to get ready, so d'you." She kissed his lips and slid out from under the blanket. Pete put his hands behind his head and watched as, naked, she flitted about the room, picking up her clothes.

"Wow," he said, "you really are something. All that training paid off for you."

"Thanks, and right back at you," she said, never pausing in her rush toward the bathroom.

Ellie consulted her watch and said, "Fifty-two minutes, Peter. We need to be there in fifty-two minutes. I need to brush my hair, and I suggest you grab a shower. You stink."

He watched her dress, getting a kick out of her reverse striptease, a self-satisfied smile on his face. Finally, she turned, put her hands on her hips, and glared at him.

"Okay, okay," he said and reluctantly climbed out of bed and sauntered past her into the bathroom.

She stopped him, put an arm around his bare torso, slid her hand down his belly and gently squeezed him.

"Listen, Peter," she said. "This is the biggest assignment I've ever had, okay? And in no small part because of you, so thank you. I just want everything to go as smooth as butter today."

He nodded his agreement, and said, "I know, Ellie, just as I know you'll nail it today. I also know a really nice hotel in London, by the way." He winked, and she raised the corners of her lips slightly.

"Get in the damn shower, you..."

He raised his eyebrows, a smile in his eyes, antici-pating a stinger.

"You... sex machine?" she stuttered awkwardly.

Pete was quiet for a moment, looking at her in amazement at her loss of words, and then they both exploded with laughter.

"Okay, that," he said, and kissed her, and turned toward the bathroom. "Hey, that's not fair," he yelped after she slapped his bare butt.

Ellie brushed her hair, standing in front of the mirror above the shabby old desk. She was dressed in a skirt and white blouse. Her suit jacket was still hung over the back of a chair. The rest of her gear: her Glock 17 Gen 5, tucked safely in its holster, along with two spare mags. Her FBI badge and creds lay on a nightstand beside the bed. It was her first assignment as SAIC: Special Agent in Charge.

Ellie, at thirty-two, was a good-looking woman: small-breasted, toned, fit, with dark brown hair that, on a good day, cascaded just below her shoulders. That day, however, she'd brushed it straight and tied it back in a ponytail.

She took one last look at herself, nodded, satisfied, put away the hairbrush, slipped into her jacket and geared up. She checked herself in the mirror once more and smiled. She didn't exactly look like a million bucks, but plenty good enough for the job in hand, so she thought. To an unobservant passerby, Ellie might've looked like any other businesswoman on her way to a meeting. Especially in this city.

A few minutes later, Special Agent Peter Donovan joined her and quickly threw on his equally bland suit and identical gear, and a minute later they were outside and climbing into yet another nondescript black SUV, unmarked, although the trained eye of a dedicated conspiracy theorist would almost certainly nail it as a Bureau ride.

"Ready to roll?" Pete said.

"Punch it," Ellie replied as they backed out of the parking lot and left their hideaway.

The motel wasn't exactly FBI protocol for their assignment, but Pete had picked it, claiming a need to be close by in case things went south on the day. In retrospect, it was a stupid, risky idea, but they were in that phase of their relationship where such clandestine assignations only added to the excitement.

It was ten minutes to eight when they arrived at the detention facility that morning. Pete parked the SUV in the empty lot—it had been cleared of civilian vehicles and was populated instead with Metro PD cruisers. A lone prisoner transport vehicle was parked close to the door, its engine idling.

"What is this, a cop convention or something?" Pete said as they climbed out of the vehicle.

"Not hardly," Ellie said. "Over cautious, is all, I'd say. Let's go find out, shall we?"

He nodded, and together they made their way past the idling transport to the entrance to the facility, where several Metro PD officers were posted, along with two prison guards.

The two agents flashed their badges and creds and received stony looks in return.

"We're here to pick up a package," Pete joked.

The officers laughed; Ellie smiled thinly.

"It just so happens that we got one all parceled up and ready to go," one of the guards said. "Come on in, guys. She'll be coming right up."

"Right up" turned out to be the better part of an hour, during which time the agents signed multiple forms and Pete once again talked the cops and the guards through the procedure. His audience listened passively, and then assured each other and the two agents of their readiness.

"Good men," Pete concluded. "Now..."

It was then that they brought her up. Ellie saw her first.

Cassandra Wu, a seemingly diminutive figure in a way-too-big orange jumpsuit, and one of the deadliest women alive, was shackled hand and foot and so restrained she could only shuffle instead of walk. Her hands were restrained within a set of VIPERTEK heavy duty hinged double lock steel cuffs; her wrists were chained to a leather belt around her waist; her ankles were shackled eighteen inches apart. The orange suit bulged and billowed over and under the belt.

"Is all of this really necessary?" Ellie asked.

"That's what I've been asking, girl," Wu said. She looked exhausted.

The news media had, over the last six months, been broadcasting Wu's mugshot to the world. It wasn't a flattering image: black leather jacket and black hair to her shoulders, but the woman in front of Ellie now had her hair cut short, and not by a stylist. It looked like it had been hacked off. If she hadn't known the woman's history, Ellie might have felt sorry for her.

"You know the protocol," Donovan said to Wu. "Let's roll, boys."

AVAILABLE AT
BLAIR HOWARD BOOKS
&
ALL GOOD BOOKSTORES

From Blair Howard

The Harry Starke Genesis Series

The Harry Starke Series

The Lt. Kate Gazzara Murder Files

The Peacemaker Series

The Civil War Series

From Blair C. Howard

The Sovereign Star Series

ABOUT THE AUTHOR

Blair Howard is a retired journalist turned novelist. He's the author of more than 50 novels including the international best-selling Harry Starke series of crime stories, the Lt. Kate Gazzara series, and the Harry Starke Genesis series. He's also the author of the Peacemaker series of international thrillers and five Civil War/Western novels.

If you enjoy reading Science Fiction thrillers, Mr. Howard has made his debut into the genre with, The Sovereign Stars Series under the name, Blair C. Howard.

Visit www.blairhoward.com.

You can also find Blair Howard on Social Media